LOVE AM(
THE DAUGH

Maureen Osborne

LOVE AMONG
THE DAUGHTERS

For Sue

Best Wishes

Maureen Osborne

Marlborough

2005

THE NIGHT OWL PRESS

Published by The Night Owl Press
West Byfleet
Surrey KT14 6DW

ISBN 0-9547368-0-X

Designed, typeset and produced by
John Saunders Design & Production, Abingdon OX13 5HU
Printed in Great Britain by
Biddles Ltd., King's Lynn

To Maurice

Foreword

Like all those who love reading I cannot pass a second-hand bookshop, car boot sale or book fair without rushing to have a look. Three years ago I found a thick volume, obviously old, with its green and gold spine torn and its pages loose. It was Volume II of *Siberia and the Exile System*, by George Kennan, published in 1891. The next week I was lucky enough to find *The Princess of Siberia*, published in 1985, by Christine Sutherland.

These two books, with their true stories of cruelty and courage, were the inspiration for my novel.

LOVE AMONG
THE DAUGHTERS

Chapter One

RUSSIA 1801

It started with a sigh. That was all. It was simply a quiet exhalation of breath in an over-heated ballroom in St. Petersburg – yet it affected many lives over many years. It filled the sails of a merchantman bound for Russia. It blew men and women in an icy blast to the snowy wastes of Siberia.

The young man who sighed was an Englishman, Richard Bingham. He had been in Russia buying furs for Marks and Company of London. Now the work was done, the furs from the great warehouse were packed into crates down in the ship's hold and he was looking forward to sailing home. He longed to see his children, Julie and Edgar and his sister Bess. And if Bonaparte was preparing to invade England he must be there to protect the family.

In the meantime he was the guest of the Count and Countess Markov. That family, he knew, had been among the first to set up trading posts in Siberia in the seventeenth century and had become rich and powerful. But now, Richard thought, the Russian aristocrats despised him because *he* was in trade. He had an unpleasant suspicion that he had been invited to the ball by mistake.

He stood apart by a window, a stocky figure with a square face and a blunt nose. Although only thirty-six his brown hair was already greying at the temples. He watched the excited young girls in their pink and white ball gowns, thinking of his own wife Isabel who died giving birth to Julie. How beautiful she would have looked if only he could have afforded to buy her such dresses. Tears filled his eyes when he remembered how short their years of happiness together had been. Then embarrassed by his weakness he quickly blinked them away, turning to watch the groups of handsome Army officers in their tightly-fitting uniforms talking together. He knew they were discussing Napoleon Bonaparte and his victory against the Austrians at Marengo. They had boasted many times about how they would deal with the ambitious Dictator of France, should he look towards Russia.

"We'll see about that," thought Richard. "They've no Navy to touch ours. And these aristocratic officers who've bought their commissions are idle, pleasure-loving fellows. None of 'em have done a real day's work in their lives. I don't suppose the Count has ever pulled on his own boots. He is no better man than I am, yet because my family owned nothing my own youth was wretched."

He could not help grimacing when he remembered the hours he had been forced to spend studying French, Russian and book-keeping so that he could join the firm of importers his father had picked out for him. He seemed to feel once again the stinging blow of the schoolmaster's cane across his hands if he so much as blotted a row of figures.

As the music swirled round him his thoughts turned to his dream of riches, of owning a big house with a park.

4

He longed for his motherless children to take their place in English society. All he needed was money.

The orchestra struck up a mazurka. Richard gazed down the long gold and white ballroom as the dancers took up their positions. The scene was lit by ten great glittering chandeliers which were reflected in the rows of gilded mirrors set between the tall windows. The light gleamed on the white columns wreathed in flowers, and they in turn filled the room with a rich, heavy scent. Between each window down the length of the ballroom stood be-wigged footmen in green and silver livery, still as statues.

Richard was uncomfortable, having eaten too much of the caviar, river trout, quails and roast mutton, and from having drunk too much vodka and champagne. Moreover he had tied his stock too tightly and had a headache. To cool his burning forehead he stepped to the window and leant his head against the glass.

And then he sighed.

"Your Excellency is sad at the sight of so much misery," came a whisper by his right shoulder.

Richard started. There was no one nearby unless he counted the footman standing immobile by the window. It was as surprising as if a piece of furniture had spoken.

"They are also God's children," went on the footman, without moving his lips. He spoke in Russian, unlike his masters, who spoke only French.

Curious, Richard looked at the young man, then peered down through the long window. Below, through the falling snow, he could see a dark mass of people moving slowly by. Cossacks on horseback rode alongside the throng, urging them on.

"Who are they? Where are they all going?" he asked quietly.

The footman continued to look straight ahead. "They are leaving their homes forever, Your Excellency. If you would see more clearly, I beg you, please to follow me."

After a quick glance right and left the footman left his post and darted through a nearby door. Richard followed and found himself in a small musty-smelling room. Through the gloom he could make out piles of spindly gold chairs and unwanted card-tables. The young man beckoned him to the window, which unlike the ones in the ballroom, had not been fitted with a second pane. This one had a large star-shaped crack in it.

Richard pressed his face to the crack, gasping as a draught of freezing air bit his cheek. Now he could see clearly the ragged column of men and women, shackled by chains fastened to their feet and waists. From the desolate throng rose a song so melancholy that it shrivelled his heart.

"Who are they, and where are they going?" he asked again, shaken.

"They are starting their long journey to exile in Siberia, Your Excellency. Some are criminals, but many are political prisoners. Perhaps they spoke too freely, or went secretly to political meetings. You can be sure that someone betrayed them..."

With a loud crash the door was flung open and the Count stood in a blaze of light. His face burned crimson with anger.

"What are you thinking of, Pavel Petrovich, you scum?" he roared. "How dare you desert your post and talk to my guests!"

The footman cringed and backed away.

"You wretch, you filth, leave here this instant! You shall be whipped for this. You shall go back to digging potatoes, that's all you're good for. Starve, for all I care! Go! Go!"

Richard tried to stop the furious tirade. "I beg you, he meant no harm..." he began, but the footman had already stumbled past him to the door.

"I beg you to forgive me. Do not send me away, my family depend on me," he pleaded. He sounded humble, although Richard saw that his dark eyes were glittering with hatred.

The Count dismissed him with an imperious wave of the hand, as if he were a troublesome fly. Then he clasped Richard's arm, smiling as though nothing had happened.

"All my serfs are ruffians," he said gaily. "Now, Monsieur Dupont, it is the Countess's name-day and we must celebrate the occasion. Come, you shall join the dancers."

Monsieur Dupont! So it was true the Count had no idea who he was.

The contrast between the misery of the prisoners trudging into exile, the Count's treatment of his house serf and the pampered aristocrats in the ballroom, made Richard feel queasy. In his overheated imagination he saw everyone in the ballroom being blown away, swirled like snowflakes in a storm high into the dark sky and vanishing forever. Then he shook his head to clear it. Isabel had been right, he was too fanciful.

As soon as was polite he bowed to the Count, pleading tiredness, kissed the Countess's hand and left. At the bottom of the wide marble staircase another footman handed him his overcoat, fur hat, gloves and cane. Then at last he was out in the freezing night. The golden lamps lit up the silently falling snow. The prisoners had gone, leaving a wide track of brown slush to show their passing. Only the echo of their dreary song seemed to remain quivering in the cold air.

In the horse-drawn cab on his way back to his hotel by the Moika Canal he leaned back with relief. Thank heaven, the day after tomorrow he would embark for home. He thought how barbarous Russia was, how dark, how vast, how cruel. He wondered what would happen to the wretched footman...

Suddenly there was a knock on the window of the cab. Startled, he saw a hooded figure running alongside peering in out of the whirling whiteness. Certain it was the footman Richard signalled with his cane to the driver to pull up. The least he could do was give the poor fellow a few roubles. He opened the cab door and helped the muffled, snow-covered figure inside.

It was not the footman. As the stranger brushed the snow from his cloak Richard noticed his long shiny boots and his blue-grey uniform. He was an Army officer. He also saw that the man was in some distress. His hands shook and there was a gleam of tears on his frozen cheeks.

"Are you ill, or has there been an accident, that you are out in such weather?" he asked the muffled figure.

Keeping his head averted the man answered a quiet "No."

As he said no more Richard introduced himself, explaining that the furs he had bought were already on board ship at Kronstadt and that now he was on his way back to his hotel, the Empress Catherine on the Moika Canal.

"Ah, the Englishman," the officer answered hesitatingly. "You may remember we met last week at Olga Shulgin's. I am Captain Dmitry Simonovich Andropov, of the Semonovski Guards."

Richard did remember, for on that particular evening some of the officers had drunk too much vodka and brandy. They had been indiscreet and had openly grumbled that Tsar Paul was a brutal bully who was ruining the Army with his harsh discipline and savage cruelty. They said he had authorised the arrest of thousands of army officers, and lately had ordered people to prostrate themselves in the street when his carriage passed by. In fact, they said, Paul was mad. That was very foolish of them, because even Richard knew that the Tsar had spies everywhere. But why was the Captain so agitated?

"What it is that troubles you, Captain Andropov? It may be I can help you, or perhaps take you to your home."

The officer brushed away a tear with a trembling hand. "I beg you, ask me nothing – " he began in a halting voice. "But as to help – if you could spare me a few moments of your time – I beg you – come home with me – my son and I live near the Admiralty on the Nevsky Prospekt."

After giving the cab driver the Captain's address Richard told his companion about the prisoners he had seen passing below Count Markov's window. Then he related the story of the ill-used footman, and how he had thought that he, Dmitry Simonovich, was that man.

The Captain sighed deeply. "My poor country suffers. The Army suffers," he murmured. "Some of us – we do what has to be done."

Soon the tall golden spire of the Admiralty came into view. The Captain lived in a white house surrounded by ornate iron railings. The two men entered a large, low-ceilinged room warmed by a great blue and white tiled stove. A little red oil lamp flickered before a silvery icon in a corner, while all around on the wood-panelled walls hung prints of sabre-wielding cavalry officers charging into battle.

As Captain Andropov poured two glasses of Vodka with unsteady hands Richard studied his face. He was a tall, handsome man, with corn-coloured hair, high cheekbones and long slanting grey eyes. Eyes that were constantly glancing at a black marble clock on the sideboard.

"Mr Bingham," he began after gulping down his vodka, "I know from what you told me that you hate injustice – "

"Indeed I do! In spite of the revolution in France, in my country we do not send people into the wilderness for speaking their minds. Nor do we kick a man when he is down."

"It is well known that all Englishmen are honourable and so I know I can trust you. Time is running out for me, and I must tell you – ask you we – that is I – need to conceal something of importance – "

Richard put down his glass. "But that is not possible. I have told you I am sailing home the day after tomorrow."

Was it the heat from the great stove that caused Captain Andropov to break out into a sweat?

"I beg you – hear me out. All I ask is that you take something and conceal it in your hotel room for this one night. You are at the Empress Catherine, you told me? Someone will call for it at ten o'clock tomorrow. The password is "fraternity." Be sure you hand it only to the messenger who knows this."

"But…" Richard began, wishing he had not come.

The Captain drew himself up. "I give you my word as an Officer and a gentleman that what I ask you to conceal has not been stolen – "

"Papa, you are home!"

A young boy hurled himself down the staircase and into his father's arms. He wore only a nightshirt and his feet were bare. He was very like his father, with the same grey eyes and the same tendril of fair hair falling over his brow. Richard was surprised at the boy's show of affection, for his own son Edgar had a cold nature.

"This is my son, Sergei," said the Captain with pride. "Seriozha, this is Mr Bingham from England,"

The boy nodded his head at Richard, staring up at his face so intently it seemed as if he were trying to memorise it.

"I have a daughter Julie who is about your age," Richard told him.

"Can I see her? Is she pretty?

Richard considered, smiling at the boy. "To me she is beautiful. She's a little wild, being only thirteen years old and always in mischief, but I love her dearly."

"Then I would like to meet her."

"She is in England, Sergei, waiting for me to come home," Richard said, warming to the boy.

"Enough talking," his father silenced him swiftly, placing a hand over the boy's mouth. "Now listen carefully, Seriozha. You must dress at once. You are to go and stay with your grandparents on their estate in the Ukraine. Platon and Mashenka will go with you. Be as quick as you can."

"No, Papa, I don't care for Grandmama. I won't go."

"Go, do as I say," cried his father desperately.

Sergei ran up the stairs. But out of the corner of his eye Richard could see a portion of white nightshirt and ten bare toes showing beneath. The boy was sitting at the top of the stairs, listening.

Richard smiled. It was what Julie would have done.

11

"You have a handsome son, Captain Andropov, as full of spirit as my own daughter. Yes, I will help you."

"Thank you." With unsteady hands the Captain unlocked a cupboard and took out a small wooden chest wrapped in a blue cloth. As Richard took it he wondered what it could contain that made the officer so anxious.

At the door he saw that Captain Andropov's eyes were again filled with tears. "Remember, keep it well hidden and only give it to one who knows the password. It was done for the Army," he went on, his face haggard. "Some will die. You are helping others to live."

Feeling he was in a strange dream Richard left the house, clutching the locked wooden chest. He shivered, for the night was still cold and the snow thicker than ever. Fortunately a sleigh, its horse and driver white as frosty statues, was waiting nearby.

As soon as he reached the sanctuary of his hotel bedroom Richard searched feverishly for a hiding place. First he thrust the chest under the high bed, then in the cavernous wardrobe. Too restless to sleep he paced the room, going over the extraordinary events of the night. What did it all mean? What was in the mysterious chest? Suddenly he felt he must know. Before he could stop himself he had retrieved it from the wardrobe and forced the lock with his knife. Then he threw back the domed lid.

It was full to the brim with Russian bank notes. There was more there than he would ever possess in his lifetime. He plunged his hands into the chest and tossed the notes into the air. Why, the money would enable him to buy him a big house and some land. It would enable his family to take their rightful places in society.

He told himself the Captain could not have come by it honestly.

Afterwards he thought of his actions as a sort of madness. Trembling as if he had the ague he jammed the chest shut and wrapped it in its blue cloth. Next he threw his clothes into his suitcase and stumbled down the echoing stairs to rouse the sleepy manager and settle his bill.

Soon he was sitting in a sleigh, his breath smoking in the chilly air, the chest and his suitcase at his feet. As the driver drove him through the cold grey dawn to the harbour at Kronsdadt he covered himself in the fur wrap and fell into an uneasy sleep. At once he dreamed he was standing in a shadowy courtroom while a goblin judge pronounced sentence on him.

"You have taken the downward path that leads to hell. You are a thief, and will never more know a quiet night."

Bathed in sweat, he woke to the shouts of the sailors and noise of the crowded dock. Stumbling on the cobbles slippery with seawater and fishscales, he pushed through the crowds, sniffing the familiar smells – tarred ropes, oak timber, saltwater, frying food and unwashed bodies. Seagulls swooped and cried shrilly amid the forest of masts. And there, thank God, among the Russian Navy ships rode the *Peter the Great*.

He was safe.

Below he found he was to share his cramped cabin with a monk dressed in a long back robe and wearing a high black headress. He had a square-cut grey beard that reached his waist. Father Gregory Bilibin looked over his spectacles at Richard, nodded, and returned to fingering his crucifix and reading his Testament.

Richard was in a turmoil. Should he try and get down into the hold, open the crates and hide the money among the sable, mink and silver fox furs? No, that would not be possible. He decided to keep the chest wrapped in its cloth in the little cabin, where the Holy Father, uninterested in worldly things, would be its unwitting guardian.

Richard leant weakly against the ship's rail, nausea curdling his stomach. If only he could turn time back! If only he could return to the Count's party – then he would go straight to his hotel and stop for no-one. But time ran on and nothing, nothing, could stop it. He was a thief and already damned for selling his soul to the devil.

The snow had ceased and a pale golden sun gleamed on the blue and gold of the churches and on the white roofs of the merchants' houses. But Richard was blind to everything but the activity on board. He felt as though his soul had split in two. He wished with all his heart he had not stolen the money, but then neither did he want to get caught. The business part of his mind began to plan how he would change the roubles into English money in London.

Would the ship never set sail?

The next morning more passengers hurried aboard, the last being a stout merchant and his be-furred wife. She was sobbing into her muff. At once Richard felt with terror it was something to do with the events of that fateful night. His heart began to pound.

"God save us all, our beloved Tsar has been assassinated!" cried the merchant. "In the Mikhailovsky Palace, too. What will become of us? Our little Father has been murdered!"

A loud wail went up from the other passengers. The sailors, however, scowled and spat over the side.

"How?"

"Who would dare murder the Emperor?"

"Who killed Tsar Paul?"

The little group jostled to get closer to the couple and the man seemed to swell with importance. "They say he was strangled by Army officers of the Semonovski Guards. It seems they tried to get away but their plans went awry. They were caught and are to be hung."

Richard staggered, his heart thudding, his face pale as ash.

"What have I done!"

"You were part of the plot to kill the Tsar. Regicide! Captain Andropov was one of the murderers!" boomed a voice in his head. "The money he gave you to hide was to help the families of the traitors."

"But the Tsar was a monster, you know he deserved to die," squeaked a second voice in his ear

"Danger! Danger!" thundered a third.

"Thief! Thief! Thief!" screamed another.

The fifth voice clanged like a bell: "The innocent will suffer. What will become of the boy Sergei?"

Distracted, Richard clapped his hands over his ears, but he could not silence the voices ringing in his head.

"I am not well," he whispered, and stumbled below.

As the *Peter the Great* sailed for London through the grey cold waters of the Baltic he lay in his narrow bunk. Father Gregory bought him soup but he pulled the coarse blanket over his head and wept.

Over and over the boy spoke to him.

"They will hang my father. Whatever he did, he trusted you and you betrayed him."

Chapter Two

ENGLAND 1802

Julie Bingham flew down the oak staircase of Starcross House and into the large kitchen, pausing only long enough to dig her hand deep into a newly baked raisin cake. Clutching the fistful of warm crumbs she ran out into the park, her brown hair streaming out behind her. As she raced towards the oak tree where she was to meet her sweetheart she glanced back to see if she was being followed by Edgar. To her annoyance her brother had taken to following her everywhere.

She climbed up into the tree, tearing her lavender-sprigged muslin gown as she went. The green leaves of the oak made a secret bower where she settled herself on a sturdy branch, stuffed the handful of raisin cake into her mouth and waited.

As she retrieved the crumbs that had fallen inside her bodice she looked through the sunlit leaves towards the house her father had bought when he came back from Russia. Aunt Bess said Starcross had been built in the time of her namesake, Good Queen Bess. Its walls of rose-pink brick were covered with ivy and the sun was reflected in its many mullioned windows. Her aunt was proud of their new house and said the family had gone up in the world. She told Julie that she must be grateful to her father for making a fortune in foreign parts.

Julie loved her aunt and glad she was happy with their new wealth. She could buy new gowns and bonnets and eat so much she was now as round as a dumpling. Julie herself was not so content. She missed the loving father who had gone away and come back a stranger.

Sighing, she twisted round to gaze across the park to the village of Wychwood. The church bells of St Lawrence began to chime, and in the still summer air she could hear the ring of the blacksmith's anvil and the lowing of cows. She could see the Manor House where Squire Ransome lived, the little river Bourne with its watermill, the village green, the Angel tavern and the road to London. Surrounding Starcross House and park were farms and fields, full of ripening corn. Over to the left was the common. She shuddered because Amy Finch, the kitchen maid, had told her that witches flew there by night.

She decided not to think of them. Instead she gazed longingly at the cottage by the village green next to the forge. This was where Jem Tulley lived with his mother. He was the farmer's boy who brought eggs to the kitchen each week, and was her own sweetheart. Of course it was a secret, but she thought he was the handsomest boy she had ever seen. His dark eyes, sunburnt skin and thick curly hair made her long to touch him. They had kissed briefly, but the cook always arrived and spoilt things. If only she was one of the village children, free to go barefoot and roam the fields as they did!

"I can see your drawers!"

Julie gave a screech of laughter and nearly fell from her perch. There beneath the tree stood Jem, who had approached unseen. He carried a bundle of faggots under his arm.

"You're a wicked boy to say such things," she called down, delighted. "Come up at once."

He threw down his bundle, spat on his hands and swung himself up beside her.

"Edgar knows about us, Jem."

"Who cares? Nobody likes your brother, Julie. He bets at the cockfights and never pays his debts when he loses. He's a weasel and a pisspot." He put his arms around her and kissed her.

She felt as she did when she had helped herself to great spoonfuls of golden honey from the larder. She kissed him back, suffused with a dreamy happiness. Presently he told her proudly how Mr Linton, the farmer, had said he was the best ploughboy he'd had.

"It's bad Moses took ill and died of the smallpox. Poor devil, it will go hard on his wife, and now they say it's come to Allerton. But Julie, Mr Linton says I'm to take his place in charge of one of the teams at harvest-time. I love them horses almost as much as I do my old Granny what lives over at Thrushfield."

"I'd dearly like to see her," said Julie wistfully. "My mother and grandmother are dead. I have no-one to love me but my Aunt Bess."

"No-one could help loving you, Julie. There's not a girl in the village can hold a candle to you – you're prettier than all of 'em. In a few years we'll get wed and have lots of babies and you can cook me apple puddings."

"I'd like us to be married now, Jem."

Murmuring endearments, neither of them noticed the lengthening shadows cast by the trees onto the grass. Suddenly they were startled by a shout from below.

"Julie, I can see you. Come down at once."

It was Edgar, his thin face angry, yet triumphant. A year older than Julie, he was slight, with a thin mouth, a sharp nose, his light brown hair pulled back in a pigtail. Julie thought his small eyes, fringed with pale lashes, made him look like a hungry pig.

As soon as they had swung down from the oak tree Edgar shouted "Leave my sister alone, you nobody!" and struck Jem a blow that sent him reeling backwards.

The boy recovered and hurled himself at Edgar, knocking him to the ground. Edgar lay still, looking frightened, his face smeared with blood.

"Get up and fight like a man," Jem taunted him. As Edgar made no move Jem spat contempteously, picked up his bundle of sticks and sauntered whistling home.

Edgar wiped his mouth. "I could have beaten him easy if I'd cared to. And I'm going to tell father you were kissing."

Julie kicked him hard on the leg. "Tell-tale-tit, your tongue shall be split. You always spoil everything."

When they arrived at the house the servants were bustling about with dishes for supper. Julie hoped to slip upstairs unnoticed and hid in the shadow of the tall grandfather clock in the hall. But Richard had seen them approaching.

He was standing by the parlour window, a bowed, grey-haired figure. Aunt Bess was sitting at a little walnut table trimming a green and white striped bonnet. She smiled at them and helped herself to a piece of gingerbread, but their father frowned.

"What is this? Why these black looks? Have you been fighting again, that your clothes are torn and dirty?"

"Father, it was all Julie's fault..." began Edgar.

As Richard gazed he saw, not his son's peevish face, but Sergei's handsome one. The boy spoke to him.

19

"You betrayed my dear father. He was hanged because you stole the money that would have helped him get away, and for that you will be forever cursed."

Richard heart hammered and he staggered, clutching at the red damask curtain to steady himself.

"Father, what is wrong?" Julie asked hurrying to him, only to be pushed irritably away as she had been so often since he returned from Russia.

"If your mother were alive you would not behave in such a hoydenish manner. Do you not know that I sold my soul for you, so you could rise in the world? You are both to go to bed without supper."

"Sold your soul! What fantastical notion is this? Richard dearest, I cannot understand you." said Bess, when Julie and Edgar had rushed from the room. "But I do know you are too stern."

Richard sat down, burying his head in his hands, trying to calm his swirling thoughts. "Bess, they need to learn manners." He knew what they needed was his love, but his heart had withered and he had none to give.

Bess skewered her needle into the green silk ribbon. "Brother, do you remember when we were giddy young things and plagued our own father with our wildness? Julie and Edgar are good children, but they need amusement. When we were poor we had such hopes of being in society. Now you have returned from foreign parts with a fortune – why cannot we be merry?"

As Richard looked over at the plump figure of his sister an exclamation was forced from his lips. Lurking in the shadows behind her chair stood Captain Andropov.

"They hanged me," the officer whispered hoarsely, putting his spectral hand to his throat. "The Tsar had to die – I did the deed for the sake of the Army. I trusted you and you betrayed me."

20

Then like a wisp of smoke he faded into the gloom.

Richard groaned. "Bess, he was here. He came to reproach me. I'm a miserable sinner – all this was got by greed, yet I did it for you and the children. I wanted you all to be happy, and that cannot be wrong. Does God judge it a sin to steal from a murderer? What the Captain did was evil – though I could not but help liking him and the boy. I believe he meant to do good by it – "

Bess looked puzzled. "Dearest, your wits are all a-jingle-jangle. You have been ailing since you came home to us, you are as thin as a reed. We are to have a beef and onion pie for supper and you must eat well and become your own self. I never liked you going to foreign parts, I'm sure, for they're all cannibals there."

Richard was no longer listening. Dabbing the sweat from his forehead he stumbled from the room.

Julie never minded being sent to bed without supper. She shared a big four-poster bed with her beloved aunt, and next to it was a small cupboard. There Aunt Bess kept a store of little cakes, treacle toffee, a box of peppermints and a tiny flask of brandy. The bedroom smelt of the lavender bags kept under the lacey pillows where they lolled and giggled together.

"I have a secret, Aunt," Julie confided that night. "I have my very own sweetheart and we're to be married."

Bess heaved with laughter. "So young too! Who is your suitor, pray? Oh, did I ever tell you of the time when I was young and considered beautiful? One of my father's clerks went down on his bended knee and asked me to be his wife."

"But you never married, Aunt."

"That was because when he knelt down he let off a great fart like a duck quacking and I laughed so much I thought I'd die. He rushed away, as red as a turkeycock, still quacking, and never came back."

Tears of mirth ran down their faces.

"Jem Tulley's my sweetheart, Aunt. He smells so good, like earth and turnips. I'm going to make apple puddings and have lots of babies. Tell me how they're made, do."

"The puddings or the babies?" shrieked Aunt Bess, her sides aching with laughter. "There's much pleasure to be got in making 'em both, and both will give you a large belly. Well, you've started your courses and it's time you knew." Then she wiped her streaming eyes, hugged her niece and told her all she wanted to know about how babies are made, and a great deal more beside. They both bounced up and down on the feather bed tickling each other.

Edgar banged on the bedroom door, as he did every night. "Let me in," he pleaded. "You're telling secrets again."

"Go away!" Julie called. "We're talking of women's affairs and we do not want you."

"Nobody ever does," thought Edgar, returning mournfully to his bed. It was strange. Everyone knew that women were the inferior sex, and yet it was he who battered on their door, he who craved their company.

Soon Jem was kept busy helping with the harvest. Two more of the men from Allerton had died of the smallpox and the farmer was short-handed. In the early morning Julie would see her sweetheart, a pitchfork over his shoulder, going to help build the haywicks. He would wave proudly to her and she knew he was happy. Whenever he could he brought eggs to sell at the kitchen door and then they stole kisses when before old Mrs Lamb, the housekeeper, arrived to pay for them. Once he brought her a posy of fragrant pink and white wild roses gathered from the hedges, and once a ring of plaited grass as a love token.

Then one hot day at the end of summer an old pedlar woman limped to the kitchen door. She looked tired and ill, and her pack was heavy. After Aunt Bess had bought lengths of creamy lace, a paper of pins and some yellow ribbons she poured the old woman a glass of Madeira.

"Fate has been kind to me. Poor soul, I pity you your hard toil on the open road. Take this shilling and may God go with you."

Within a few days Aunt Bess was hot and feverish. Julie cooled her burning forehead with wet cloths, but it made no difference. Soon her aunt was delirious, seeing visions of the devil at the foot of the bed. When the doctor lifted her nightgown he found angry red spots all over her body.

"An old woman with a pedlar's pack was found dying in a ditch outside the village," he told Richard. "She sold her wares here, did she not? Now your sister has the smallpox and will die soon. Your daughter, who attended her, is in great danger unless I treat her at once. Send her to me."

The following weeks were a nightmare for Julie. As her aunt lay dying, Doctor Jason cut her arm and rubbed pus from Bess's sores into the wound. Then she was shut away from the family, bilious from the smell of vinegar that disinfected the room. Her arm itched and she thrashed about on the narrow bed, calling for Jem.

When she recovered Aunt Bess was dead. Julie, weak and wretched, cried bitterly. She had not been able to go to her aunt's funeral, listening from her sickbed to the mournful tolling of the church bell. It rang not only for her aunt but for the miller's wife, the post-boy, the wheelwright and his apprentice, and the rat-catcher and his family, all cut down by the terrible disease.

Julie's father did nothing to help her distress. It was as if a hoar-frost shrouded his wintry heart.

Edgar sat beside his sister and wiped her tear-stained, swollen face. "You have only a few pockmarks," he told her, lifting the curtain of hair that covered her right temple. He stroked the small constellation of pits with his finger. "Though I doubt you will find a husband to marry you now."

The idea seemed to give him pleasure. Julie cried harder than ever, burying her face in the cushion. Edgar stroked her long brown hair and although she did not like it, she felt she had no strength to stop him.

"Sister," he went on softly, "let us be friends. We have only each other to love now."

Julie craved affection. She thought of Jem, whom she had not seen for so long, and she sobbed bitterly.

Edgar bent closer. "Julie, you shared Aunt Bess's bed and told secrets together, but now we can do the same."

That night he came to her room and climbed in beside her.

"Let me put my arms round you," he whispered, breathing fast. "I have no one to love me but you." She was too sad and weak to protest. Before she could stop him he pushed her legs apart with his knee and entered her with a grunt. Afterwards he collapsed, then rolled away from her.

"It was nothing – all the fellows do it, but this must be our secret," he mumbled, wiping himself with a corner of the sheet. Unable to look her in the face he covered her with the quilt and slipped away to his own room, leaving Julie aching and bleeding.

"Aunt Bess," she cried silently into the shadowy

room, "I didn't want it. Why did you have to die? Why were you not here to protect me?"

The next day Edgar crept around the house, avoiding her. If Julie was quieter than ever her father thought it was grief that made her so.

The next month she missed her courses and her breasts hurt. Then she knew with dreadful certainty that she was pregnant with Edgar's child. She was fourteen.

Chapter Three

RUSSIA 1801

With every mile of the flight south Sergei felt more miserable and confused. Why was he being hurried from his home, his father, his schoolfriends – everything and everyone he loved? Was it something to do with the Englishman, the one who had a daughter called Julie, the one who agreed to hide something for his father? And when would he see his father again?

"I know nothing," Platon answered when Sergei questioned him. The old man stroked his beard. "We are all in God's hands, little Master."

"Perhaps it is a holiday," Mashenka suggested, her moon face breaking into a smile. "You'll see, we'll be back in Petersburg with your papa by Easter. Then I'll make you pashka and we shall all be happy again."

Easter had always been a specially joyous time for the household – the exchange of red-painted eggs, the special food, the glorious singing at the church services, the candlelit processions, the cries of "Christ is risen!" and the Easter kisses. But memories of happy times did nothing to stifle Sergei's feeling of dread. His fear was increased when they stopped at an inn to change horses.

"They say Tsar Paul is dead, and heaven be praised, his son Alexander is our new Emperor," the ostler told them. "It's been put about he died of apoplexy." He tapped the side of his pockmarked nose and winked. "But everyone knows he was murdered."

It was clear nobody mourned the dead Tsar.

His grandparents' estate on the River Tamsin in the Ukraine was large and prosperous. Sergei had visited it several times when he was a child. He remembered the beauty of the white porticoed house, the apple and cherry orchards covered in snowy blossom in the spring, the flower gardens that sloped down to the lake, the vineyard, the song of nightingales. He also remembered the stern grandmother who had scolded him for crying when he lost one of his toy soldiers. Now his spirits sank even lower as the troika drove up the long curving drive. He wished with all his heart that he was back in St Petersburg. When would he see again its many canals, the gold and blue of the churches, the elegant summer and winter palaces and his beloved great bronze statue of his hero, Peter the Great?

"He wanted a gateway to the west, Seriozha," his father had told him. "That is why he built our great city. In every way he was a giant of a man."

Sophia Petrovna greeted her grandson without emotion, banishing the two serfs to a log hut beyond the apple orchard. Sergei tried to like his grandmama, but he could not. She seemed to find him a nuisance, rarely speaking to him and then only to correct his manners. He became silent and clumsy. He found he could not eat under her critical eye, and was only at ease with Platon and Mashenka. As often as he could he escaped through the orchard to their small wooden house and together they would talk of his father and of home. Platon sang the mournful songs beloved of all Russians, and old Mashenka cooked him his favourite supper of blinis with sour cream. She mended his breeches when he tore them, so that he did not get into trouble, and when he was sleepy told him wonderful stories. But somehow his grandmother came to hear of his visits. She made it clear she did not approve of him wasting his time with serfs and told him sternly the visits must cease.

Sophia had served for many years as First Lady of the Bedchamber to the Dowager Empress Elizabeth, mother of Tsar Paul. For this service she had been awarded the Order of St.Catherine. Loyalty to the monarchy overrode all her other feelings. Portraits of Peter the Great, the Empress Catherine and the Empress Anna stared down haughtily from the walls. Now too lame from arthritis to travel to St.Petersburg, she lived on her royal memories.

Nikita, her husband and Sergei's grandfather, was often away from home. So it was Sophia who summoned the boy one afternoon to attend her in her sitting room. Standing erect and still as an iron statue, she informed him that his father had been among the group of traitors who had assassinated the Tsar. She added grimly that as a result he had been executed.

"No!" Sergei screamed, rushing at her with clenched fists. "It is not true. He is not dead. My father is an Officer and an honourable man. He would not kill the Tsar. You are a wicked old woman to say such things!"

Pride forbade any emotion to soften Sophia's stony face. She held the boy away from her, and picked up a letter from her writing desk. "Dmitry broke his solemn oath to his Emperor," she said impassively. "It was unfor-givable. From henceforth I have no son and you have no father. He is not to be talked of again."

Disbelief, anger, and at last a terrible grief overwhelmed Sergei. He knew that the Army hated Tsar Paul, but how could his father have killed him! Every night he tried to pray for his father's soul, but he no longer believed in a God who could let such things happen. Under his quilt he wept bitter, scalding tears.

It was as though his old life, his happy childhood, was gone forever. His only friend in this cold, rigid household was his tutor, Marcel Laval. The young Frenchman had been engaged by Sophia after a lengthy interview. Fearful of the new ideas circulating she had expressly forbidden the study of books she thought seditious. However, upstairs in the privacy of the schoolroom Sergei and Marcel were able to discuss the new ideas of liberty, equality and fraternity abroad in the world since the revolution in France. On their walks by the lake and through the meadows they debated how Russia might be governed without corrupt officials, serfdom abolished, the peasants educated and poverty banished. Although Sergei could not bring himself to tell his friend of his father's part in the assassination of Tsar Paul, they even dared to discuss if it would need a revolution in Russia to bring these changes about.

Later Marcel smuggled in stories of the early rebellion of the Cossack Pugachev. Together they read "The Journey from St.Petersburg to Moscow" by Alexander Radischev. Becoming careless, they sang the stirring lament for Sten'ka Razen.

As her arthritis worsened Sophia had taken to using a stick. Suddenly the young men heard its tap-tap outside on the stair. She had heard their singing and now flung open the schoolroom door. Embarrassed, Marcel and Sergei rose and kissed her hand in greeting. At the same time Sergei tried to push the incriminating books out of sight behind his back.

Sophia missed nothing. "Show me those books, if you please."

She examined them in silence. "And this is what you have been teaching my grandson, Monseiur Laval! Lives of traitors such as the rebel Pugachev, who proclaimed himself Peter III. And Radischev, who had the impertinence to say the Tsar should free the serfs and was rightly exiled to Siberia! How dare you!"

Marcel was unabashed. "But Sophia Petrovna, surely such an enlightened person as yourself cannot deny that all men are equal in the sight of God? And thus it follows that the peasants should have the same rights as we have."

The old lady drew herself up. "I will not have someone tainted with such ideas in my house. I should have known better than to employ a Frenchman. You are dismissed. You are to leave at once."

Anger, hot and red, shot through Sergei like a knife. "Grandmama, that is unjust. Marcel is right. Do you not see that the outside world is changing? Mother Russia must change as well, or we shall be left behind."

"Loyalty and respect for one's betters is all that is needed in Russia," she answered icily. "It is a lesson you appear not to have learnt, Sergei."

After gathering up his pens and notebooks the tutor bowed to Sophia. "Farewell, Sophia Petrovna. These books I leave to you, in the hope that you may read them, and perhaps even think a little. A body stiffened by arthritis such as yours is a misfortune, but a mind stiffened by prejudice is a disaster."

It was a speech he had prepared some time before, when he had found that Sophia considered him little better than a servant. Pleased with himself he smiled ironically, bowed and left.

The silence in the stuffy schoolroom was oppressive. Then with a violent gesture Sophia swept the offending books to the floor. "The servants shall burn them," she hissed.

Sergie gathered up the books in a fury. "But Grandmama, think what a disgrace serfdom is to Russia. It cannot be right that a landowner should be able to buy and sell men and women, or have them flogged to death."

"Silence!" Sophia cried. She touched the scarlet ribbon and star of St.Catherine pinned to her large bosom. "You have deliberately disobeyed my orders, in this and in other matters. I have decided that as a punishment you shall join the Army. There you will learn the virtues of loyalty and discipline. I shall speak to General Raevsky tomorrow."

The door closed behind her. Sergei put his head in his hand and wept tears of rage. His only friend had been dismissed, and now he was to be a soldier.

Nikita Davydov, Sophia's husband, was a small, lean man with the brown leathery skin of a peasant. He had arranged his life very agreeably so that he spent most of his time away from his wife. He loved the hunting, shooting and other rural delights of their estate at Orenburg in the foothills of the Ural mountains. He also loved his mistress, Elena, and their three sons.

Now he was on one of his rare visits home. On hearing the sound of sobbing he bustled into the schoolroom to find the cause.

Sniffing and wiping his nose on his cuff, Sergei stammered out the whole story. The old man lifted his grey wig and scratched his head with a pen.

"Here's a to-do. She's a strong woman, your grandmother, and likes her own way. But that's not to say she does not grieve for our son, as I do. Well, dry your eyes and wait for me to think of something. Then we shall pay her a visit. Only remember to look unhappy at whatever I suggest."

Downstairs they found Sophia sitting by the samovar drinking a glass of tea and reading a novel.

"My dear," began Nikita, "it pains me beyond measure to learn Sergei has displeased you."

"The boy needs discipline," said Sophia distantly.

"Of course he does, quite right. And I have devised the severest punishment for his disobedience. He shall spend a year, a cold, hard year, on our estate in the Urals."

Sophia looked at her husband with distaste. "You know I dislike the mountains, Nikita, they are not civilised."

"Of course, my dear, I would not ask you to leave this house where you are needed. No, I alone must be the boy's stern taskmaster. He will have no luxuries such as we enjoy here, but coarse food and rough clothes. He will have to learn to hunt and shoot and fish. It will be the making of him."

Sophia stared. "But the Army..."

"Oh, there will be time enough for that when we return. My dear, what unhappiness it gives me to be away from you, but for the boy's sake I must make this sacrifice."

The old man turned his head and coughed to stifle the spurt of laughter welling up inside him. As for Sergei, he could hardly contain his joy.

That evening his grandfather invited him into his private study. It was a dim, cobwebby room which smelt deliciously of dried plants, earth and tobacco. Scattered over a large table were books on farming, a broken clay pipe, a clock in pieces, a stuffed owl and the skull of a wolf. Hunting guns were propped up in corners, together with rolled-up cloth maps in various states of decay. With a sweep of the arm the old man cleared a space and unrolled one of them. On it he showed Sergei the rivers, the steppes, the tundra, the forests and the mountains of Russia. He stabbed a grimy finger at the barrier of the Ural mountains, to the east of which lay the vastness of Siberia.

The boy leant over the map, memorising its main features as he had memorised the face of the Englishman.

On the evening before he was to leave Sergei stole through the apple orchard to say goodbye to Platon and Mashenka. After embracing they sat down to a supper of borsch and bread followed by his favourite jam suet pudding. They toasted the future and wept a little.

"When I come back from the mountains I shall be fifteen," said Sergei. "Then my grandmama wants me to go into the Army, but I hope I can take you with me. I do not want you to stay here with her."

"Then let us drink to a happy future together, my dear," said Platon, filling their tankards with strong home-brewed beer. "It will be as God and the Tsar wills."

They drank many toasts, talked of Dmitry and wept again. Sergei, not used to the strong beer, later fell asleep with his head in Mashenka's lap.

He dreamed that he was ten years old again, riding his pony Sultan on the frozen River Neva. Steam rose from the animal's warm body and its harness jingled in the clear, cold air. Then they passed the grim bulk of the Peter and Paul Fortress and he was filled with a terrible desolation at the thought of all the prisoners who were shut up behind its forbidding walls.

He woke to find he was not on Sultan's broad back, but on Platon's. The good old man was carrying him back through the moonlit orchard to the house, hoping to get him to his bed before his grandmother found out he had disobeyed her orders and visited them.

It was not until years later that Sergei discovered that they had been seen that night.

His year in the mountains was a happy one. He came to love his Grandfather's mistress Elena and their boys, Vasily, Petya and little Gregory. He learnt to fish, to track and to hunt, and even shot a bear. He danced at village festivals and tried to learn the balalaika. He felt he could live there forever.

Not a day went by, however, when he did not grieve for his father.

Chapter Four

ENGLAND 1802

Julie seized the water jug from her chest-of-drawers in her room and hurled it in a fury at the wall. There was a deafening crash as it shattered into pieces while she damned Edgar to freezing and scorching torments in hell.

Later her rage gave way to panic and she tried everything she could to dislodge the new life in her belly. Aunt Bess had told her that in such cases women jumped off a chair or fell down the stairs. She tried both, but only covered her legs in painful plum-coloured bruises. Her father, sunk in his private anguish, did not notice her pale face and distraught manner. To tell Jem was not to be thought of. In any case he was kept busy on the farm. Edgar kept out of her way, to her relief. Her revulsion was so strong she could not bear to look at him.

It was only when Amy, the kitchen maid, found her vomiting outside the privy one morning that she got any help.

"Ah, young mistress, I see how it is with you." she said, taking her into the kitchen and wiping the girl's damp face.

Julie retched. "What must I do? I dare not tell my father."

"There's a wise woman, Mother Ferry, lives on the common. She has a hovel by the brook near a willow. Go tomorrow night and say I sent you. She has a rough tongue but don't be afeared. You must take a shilling to pay her. I'll say nothing to anyone here."

"I couldn't go alone," said Julie, with a shiver. "I'm afraid of the witches that fly there at night. Will you come with me?"

Amy shook her head. "I can't. Go with your sweetheart, as I did."

Julie looked at her in surprise. Amy's skin was blotched, her front teeth were crooked, and her breath smelt sour, yet she had a sweetheart! And she had once been with child and needed Mother Ferry's help too. Under Aunt Bess's care the household had been so well managed that Julie had never thought of the servants' lives.

"I cannot go with anyone," she answered, guessing that Amy thought Jem was the father.

"Then take a twig of rowan, 'twill be a charm against the evil ones," the girl advised.

The next day was wet and windy. Julie spent it dreading her journey across the dark common, yet willing her father to go to bed. As soon as the grandfather clock in the hall chimed eleven she heard him close his bedroom door. After waiting until she heard him snore, she fastened her dark cloak and put on her boots. Clutching the shilling and the rowan twig she had picked during the day she crept down the stairs. The servants had gone to their beds and Edgar was out, she knew, on one of his mysterious night errands. Once in the shadowy kitchen she lit a lantern with a spill from the fire and then wrenched open the front door.

The wind had risen to a gale and was blowing round the house with a high whistling sound. At once it snatched at her cloak, blowing it over her head. Julie had never ventured out in the dark alone and she stumbled, almost losing the coin clutched in her fist. But dread of carrying her hated brother's child drove her on.

The tiny golden light of the lantern lit her way as she turned south across the park and climbed over a stile into a field. The barley had been cut and the stooks stood dark and sinister, like the corn kings of old. Frightened, Julie kept close to the hedge, trying not to look at the regal figures who called after her, shaking their tasselled crowns.

"These are our dominions. We are the Lords of the earth. We rule the land... " The rest was lost in the shrieking of the gale.

She hurried on, tripping several times in her haste to escape the menacing kings. She flung herself over the next stile into a field of wheat stubble, dropping the branch of rowan in her haste. Beyond this field lay the common. Before the enclosures it had been four times the size, but to her it seemed to stretch as wide and pathless as the sea. With her little light she felt like a lone ship riding the waves in a storm.

As she picked her way among the dark shapes of the furze bushes she found the rowan twig was gone. Suppose the witches got her! She turned back to find it, shuddering with fear.

At the same moment that she knew she would never find the charm, she also realised that she was lost. Which way was the old woman's cottage? She had turned round and round and now everywhere looked the same. Despite the cold Julie felt sweat trickling down her back. Then the wind blew the clouds from the moon, lighting up a pale threadlike track that wandered southwards.

With a gasp of relief she hurried on. After a while the wind died down and in the silence she heard the sound of water babbling over stones. She almost fell down into a hollow where a willow tree grew beside a brook. And there was Mother Ferry's dark hovel.

Suddenly there was an uproar as a flock of geese approached, gobbling loudly and beating their wings. Julie was about to run away when an old woman approached and grabbed her by the arm.

"So you've come," she said in a deep, rusty voice, pushing her into the tumbledown cottage. The floor was of beaten earth, with a fire flickering in a circle of stones in the centre. She motioned Julie to sit on a stool and peered into her face.

Mother Ferry was old and bent, with a cluster of warts on her dirty cheeks. She smelt strongly of fish. When she thrust her face into Julie's it was all the girl could do not to recoil. She looked like a witch and it would not do to offend her.

"Well, what are you waiting for? Hand over the shilling."

Once she had the money she asked Julie how long she had been carrying.

"Highborn or low, you young girls are all the same," she said contemptously. "On your backs as soon as a man looks at you. And I'll wager you've been jumping downstairs and suchlike?"

Julie nodded, biting her lips to keep them from trembling. She watched as the old woman boiled water on the fire, adding juniper, pennyroyal and other dried herbs from a bunch hanging from the thatch. When the brew had cooled she poured the girl a cupful of the syrup and told her to drink. It was black as pitch and tasted foul, but Julie forced it down.

"Well, don't sit there, child," the old woman scolded. "Get up and go home. Things will right themselves tomorrow and then you must rest a while. And say nothing of this to anyone or it will be the worse for you."

Feeling dizzy, Julie took the lantern and stumbled back across the common. The wind was blowing fiercely and clouds were racing across the moon, so that she was afraid of losing the track again in the darkness. Suddenly she was forced to stop, doubled over by violent griping pains in her stomach. She began to retch and with a agonising spasm vomited up a fountain of sour-smelling black mess. As the painful cramps continued she collapsed onto the cold earth, overwhelmed with despair. She had voided Mother Ferry's syrup and it had all been for nothing.

The wind increased in strength, howling and shaking the trees as the darkness seemed to thicken around her. Black clouds, like midnight hags on their broomsticks, hurtled across the inky sky. A sense of desolation overcame her and she began to cry with great racking sobs.

"What will happen to me now? I daren't go home and if I stay here the witches will get me. I shall die and nobody will know or care."

Weak and ill, she curled up, covering herself with her cloak against the cold wind. Around her in the grass she could hear little rustlings of rabbits and mice on their night errands, but there was another unearthly sound borne on the wind. It rose and fell, like a faint human voice.

"Julie, don't be afraid," it sighed, "I am with you. Take heart – wait for me to come..."

She raised her head, listening to the faint call. She knew it was the voice of her child imploring to be born, and a great love welled up in her heart. Like the turning of a tide, all the courage that had been draining away from her began to flow back into her soul. At that moment, alone on the dark common, she stopped being frightened. She would keep her baby and love it forever.

"Julie!" called a voice. A lantern bobbed into view and to her great relief Amy appeared.

"Oh Amy, I'm so glad you've come – "

"Poor girl," said the kitchen maid, helping her to her feet. "I was fearful for you, so I stole out to find you and have been calling for you."

Julie was too preoccupied to ponder Amy's words, although she did so many years later. They linked arms and braved the dark common together. Amy made a face.

"I see Mother Ferry's cordial has not worked, it is all over your boots and you smell like a privy."

"I know. At first I minded, but not any more. I feel so very sick, but it's strange. I feel – changed. My mind is made up. I shall have my baby."

Amy stared at her. "Well, you've got some courage, I'll say that for you. What will you do? How will you live?"

"I shall run way. Promise you'll say nothing."

"Cross my heart and hope to die."

Amy's family had kept cattle on the common and she knew it well, by day. By night she feared the evil ones and had herself brought a twig of rowan for protection. They crossed the field of stubble and then the field of barley keeping their eyes averted in case the dreadful kings demanded homage.

At the door of the house Julie kissed her friend. "Thank you for coming to fetch me home, Amy. Whatever happens, I won't forget you."

Her mind was made up. She would go to Jem. They

must lie together so that he must think the baby was his, then they would get married. Only she must hurry.

As soon as she had tiptoed up to her bedroom Julie threw off her soiled clothes, washed her face and climbed thankfully into bed. At once she was asleep and dreaming she was lost in a strange frozen country, deep in winter snow.

Starting awake, she slid out of bed and went over to the window. A pale sun was rising, and the trees were casting long shadows over the park. Her queer dream melted away, not to be recalled until half a lifetime later. Meanwhile she knew she must pass the day at Starcross so that no one would suspect it was to be her last there.

After eating breakfast with her father she went to her room, packed a small bag and wrote him a letter. In it she told him she was going away and asked him not to try and find her. The rest of the day she spent impatiently waiting for nightfall.

"Goodbye, Father." she said silently as they sat at their quiet supper together. He ate slowly, without speaking. Once or twice he started, staring behind her with haunted eyes. Occasionally he muttered about a Russian boy called Sergei, whom he'd wronged. He spoke about seeing him sitting on the stairs, his bare toes showing beneath his nightshirt. As he lifted his wine glass to drink he started violently, staring behind her into the shadows, addressing someone as "Captain." He did not notice when she rose to return to her room.

Frightened yet elated, she waited for the clock in the hall to strike eleven and for his bedroom door to close. Once more she listened as rain began to drum on the window pane, once more she lit a lantern and stole away. Only this time as she left she whispered her goodbye to her old life.

41

Outside the rain blinded her, so that as she ran she often slipped and fell into the mud. The swaying lantern made her shadow flicker, but was it hers alone – or was she being followed? Not daring to look behind she floundered on across the park to the north, over the fields and into the sleeping, darkened village. There was the road and the river, and there at last was the forge and next to it, Jem's cottage, its slate tiles gleaming in the wet. As she hammered at the door she prayed she would be made welcome.

A sleepy Jem opened the door. His hair was tousled and he was clad only in his nightshirt and breeches. Holding a lantern high he peered down at the small rain-soaked figure.

"B'Jesus, it's Julie. Come in, come in, sweetheart. What are you doing out on such a night?"

He led her into the little kitchen, taking off her sopping cloak and poking the fire into a blaze. "My poor girl," he said, settling her into a chair and kissing her wet cheeks.

Julie kissed him back, her heart overflowing with gratitude. How very handsome he was, and how good he smelled! Now all would be well with her.

"What's this, Jem?"

His mother came down the stairs into the kitchen, her grey hair loose over her shoulders. She had a thin, pinched face, with deepset black eyes. Julie saw no spark of kindliness in them and her heart sank.

"It's Julie Bingham, Mother."

"So I see. And why have you come at this ungodly hour to trouble decent folk, girl?"

"My – my father beats me," Julie lied, her voice trembling. "I'm in mortal fear of him."

Mother Tulley stared at her as though she could see

right into her wicked soul. Tears ran down Julie's cheeks, and this time they were borne of fear.

"Where's the proof? You have no bruises and 'tis the first time I've seen a muddy gown taken as evidence of a beating," the woman said sharply.

"It would be more Christian to help the poor girl get dry than to question her like this," Jem retorted equally sharply. Julie felt there was no affection between mother and son.

"Well, she can't stay here," Mother Tulley went on. "It'll bring us nothing but trouble."

Julie sobbed even harder and clutched at Jem's arm. "Take me away, I do so fear my father will find me."

He bent and kissed her again. "No, indeed he shan't. I'll take you to Granny Forrester's over at Thrushfield. I'll borrow Lewis's mare and we'll be there afore morning."

Mother Tulley turned on him. "You're naught but a boy. Too young for a sweetheart."

"I'm fifteen," said Jem shortly. He draped a sack round his shoulders and went outside to saddle Bridie, the blacksmith's mare. Afraid to meet his mother's scornful gaze Julie covered her face with her hands and forced another sob.

"Leave my boy be," Mother Tulley said sourly. "I need his wages."

It was true, the room was bare and cheerless, and Julie felt a faint prick of conscience. It was a relief when Jem came back. Soon she was mounted behind him on Bridie, her bag tied to the mare's saddle, her arms clasped tight round his waist. Jem's mother, grim-faced, her arms akimbo, stood at the cottage door to watch them go.

Julie never forgot that ride by night. The rain had

stopped and the clouds had drifted away so that over-head the dark sky was filled with a dazzle of silver stars. As they trotted over the fields the moist earth gave off a pungent smell like a rich spice cake. A dappled horse nodded at them over a gate as they passed, and sheep huddled like grey shadows by the hedgerows. Julie had never been so far. Up hills and down into valleys they rode, the farms and fields gilded by the silvery starlight. As Bridie waded through a stream her hooves churned the water into foam until it sparkled like diamonds. On the other side the track turned white with chalk and beech trees replaced the oaks, and then they were out into open country once more. It seemed to Julie that she and Jem were riding to a magical fairy kingdom where they would be happy forever.

At last they rode up a hill to a small hamlet. There were seven cottages set around a greensward and sur-rounded by huge elm trees. Granny Forrester's home was a low whitewashed cottage topped by a sagging thatch. Next to it, shaded by an ancient apple tree, was a muddy sty where a large pig snored contentedly.

The old woman answered their knock, shielding a candle in her thin hand. She was small, with pale wrin-kled cheeks and wispy white hair.

"What ails thee, Jem that you visit at this hour?" she asked, beckoning them in. "Tis not yet day."

"My sweetheart Julie has run away, Granny. Can she bide with you a while?"

Granny Forrester smiled at Julie. "She can and wel-come."

"I'm safe, safe!" thought Julie, thanking her. She was grateful to the old woman for not asking questions. And she liked the little kitchen, which smelt of the dried lavender and mint hanging in bunches from the ceiling.

The small room was warm and clean. Pewter gleamed on the dresser and the firebars shone, reflecting the red and orange flames. There were dried beech leaves in a jug on the windowsill and a yellow and blue rag rug on the beaten earth floor.

As they ate bread and dripping and drank milk the old woman told them that Noah, another of her grandsons, had joined the Army to fight the Frenchies. So there would be a bed for Julie. Jem, she said, could bide in the kitchen by the fire.

With every aching bone in her tired body Julie craved sleep. But she knew she and Jem must make love before the night was past. Now it seemed as if the old woman would never go back to her bed. Julie sat shivering in her shift waiting until she heard gentle snoring. Then she crept down the creaking stairs to the shadowy kitchen.

Jem was awake, lying with his hands behind his head staring at the ceiling. When he saw her he held out his arms.

"My little sweetheart, my darling…"

She slipped under the patchwork quilt, overwhelmed with gratitude.

"My beautiful girl," he murmured, covering her with kisses.

After they had made love he fell asleep, his curly head heavy on her arm. Julie sighed with relief and pleasure. It was all so different from that dreadful time with Edgar. Why had she not had the strength to push her brother away? Well, she would not think of it any more. Now all was well – her baby would have a father and she would have Jem. She stared out of the little window, watching the sky become grey, then flush with pink as the new day, and her new life, began.

The next morning Granny Forrester smiled at them

curled up together under the quilt. "Happen you'll be getting wed, my dears."

"Aye," said Jem proudly. "I'll walk over to see Parson this morning."

Julie remembered her aunt's suitor, who had gone down on his bended knee. Sometime she would tell Jem the story. But this was Jem's proposal of marriage, and it was enough for her.

Chapter Five

ENGLAND 1802

Julie and Jem were married in the little church of St.John over at Foxton, the village two miles from Thrushfield.

Faith, her neighbour, lent Julie a blue gown trimmed with velvet buttons, a gift from her mistress when she left service. For a nosegay Granny twined scarlet hips and briony together and tied them in a bow with a ribbon of her own hand-made white lace. After the simple wedding ceremony they walked home across the bare brown fields to tea. For a bridecake there was Granny's freshly baked seed cake, and to drink healths they had her cowslip wine.

Jem had been to see Mr Elworthy, the farmer at Foxton, and had been taken on as a farmhand in place of Noah, at the usual wage of four shillings a week. With the pig and the vegetable plot, they could manage.

Julie had never been happier. She loved the hamlet with its little green, its great elm trees and flying rooks. The strong clear air was like wine. With the clean washing billowing on the clotheslines on the green the hamlet reminded her of a sailing ship at sea. The past was behind her and, bursting with energy, she almost danced as she worked. Her only worry was that the baby was due in eight month's time and she still had to tell Jem. When she did he picked her up and kissed her, delighted and proud.

"It will be a big strong lad, Julie, who'll work alongside me on the farm."

Although she was relieved that he suspected nothing, she could not help feeling a twinge of alarm. Surely Jem wanted something better for their child? Faith had told her that when they were old enough the hamlet girls went into service and the boys worked on the land. But not her child, she vowed to herself. Her child would have a better future.

At Christmas Jem brought in boughs of holly, rich with shiny red berries, to twine above Granny's picture of King George, and she picked ivy to twist round the candlesticks on the mantel. Granny cooked a big joint of ham and Julie helped her make a plum pudding.

Julie came to love and admire the old woman. She was born in 1722, had been sent into service when she was only ten and had been working ever since. Now eighty she suffered from arthritis, but although her hands were often painful they were never still. No longer able to make the delicate lace she loved she still knitted coarse stockings and rag rugs to sell to the travelling pedlar. She taught Julie how to clean and sew. Best of all, she showed her how to cook and keep house thriftily. A large pot of boiling water was slung from its hook over the fire. Into it went three nets, one containing bacon, another potatoes, with green vegetables in the third. A suet pudding wrapped in a cloth also went into the pot. Julie was always hungry and found this one big meal of the day delicious and filling.

Once a month Jem fetched them water from the well and she and Granny washed the clothes. Although her pregnancy made her slow Julie found great satisfaction in her work. Jem worked long hours on the farm, often returning home wet and cold, and she could see how happy he was in the warmth and comfort of the cottage.

Harry was born in May. A neighbour, Widow Jordan, acted as midwife, while Faith helped with the housework. The fresh air and good plain food meant Julie was blooming with health and her labour was quick. Harry was small, too, which made it easy for her to pass him off as an eighth-month baby. Her only concern was that his mop of black hair grew down into a peak low on his forehead, as Edgar's did.

"Look at the little man," said Widow Jordan admiringly as she placed him in Julie's arms. "A regular little fuzzy-wuzzy."

"He's the very image of my father," Julie told her, quickly smoothing the baby's hair forward over his brow.

The three of them doted on little Harry. Jem loved to dandle him on his knee, however tired he was from his hard work on the farm. Granny rocked the cradle with her foot as she knitted him a shawl. Julie loved to bury her face in his neck, smelling his delicious baby smell and kissing his fingers, whispering "You called to me that night on the common. You wanted to be born."

The life of the hamlet suited her. She enjoyed the rhythm of the seasons – rising early in spring and listening to the birds as they greeted the dawn, delighting in the diamond beads of dew that glittered on the grass, picking cowslips for winemaking, sitting in the meadow making daisy chains for their babies with Faith and her children in summer, gleaning the stubble after the harvest in autumn, seeing the silver-spangled cobwebs on the hedges in winter. She felt she had never noticed the countryside before, and now its beauty filled her with a keen and secret delight.

If Edgar's face occasionally appeared to her when she and Jem made love she quickly dismissed it. Sometimes she remembered her life at Starcross, with the elecution and dancing lessons she had to endure because her father wanted her to be a lady. What would he say if he could see her now? Holding up baby Harry to see the pig, planting vegetables, scrubbing on her knees, tending Granny when she grew too stiff to leave her bed?

As time passed and her father did not come to find her the image of him faded, like the ghost of someone she had known long ago.

Her second child was born in February 1804, another boy, whom they called George. He was a sturdy baby, unlike Harry, and this time he was the image of Jem. Faith had told her she would not conceive while she was breastfeeding him, but to her surprise she found was pregnant again almost at once.

Granny was becoming weaker. Her old bones were so cold that even a brick wrapped in flannel could not warm her. Julie fed her gruel and milk toast and brought bunches of dried lavender to scent her pillow. Jem wrapped her in a shawl and carried her downstairs to sit by the fire where she nursed the children on her lap, mumbling songs from her childhood when the first King George was on the throne of England.

In March they knew she was dying. Julie sat by the old woman's bedside combing her wispy white hair.

"Granny, I'm expecting again," she told her. "It's sooner than we thought but we're happy. Jem and I would dearly like a girl this time."

Granny smiled at her. "I'm happy for thee, my dear. You are a good mother, and a fine wife to Jem."

"I love him, Granny."

"So you should, dearest, for he loves thee well. He

50

works hard and is as honest as the day." Her voice became so faint that Julie had to bend closer. "Did you hear the owl screeching outside the cottage last night? It was telling me that my time has come. I'm not afeared, for I've had a good long life. But there's something I must say to thee – do not thou be as honest as Jem."

"What do you mean, Granny?"

"Why, that you must never tell him that Harry is not his own son. Now do not you be sad, my dear, I've known a good while, and no one is the worse for it."

Julie buried her head in the patchwork quilt. "I was so afraid…"

"Hush, my dear. I love thee and would not see thee unhappy. Thou art closer to me than my own daughter over at Wychwood, who's my flesh and blood. Now dry thine eyes and do not grieve."

Julie blinked away her tears and taking the thin old hand in hers held it to her damp cheek.

Granny Forrester died the next night and was buried in the churchyard beside her husband. Julie and Jem missed her sadly and often took the little ones visit her grave.

This time Julie's pregnancy seemed endless. With no Granny to help she and Jem had to work harder than ever. They rose earlier and went to bed later, so that her back ached and she was always tired. They also missed the little money Granny had made from selling her knitted stockings and rag rugs.

Then one autumn day Jem came home from the farm with good news. Mr Elworthy was so pleased with his skill at the plough that he had entered him into a ploughing contest over at Birchington.

"I'll get a whole guinea if I win, sweetheart," he exclaimed, smiling happily. "Think of that! I'll buy toys for Harry and George and the baby to come, and a shawl for you…"

Julie kissed his eager face. "I know you'll win, Jem, you plough such a straight furrow. I shall be so proud of you."

On the day of the match they rose at five, while it was still pitch dark. Jem polished his boots till they shone and put on his best smock. Julie, slower than ever because of her huge stomach, prepared his midday meal of bread, cheese and onion. Soon the little ones woke and while she fed them Jem filled a tin bottle with cold tea. Then he was off.

Although she did not show it, Julie was troubled. Birchington lay south of the hamlet, five miles nearer to her old home. Suppose her father met Jem? He had not come looking for her and she had always felt safe at Thrushfield, but as she waved goodbye to Jem she felt a shadow fall across her happiness. But it was washing day and she forgot her worries in a cloud of steam. The wind began to blow.

"A good drying day," the women called to each other as they pegged out the damp linen.

At eight months pregnant Julie was too heavy to romp with Harry and George as she used to do. Instead in the afternoon she told them the story of Tom Thumb and sang them Mother Goose rhymes.

When she went outside to bring in the washing she saw to her dismay huge grey clouds like snouty monsters filling the bilious yellow sky. As the north wind blew their jaws gaped, their bodies elongated and their tails were teased out like great fins. She watched them moving in menacing procession across the evening sky and felt their evil.

Jem should have been back from the match by four

o'clock. It began to rain, the wind blew violently and thunder rolled round the darkening sky. Putting a sack over her head she struggled back out through the gusty wind to the garden gate. The elm trees were waving violently and as she watched a large branch cracked and broke off.

There was no sign of Jem. Not wanting to be alone in the storm Julie called on Faith and the two women placed a lighted candle in the window to guide him home.

The hours went by. Julie put the children to bed while Faith made camomile tea. At eight o'clock they heard voices outside. It was Mr Elworthy and his son, Jonas, their usually ruddy faces chalky white.

"'Tis Jem, Missus," said the farmer, looking down at his boots. "Bad news, I fear."

Julie's chest tightened. "What has happened?"

The farmer's son looked at her piteously. "Dead, Missus, dead and that's the truth." His eyes filled with tears.

"It grieves me sorely, Mrs Tulley," went on the farmer, "but as he was coming home the storm toppled one of them beech trees. Jonas, my boy here, he found him with his back broke."

"It's not true," whispered Julie, "No, it cannot be. Not Jem." She felt dizzy and held on to the Faith's arm.

Mr Elworthy twisted his hat in his hands. "I'm mighty sorry, Mrs Tulley. He won the ploughing match and this is a terrible end to it. Here, the guinea's yours."

He laid the coin on the table, anxious to be off. "I'll pay you another visit soon. We'll talk of other matters after the funeral. Come, Jonas. Goodnight to you both."

It could not, must not be true. It was not possible, thought Julie, that Jem was dead, her children fatherless and she herself a widow eight months gone with child. She looked at Jonas, his dirty face streaked with tears.

"Poor lad," she said to herself, "he has found a man dead and thought it was my Jem. Still, it must have been a great shock for him."

She went to the larder, handed the boy a small jam tart and stroked his untidy hair. "Don't weep for Jem, lad, he'll be home soon, you'll see."

"Come along, Jonas," repeated the farmer, looking uneasy

Julie stood watching for Jem by the window, refusing to move in spite of the sorrowful neighbours telling to her to rest. At last Faith asked them to leave her and go home. She sat gazing at Julie's still figure as the night wore away. It was only when the sky began to lighten in the east and Jem had not returned that Julie left her post, knowing he was gone forever.

The hamlet women did what they could for her, cooking, cleaning and caring for the children. Julie passed her days grieving for a life that had been so tragically cut short. Just before the funeral she remembered to send a letter to Jem's mother at Wychwood, but the old woman did not reply, nor did she come to her son's funeral. Jem was buried next to Granny in the little churchyard, mourned by his fellow farm-workers,and the neighbours from the hamlet. Julie said her last good-bye and strewed michaelmas daisies from the garden on his coffin.

Harry asked constantly for his father and the baby kicked savagely. This time her pregnancy gave her no pleasure.

A week after the funeral there was a knock at the cottage door. Mr Elworthy stood outside again, twisting his black hat in his hands.

"Missus," he began, settling into the chair Julie offered him. "I'm deeply sorry to worry you at a time like this."

She sat opposite him, with George asleep on her knee. "Worry me about what, Mr Elworthy?"

His brick-red face turned even darker. "Well, I wondered when you would be moving out of the cottage."

"Move out? Why should I?"

He coughed. "See here, your Jem was a fine boy, none better at the plough-tail. But I have to replace him and I've engaged a young fellow with a family of his own. I need the cottage."

She looked at him blankly. "But this is our home, Mr Elworthy."

"Now, don't tell me you didn't know this place belonged to the farm, Mrs Tulley. It goes with the work. No work, no cottage, and that's a fact."

The colour drained from Julie's face and she shivered.

"Have you never wondered why you paid no rent these three years?" he went on.

She shook her head. If she had thought of it at all she had imagined the place belonged to Granny Forrester, or Noah, and then to Jem.

The farmer rose. "I've heard you come from gentry, my girl. And although you've put on no grand airs since you've come down in the world, I'm told you scorn to curtsey when our Squire and his wife go by."

Julie stared at him. "I see so reason to. And what has that to do with the matter, pray?"

"Mebbe it has somewhat," he replied, his voice hardening. "Now, seeing as you have folk with money, my advice is to get you back home. They will not turn you away in your condition."

"No!" she cried. "I'd rather starve."

"Please yourself," he told her harshly. "You've got somewhere to go to, which is more'n most folks around here. I'll send Jonas with the spring cart one month from today and he will take you and your children back where you came from."

Chapter Six

RUSSIA 1804

When he was fifteen Sergei left his grandfather's estate in the Urals and joined the Pavlograd Hussars, as his grandmother had wished. He had grown during his year in the mountains and was now six feet tall. Even if he had wanted to, he could not forget his father, for each morning he saw in his shaving mirror Dmitry's high cheekbones, long slanting grey eyes and fair hair.

He had learnt that his father and his co-conspirators had not killed Tsar Paul to gain freedom for Russia, but to save the Army from a cruel despot. The Tsar had tried to run the Army on Prussian lines, with constant drilling, harsh discipline and random cruelty. Sergei also heard the story of the Englishman's theft of the money from his father, money intended for the assassins' escape. With it, he knew, his father might have gone abroad and lived. By then Sergei no longer felt any bitterness, but he wondered what made the Englishman succumb to temptation. He also wondered what had happened to him and to the daughter he said he loved.

Sergei was a clumsy and absent-minded soldier, but owing to his time in the Urals, a good marksman. He was surprised to find that he liked Army life and enjoyed the company of his fellow officers. Napoleon was on the march through Europe and they were in a fever to stop him.

In camp Sergei shared a tent with his friends Boris, Ivan and Misha. It was never mentioned, but he realised that his father was a hero to many Russian officers, who had detested Tsar Paul.

In 1805, Sergei's regiment fought against the French army in Poland. At Melk he lost his companions in the confusion of the fighting, and was thrown from his horse at the battle of Amstretton.

His fellow officers laughed and nicknamed him "unlucky Andropov."

"I shall never get used to killing," thought Sergei, as he rode with his regiment into battle at Shön Graben "I shall never make a good soldier like Mischa or Boris or Ivan."

As before, no one knew what was happening. Men shouted orders, others cursed, horses screamed at the smell of gunpowder, muskets were fired and cannon boomed. Suddenly there was a thud and to Sergei's horror a soldier's head, still wearing its yellow shako, flew past him and landed with a sickening splash onto the muddy ground. At once his horse reared, neighing with fright, then bolted. Splattered with blood, earth and his own vomit he hung on to the saddle as the terrified animal raced through the gunsmoke towards the enemy.

"Turn back, you fool, we're retreating!" a Cossack shouted at him above the roaring cannon. Sergei tried to follow but could not control the panicking beast's headlong flight. Then he heard someone shout "Come on, forward with the Lieutenant!" and to his surprise he found himself at the head of a cavalry charge. A group of

French soldiers at a gun emplacement heard the yelling and took to their heels, leaving it to be captured by the Russians. So Sergei became an unwilling hero.

After the battle Sergei learned that Mischa had been killed and that he was to be awarded the cross of St. George for bravery. To the Staff Officers' anger he refused to accept it. Later, at the review of the army the Tsar and the Austrian Emperor rode up and down the assembled ranks stopping occasionally to talk to the men. Sergei wished the parade ground would open up and swallow him.

"My father killed your father," he said to himself, as he watched Alexander riding towards his regiment. The young Tsar was slim and elegant in his tight-fitting Guards uniform and plumed hat. He was the darling of the Army and every soldier hoped to be noticed by their hero.

"And here," said the General, pausing in front of Sergei, "we have the Lieutenant of the Pavlograd Hussars who refused the medal for bravery awarded at Shön Graben." He looked at Sergei with contempt.

"I shall never be made a captain now," Sergei thought ruefully.

The Tsar reined in his grey horse, his blue eyes smiling. "And why was that, Lieutenant? The cross is an honour and reflects well on your regiment."

"It was all a mistake, Sire." Sergei replied, flushing with embarrassment. "If anyone deserves a medal it is my horse. He bolted towards the French."

The Tsar threw back his head and laughed. "Well, you are an honest fellow! Please inform your horse his Emperor awards him an extra ration of fodder. And General, I recommend this young man be promoted to Captain."

Sergei was so surprised he could only mumble his thanks. The General narrowed his eyes, gazing at him with distaste.

To Sergei it was clear that the Tsar cared for his army and was much loved. They nicknamed him "their angel." Everyone knew that he wanted to reform his country, but still nothing changed. Sergei was forced to watch an orderly savagely flogged for stealing five roubles and a young drummer boy shot for running away. It was common knowledge that the quartermasters stole the mens' rations and the paymasters collected for themselves the pay of men killed in battle. Sergei loved his country dearly but hated the corruption he saw everywhere.

At the battle of Austerlitz Sergei's horse was shot from under him and as it fell, screaming, it rolled heavily onto his right arm. The pain was so intense he thought he was going to die, but Ivan galloped up and managed to pull him free. After having his arm set by the Company Surgeon Sergei stayed in camp helping the adjutant. Then one day he forgot to find forage for the horses.

"You're a good fellow, but you're more trouble than you're worth, Andropov," said the Major, with good humour. "For God's sake take some sick leave before our poor beasts starve to death."

As he was packing to stay with Ivan in Moscow he received a letter from Sophia Petrovna telling him that his grandfather had died. He had not been back to the Ukraine since he had left for the mountains, for the place held unhappy memories. But he had been fond of his grandfather and felt it was his duty to visit his grandmother.

It was autumn when he reached the estate on the Tasmin. The white birch trees were spangled with golden leaves and most of the orchard trees were already bare. It still looked beautiful, with its porticoed white house and its terraced garden sloping down to the lake. But something was different. There was a quiet, lifeless feeling everywhere and no servants were to be seen.

As his grandmother was not in her sitting room Sergei clattered upstairs to her bedroom. There he found her lying rigid in her great mahogany bed, propped up against a cushion of ivory-coloured silk, her iron-grey hair hidden under a lace cap. She looked regal, but the room smelt stale and Sergei was reminded uncomfortably of a corpse. Her elderly maid had been feeding her spoonfuls of soup, some of which had dribbled onto the black and red embroidered quilt.

"Grandmama, I have come to pay my respects," said Sergei. "How are you?"

She looked at the tall young man in his Hussar's uniform, her eyes like bright pebbles. "I am as you see."

He shifted uneasily from one foot to the other, feeling as if he was fourteen again. "I was sorry to hear of grandfather's death, Grandmama. I was fond of him."

"It was unfortunate that he died away at Orenburg. But enough of that. I was right about the Army, was I not?"

"Yes, Grandmama. I am not a good soldier, but the life suits me. Has your arthritis become worse, that you are in bed?"

The maid dabbed roughly at the old woman's mouth. "She can do nothing for herself, Your Excellency."

Sophia waved her away impatiently. "I am as I am and do not complain. The Tsar must be very concerned for me, but tell him I accept my fate."

Sergei smiled to himself. Did she really think that in the midst of the war against the French the young Tsar

61

worried about an old woman, or even knew of her existence?

"I will do what I can for you," he said, feeling sorry for her in spite of himself. "But first I want to visit my old friends, the serfs Platon and Mashenka."

"They are not here."

"Not here? Why not?"

He came closer, filled with dread.

"I needed to raise money. They were sent to Omsk, or was it Tomsk? I cannot be expected to remember everything."

Sergei stared at her, filled with a violent, poisonous, hot rage. "You sold them! You sold two loyal, kind old people as if they were cattle! How dare you! You disgust me – you are a monster!"

He clenched his hand onto the hilt of his sword to stop himself striking her.

"They were merely serfs. I cannot see the reason for this fuss. And they were neither loyal or obedient."

"I will kill her," thought Sergei in a fury. "I will run her through, now, this minute."

"So you punished them for comforting me when I was a lonely, unhappy boy grieving for my father. May you rot in hell for what you have done!"

Breathing fast and raging, he turned on his heel and left. At the door he turned. "You know, of course, that Grandfather died with his mistress Elena and their three sons. He loved them all very much."

He hurried downstairs, anxious to be gone. At the door he felt someone clutch his arm. It was the maid, who had followed him.

"Take me with you, Your Excellency. I am trapped here with a hateful old woman. I wish she would die. Let me serve you instead."

Anger had tightened his chest so that he could hardly breathe or speak. He shook the servant's arm away roughly and strode on.

He walked through the orchard and reached the birch wood. The little wooden house where Platon and Mashenka had lived had been pulled down and only the rows of decaying cabbages in the black earth of the vegetable garden showed where they had lived. He sat down, leaning his back against a birch tree, tears running down his cheeks.

He wondered where they were. It was all his fault – if only he hadn't stolen out of a night to be with them! He remembered how they used to wait for him, putting a candle in the window to guide him through the dark orchard. He thought how they had welcomed him, how Mashenka had made him his favourite soup because he could not eat under his grandmother's disapproving eye, how they had sung folk songs together and talked of the old days in Petersburg. He remembered how they had wept together because there was no word from his father and how he had fallen asleep with his head in Mashenka's lap. He had woken to find Platon carrying him to the house on his back through the orchard, with the moonlight glinting on the apples. That night he had dreamed of the firebird.

Why had such simple, good people been treated so cruelly? And why had an honourable man like his father killed his Emperor? Why had the new Tsar still not freed the serfs? He, too, was a good man, yet he did nothing.

Sergei began to nod. He could not solve the problems of life and his anger had exhausted him. His head fell onto his knees As he slept the birch leaves, like fragile golden coins, whispered down into his lap, onto his fair head and all around him.

Many years later Sergei told Julie that while he slept he had dreamed that he could fly high above the branches, looking down on the sleeping Hussar in the enchanted wood as if he was in one of Mashenka's fairy stories. He could see himself leaning against the black and white trunk of a birch tree, his long legs bent, his head fallen on his chest, his shako beside him. Then he soared higher still among the cottony white clouds. Looking down he could see all the vastness of Russia, the forests, the mountains, the steppes, the slow-moving rivers, the gleaming domes of the churches. From below rose up the mingled cries of the peasants, the clanging of the monastery bells, the singing of the Priests, the screams of wounded soldiers.

He woke with the clamour still ringing in his ears.

"I was a different person after that," he told her.

In 1807 Sergei's regiment was present at the historic meeting of Tsar Alexander and Napoleon at Tilsit, by the River Nieman. While the two Emperors discussed peace in the pavilion on the river their troops were able to talk to one another.

"It seems to me," said Boris in their billet one evening after a game of cards, "that these Frenchies are very decent fellows." He helped himself to a sausage from the dish in front of him and leant back in his chair, his boots on the table. "Although of course, Bonaparte can't compare with our own glorious Emperor."

Ivan nodded, pouring his friends glasses of champagne. "This is good, I bought it off the French Quartermaster."

They drank healths to the regiment and to the Tsar.

"You must agree Napoleon Bonaparte is a military genius," Boris went on, holding his glass up to the light. "And see how well he treats his soldiers. The lowliest of 'em can rise through the ranks, and there is no flogging."

"And there are no serfs in France," added Sergei. "The Tsar simply must free ours. The system is barbaric. I know only too well how they suffer from the oppressive landowners."

The fourth cardplayer, Mikhail, jumped to his feet, scattering the cards onto the floor.

"What nonsense you fellows talk," he cried angrily. "The peasants don't want to be free from oppressive landowners. What they want is to be landowners themselves, so they can oppress others. And watch how you criticise our beloved Emperor!"

He rushed out, shouting for his horse. They listened to the jingle of his spurs as he rode off.

Then Boris said quietly, "He is not to be trusted."

Sergei tugged at his fair moustache, frowning. "Mikhail is a perfect example of what is wrong with our country. He will hurry to tell the General. No, we cannot speak freely of liberty, equality and brotherhood, as the French do. So it follows we must speak in secret."

Boris and Ivan nodded and raised their glasses.

"There are many others in the Army who think as we do, my friends," Sergei went on. "I have heard there are societies all over Russia. If you are with me I will sound them out and arrange a secret meeting."

"It will be dangerous work," said Boris. "And we shall need funds."

Sergei nodded. "If I can collect a debt we shall have some funds for our enterprise. Give me your hands on it, my friends."

The three men clasped hands, and the die was cast.

Chapter Seven

ENGLAND 1804

"Papa, Papa!" babbled Harry, as Faith lifted the children into the cart. He was just over a year and a half, already tall for his age. George, a plump nine months, nodded vigorously and stuffed his mouth full of lardy cake.

"No, dears, papa is in heaven," Julie told them, buttoning up their coats against the chilly November day.

"Poor lambs" Faith whispered to Julie "'Tis a sin and a shame to turn you out, and you so near your time. But soon you'll be safe back with your own people, who'll care for you. You'll be a lady again and forget us humble hamlet folk."

"Never, never!" cried Julie, kissing her. "You have been as good a friend to me as I could hope to find. If Jem had lived I would have been happy to stay, but..." She bit her lips to stop herself crying in front of the children.

At last their belongings were stowed in the cart, including a dinner of bread, cold bacon and a bottle of blackberry-leaf tea for the journey. Julie was dismayed to see how few possessions they had. There was the money from selling the pig and the guinea Jem had won, but they had never been able to save.

"Ready, Missus?" asked Jonas, the farmer's son. He stared at her bulging stomach. "I'll go extra careful, see if I don't. Our sheepdog Jess is in pup and I be looking after her, too."

Julie ruffled his hair, smiling wanly at the nine-year old. "You're a good boy, Jonas."

The boy climbed into the driving seat. The men were away working in the fields, but there was a little knot of women outside Julie's door to wave their handkerchiefs in farewell.

Julie waved back, gazing for the last time at the little hamlet with its white-walled thatched cottages gathered round the green. The washing lines were pegged with clean washing which billowed out, blown by the gusty wind. The great elm trees were bare, the rooks were fly-ing and the white feathery clouds were racing in the bright clear air. Nothing had changed and she felt she loved it all.

Then Jonas slapped the reins on the horse's back and the cart trundled down the hill. Harry laughed at the jolting but Julie was in great discomfort.

"It can't be born yet, it can't. I won't have my baby in a cart like a tinker," she worried. "And I hope to God Edgar isn't at home, I couldn't bear it."

The sky turned iron-grey and it become colder. The keen wind whirled the brown autumn leaves high in the air around them. Julie held onto the side of the cart, shiv-ering. How wretched it was to travel back over the same ground she had ridden that night with Jem! They had to pass the great beech tree that had killed him, lying like a fallen giant on the chalky earth. She turned her head away quickly.

There were the same hedges, lanes, fields and farms. Three years ago she had ridden behind her sweetheart, bewitched by the magical, starry night. She recalled the rich smell of the moist black earth, the starry sky, the stream's diamond foam. She remembered how she had clasped Jem round the waist, lost in a dream of safety, love and happiness. It seemed a lifetime ago that she had run away from home, and now she was returning to throw herself on her father's charity. How could her life have changed so quickly because a tree had toppled in a storm?

She was jolted out of her reverie as the cart bumped over the uneven ground. Harry screamed with laughter, but Julie had to stifle a cry as a sudden pain tore through her swollen belly.

"It's starting! Oh, please, please, not yet," she cried silently. She chewed her hand to stop herself groaning aloud. The births of Harry and George had been quick and she had had kindly neighbours to help her. She longed to be in her clean bed in the cottage. Then to her great relief the pain gradually subsided.

She dozed, waking when Jonas drew up the horse and cart, hinting it was time for their dinner. They ate in the shelter of a large oak, then in turn they disappeared to relieve themselves. She changed George's wet napkin while Harry pissed in a high glittering arc to make his little brother gurgle with amusement.

As they resumed their journey the lowering clouds grew inky black and it began to rain. Julie pressed the children to her side and covered them with her cloak. Soon they fell asleep, little George with his thumb in his mouth and Harry leaning against her knee, murmuring in his dream.

The cart rumbled onwards and with every mile Julie

felt more frightened. It seemed as if a cruel hand was reaching in and ripping at her insides. As the pain clawed at her she cried aloud and the boys woke.

"I'm mighty sorry for you, Missus dear," said Jonas. "Take heart, journey's nearly done."

And there was the parish of Wychwood, just as she had left it three years before. There were the farms, fields, common, river, watermill, little shops, church, the Angel tavern, There was the village green, with Mother Tulley's cottage by the forge. And there was the park and Starcross House, its rose-pink walls covered in ivy, with its tall chimneys and gables.

When they reached the door Jonas lifted the boys down and carried her boxes to the door.

"I'll remember you when I say my prayers on Sunday," he mumbled. Julie gave him a penny and kissed his cheek. Then he was gone and with him her last link with her old life.

"Papa!" cried Harry."

"Hush, dear," she murmured, wondering how she could make him understand that he would never see Jem again.

Her pains were now coming regularly. As she knocked at the door she wondered desperately what she would do if no one was at home. After an agonising wait an old woman in a stained apron answered. She stared contemptuously at the bedraggled group before starting to close the door.

"No beggars, Master Edgar won't have 'em," she shrilled.

"Beggars!" Anger exploded in Julie's head like a firecracker. Clasping Harry by the hand and carrying George she pushed past the old woman, who shrieked and ran for Richard.

As Julie stood in the hall she noticed the air of neglect, the dog's mess on the floor, the cobwebs, the dust, the smell of dirt and decay.

Her father came slowly towards them through the shadowy hall, his hand clawing at his chest. Standing by the grandfather clock he saw, not his daughter, but the tall figure of the Captain Andropov.

"Father!" Julie's heart went out to the white-haired, stooping figure. How he had changed! She longed to run into his arms as she had so often done as a child. Richard started. The mist cleared from his brain and for one heartbeat he, too, longed to embrace her. But remembering that God had cursed him for his sin he paused, and the impulse died.

They faced each other. It seemed as if time stood still. It was a moment when their lives could have changed forever. Then the clock struck the hour and the moment passed.

"I mean nothing to him," Julie thought bitterly. Her pains were coming so rapidly that she knew her baby would be born soon. All at once she felt cold but strong, her soul stiffening as though encased in thick ice.

"Father," she said sharply. "I have come home. These are your grandsons. We are wet, tired and hungry. Is there to be no welcome?"

Harry began to whimper and glancing down Julie saw a yellow pool glistening at his feet.

"Never mind, dearest," she comforted him. He clutched her skirt, hiding himself in the folds.

Richard peered at Harry and George as though, thought Julie, they were some kind of strange species.

"I did not expect you to return," he said slowly. "Of course, you must come into the parlour."

The room also had an unpleasant, stale smell. To

Julie's dismay Edgar sprawled before the fire, an empty wineglass dangling from his fingers. A shudder of revulsion and fear went through her. He must never know the result of that dreadful night.

"Your sister has come home," Richard told his son.

Edgar stared at the little group, a sneer on his thin face. "And with her bastards, I see."

Julie's face burned. "How dare you call them bastards, Edgar!" she cried. "Jem and I were married in church…"

As she spoke an even fiercer pain stabbed her, and then another. She quickly sat George on the floor beside his brother and collapsed onto a chair, her hands pressing on her swollen belly. The baby in her womb had not moved since early morning. It could not be long now.

"Two children and one to come. Fast work indeed, sister."

"And one is yours, Edgar," Julie said to herself. "Though you will never know it." She drew Harry to her and brushed his hair over his forehead to hide the telltale likeness. Then another pain dragged at her insides and she cried out. Suddenly a flood of warm liquid drenched her legs and she knew her waters had broken.

Her father appeared neither to hear nor to see her distress. "It is three years since you left, but you sent no word…"

"You ran off like a thief in the night," broke in Edgar. "You preferred a village yokel to me."

Even in her agony Julie knew that her brother's behaviour was rooted in his jealousy.

"I need help…" Julie whispered desperately. "Help me, help me."

Just then a stout, middle-aged woman carrying a

71

lighted lamp came into the parlour. By the bunch of keys dangling at her waist Julie knew she was the housekeeper.

"Why have you not drawn the curtains? You do nothing all day." she scolded the two men, banging the lamp onto the table and wrenching the torn curtains closed.

As the room glowed with light Julie could see how very dirty it was. Plates of half-eaten food lay in pools of grease and puddles of red wine gleamed on the oak floor. A wave of nausea swept over her.

Richard noticed her grimace. "The house has been neglected somewhat since your aunt Bess died. The servants will not stay…"

Edgar jumped to his feet. "Let Julie be our servant, Father! She shall stay here if she put the house to rights." He stood before her triumphantly. "Yes, if we are to feed and clothe you and your brats you shall work to earn your keep."

She was to be a servant in her own home! The bitterness of her humiliation was so strong she could taste it. But they had nowhere else to go and her baby was about to be born. As yet another scalding pain dragged at her insides she nodded and groaned aloud. Harry pressed against her and began to whimper.

The housekeeper hurried across the room to Julie and stood staring at her. Her face was round and doughy, like an uncooked bun, and her eyes were uneven, the left being small and right one large. As Julie looked the woman's right eye drooped in a wink. Julie shuddered.

"Shame on you both," said the housekeeper, "Are you both blind that you cannot see this girl is near her time?"

Richard looked confused. "This girl – she is my

daughter – near her time, did you say? I did not realise – Mistress Wardle, do what is needful, put her to bed ..."

"Put her in one of the servants' rooms," Edgar added spitefully. "That is where she belongs."

The two children wailed loudly as the housekeeper helped Julie from the room.

"They need comforting," said Julie. "They are hungry and tired."

"Never you mind that," the older woman told her, ushering her into one of the small rooms off the kitchen and helping her onto a narrow bed. "I've had five of me own and grandchilder. Now just you bite on this bit of cloth when the pains come." Her eye winked.

Left alone, with the searing contractions becoming more frequent, Julie lay in torment. The cramped room was dirty and the stained sheets smelt sour, as though someone else had just slept in them. Above her head loops and strands of grey cobweb trembled in the draught. Suddenly she heard a scrabbling noise and a large black rat scuttled across the filthy floor. It paused to stare at her with its little beady black eyes and she saw that it, too, was pregnant. It was the final horror and she screamed.

At once Jem appeared, stepping through the wall as lively as ever. He smiled at her.

"Jem," she wailed. "Take me back to Granny's cottage! Do not leave me here alone in squalor among people who do not love me."

He bent over her, smoothing the damp hair plastered to her forehead. "Be brave, my little sweetheart," he murmured, and then melted away.

At once the gloomy room was filled with radiance as Aunt Bess came to the bedside with a candlestick in her plump hand. "Remember, little wench, that it is better to light a candle than to curse the dark." She kissed her niece and dissolved into the sinister figure of Mistress Wardle.

"Now, my girl, you must do your part and push hard. 'Tis about to be born."

After one last agonising contraction, when she felt as if her insides were being torn out, Julie pushed and felt the baby slither from her. At once she burst into a torrent of weeping.

"No need for that noise," said the housekeeper impatiently. "You have a daughter." She cut the pulsating purple cord, wrapped the baby in a cloth, then massaged Julie's belly until the afterbirth came away. Julie held out her arms for her baby, but to her dismay the woman picked up the child and hurried with her to the door.

"Bring her back!" Julie called. "Where were you taking her?"

"A baby must be taken upstairs first so it will rise in the world," the woman told her in a resentful tone, coming back. "But I see I am to get no thanks." She thrust the child at Julie, winked at her and flounced from the room.

"She is nothing but a superstitious old woman," thought Julie, dismissing the housekeeper from her mind. She was exhausted, but overwhelmed with love for her newborn baby. Unlike her sons, who had been red and wrinkled like old men when they were born, her daughter had a smooth pink and white skin, with a fuzz of fine golden hair. When she opened her eyes Julie saw they were a deep violet blue.

Later Harry and George came in to see their little sister. They kissed her and poked her with their fingers.

"Her name is Isabel. That was your grandmama's name," Julie told them, putting her nipple in the baby's tiny pink mouth.

"Papa, papa, papa!" persisted Harry, looking into her face.

"Papa is with the angels, dearest." She longed for him to be happy and promised him that when she was stronger she would make him his favourite suet pudding with treacle.

She craved sleep but she knew she had to keep up her strength. She forced herself to eat the bread and soup brought in by Mistress Wardle, although it was swimming with globules of fat.

At last as night came on and with Isabel nestling beside her, she fell into a deep reviving sleep. At midnight she woke. Through the window she could see Orion shining in the dark sky. The baby stirred and woke and Julie fed her again. She stroked the downy head tenderly.

"Aunt Bess," she cried silently, "come and see my children. I know you would love them. And Jem, we have a beautiful little girl." She gazed longingly at the wall where in her delirium she had seen them. "Come again, come and see her. You left me all alone with three children to care for.... please come back."

But they did not return.

When Julie awoke again the walls of the grimy room were pink with reflected sunrise. The baby snuffled but did not wake and Julie lay staring out of the window, thinking hard. It was clear that she had no one to rely on but herself, and that she was responsible for three other lives. So if she was to be a servant she would be a good one. Never, never, she resolved, would she and the children suffer the dirt and bad food they had been given. She vowed to herself that the boys would go to school and become professional men and that Isabel would be educated and happy and marry well.

She smiled as her thoughts raced on towards the future. But first she would insist on having three rooms that would be hers alone.

As soon as she was strong enough Julie nursed the baby sitting in an old rocking chair in the big kitchen. She cut animals out of paper for Harry and George, who disappeared under the table to play. Then she made a list of work to be done, and put the tasks in order. The housekeeper watched her resentfully. She knew Julie was the Master's daughter, sentenced to be a servant because of her sin. Yet the girl would not obey her as a lower servant should. She hinted that Julie was not grateful for her kindness.

"It's true, she was good to me in her way, but a more slovenly creature I have never seen," Julie thought. "Aunt Bess would never have suffered her dirty ways, nor Granny, neither, though she was as poor as a church mouse. And I do not like her winking right eye."

Julie scrubbed the kitchen table until it was white, then swept and cleaned the room. The next day she polished the copper pans lining the walls and rubbed up the firebars till they shone. Soon the whole room gleamed warmly, the pans winking with sparks of reflected light.

Christmas 1804 came and went. Julie was not able to do much to make it a special day for Harry and George, but she made a plum duff.

Two servants left, including the old woman who had answered the door to her, not liking the new order. With the hard work, feeding Isabel and caring for the boys Julie was always tired. Her legs and back ached. Mistress Wardle became increasingly unpleasant, and Julie longed for a friendly face.

As she feared, each night Edgar knocked at her bedroom door, begging to be let in.

"We were close once, Sis, let us be friends again," he called.

She pushed a chair under the handle, so he could not open it and refused to answer him.

Then one afternoon in spring she had a visitor.

Chapter Eight

ENGLAND 1805

At the kitchen door stood Jem's mother, tall and forbidding as ever.

"I have come to see my grandchildren," she told Julie, "as you have not seen fit to bring them to me."

Julie flushed. "I would have come, but I was brought to bed with the baby. I meant to come and tell you of Jem's sad end. I wrote you a letter, but you did not reply."

Mother Tulley came in, bringing with her a whiff of earth and turnips and tobacco that reminded Julie of Jem. She took off her faded blue bonnet and sat down at the table. Julie sat opposite, the potatoes she had been peeling scattered on the table between them.

"Aye, well you might tell me of his death, seeing that you were the cause of it."

"That is cruel, I was not to blame," Julie cried hotly. "It was an accident and we have both lost someone we loved."

Mother Tulley stared at her with her dark, deepset eyes, which Julie saw were full of a terrible grief. "Aye, I loved him well, though I was never one for kisses and caresses." Her hoarse voice cracked. "Well then, let me see his children."

Julie called the boys, who stood before the gaunt old woman holding hands. She felt in the pocket of her long flowered skirt and gave them each a small wrinkled apple. As they scampered away to eat them she peered into the cradle where Isabel lay asleep, her golden curls spread over the pillow and her thick lashes shading her pink cheeks.

"The boys are handsome, but this baby has the look of a fairy child."

Julie was pleased. No one else had taken any notice of her children, who seemed so beautiful to her.

"The boy Harry is like his father," Mother Tulley went on.

"No, it is George who favours Jem."

The old woman smiled, her white teeth gleaming in her lined brown face. "Oh, my girl, do you take me for a fool? I know well you did not run to my son through the rain at night because of a beating. No, I mean he is the image of your brother Edgar."

Julie gave a shiver.

"Well, what's done is done, my girl. I think perhaps that you and my boy Jem loved each other, and that you were a good wife. Your secret is safe with me, for I'm leaving Wychwood."

"But why?"

"Before most of the common was enclosed I could keep three cows. After the common was took I had but one and that got the staggers and died. Folk said Mistress Wardle had put the evil eye on it. So we fell on hard times. When I lost Jem's wages I took in washing, but still could not pay my rent. Now I am to be turned out."

Julie frowned. "I know what it is to be homeless. I will speak to my father..."

Mother Tulley gave a bitter laugh. "So you do not know it is by your brother Edgar's orders. 'Tis said he's in debt from his gambling folly. And having no wish to end my days in the workhouse, I shall buy me a pedlar's pack and travel the open road."

Impulsively Julie leant across the table and took her mother-in-law's lean brown hand. "It will be a hard life for you. I mind me of the poor pedlar woman who brought the smallpox. Will you sleep in ditches, as she had to, Mother Tulley?"

The older woman's face softened. "No, my bed shall be a barn or a hayrick, for summer is coming. I shall survive, as you will, my girl."

Reaching up, Julie fetched a little box from the mantel. "Please, take this guinea that Jem won at the ploughing. It will serve you for bed and board when it rains."

Mother Tulley bit the coin before putting into her skirt pocket. She fell silent and Julie knew she was sorrowing for her son. To give her a moment alone she brought them both a mug of cider from the brewhouse.

"So you have come down in the world and have to work as a servant?" the old woman said, drinking.

"It is my father and brother's punishment for running away and marrying Jem. I have no choice, but must earn my keep. I am thankful I can cook and clean and sew clothes for the children, for Granny taught me."

Mother Tulley looked out of the window. "Aye, she was a good woman, my mother, and I was a bad, wayward daughter to her. Did she speak of me afore she died?"

"Often," lied Julie, "and with great love."

This time it was the older woman who reached

across and clasped her daughter-in-law's hand. "The open road may be hard, but my heart will be lighter for knowing that."

Isabel woke and began to whimper with hunger. Julie picked her up and opening her bodice, began to feed her. Mother Tulley touched the golden head with unexpected tenderness.

"I did not expect kindness from you, Jem's wife. I have nothing to give you in return. But here is something to think on. How has Mistress Wardle saved enough money these three years to pay for her boy's apprenticeship to the baker? And how is it, daughter, that she has waxed so fat and the goods in your father's house grown so very thin?"

Julie warmed to the old woman. "Thank you, it has been a great puzzle to me. I have never liked or trusted her. But will you not stay with me here? You called me daughter, and I would wish to be that to you."

Mother Tulley's dark eyes glowed. "I cannot, but I will be a friend to you and yours. I have not had much affection in my life, child, and I am glad of it now." She drained her mug and wiped her mouth with the back of her hand. "Tell me, did your brother force you?"

Julie bit her lip. "N-no. I think now I could have fought him harder, but I was ill and grieving sorely for my Aunt."

"You were a child. Does he trouble you still?"

"Every night since I have been at Starcross he has tried to share my bed. I cannot rest for fear he will break my door down."

The old woman nodded. "Well, he will not do so for much longer, that I can promise. Now, farewell, my daughter."

After she had gone Julie felt she was no longer alone.

The next day she waited until she saw her father and Edgar ride out through the village. Then, notebook in hand she and the boys inspected the house. When her father had first bought Starcross she had been a careless girl who gave no thought to the running of it. Now in each room she noted down the signs of neglect and decay. Dust flew out whenever she touched the hangings. She found candle-ends nibbled by mice and in one bedroom she retched on finding an unemptied chamber pot. Everywhere stank of stale food and dirty clothes. Worse still, the great linen press was almost empty and in the dining room most of the silver cutlery was missing.

How had her father not noticed?

The next day, as she was bathing Isabel before the fire, Richard came into the kitchen. He looked ill and tired, older than his years, so changed from the affectionate father who had sailed away to foreign lands.

"You have done well," he told her, peering vaguely round at the shining pots glinting in the firelight.

"And you have not," Julie retorted sharply. "You have been robbed these three years and live in squalor. I should be ashamed to do so."

He looked at her sadly. "Ah, times are changed indeed. Now Edgar gambles away our wealth. He does not manage our affairs well..."

"He turns decent folk from their homes," said Julie furiously, drying the baby. "And as to money, you have seen fit to make me a servant in my house. Give me wages then, and money to replace the things you have been robbed of. And I must be free to engage and dismiss the servants..."

He nodded. "Do as you please. Place all bills on my desk and I will settle them."

Isabel held out her little arms to her grandfather, smiling. Richard touched her cheek.

"Your child is beautiful, as your mother was."

"I have called her Isabel, after my mother. Do you wish to see Harry and George?"

"Not now. I see them playing from the window."

He turned to go. Nettled by his lack of interest in her beloved boys Julie sprang up and barred the way.

"Father," she said fiercely, "there is another matter. I know I am not welcome in the dining room or parlour, having sunk low. But these are my rooms. You in turn are not welcome here unless I ask you."

He stared at her dully. Was this hard, determined woman his daughter? Well, if she had altered it was his own fault. If only he had not become a thief, cursed of God. Once more his mind clouded and he saw the hanged man before him.

"Julie," he began in a faltering voice, "He is here, in this room. He was an Officer in St Petersburg – I did it on an impulse – he had a handsome son your age who loved him, a good boy, Sergei, who sat on the stairs in his nightshirt – his toes were bare I remember – yet I did it so you all could live in comfort, and now God has punished me – "

"Father, your mind is wandering – "

"Mama, Mama, me and George are horses!" shouted Harry as he and his brother galloped into the kitchen and cannoned into her legs. To save herself from falling she sat down and when she looked up her father had gone.

Armed with her father's permission to dismiss the servants, Julie waited until Mistress Wardle came into the kitchen. She looked at Julie and her right eye drooped. Then without a word she filled a basket with tea, cake and a loaf from the larder. At the kitchen door she handed the basket to her little grandchild, Fanny. Julie had often seen the red-haired little urchin calling for her grandmother, but had thought nothing of it. Now she followed the child and looked into the basket. Hidden under the loaf were the last of her silver spoons.

Bracing herself, for the woman was old enough to be her mother, Julie confronted the housekeeper.

"Mistress Wardle, you were kind to me when I came home, and for that I thank you. But I know that you have robbed this house the three years I was gone. Linen and silver are missing. You have grown fat and prosperous and paid for your boy's apprenticeship – "

"How dare you accuse me!" The housekeeper began to sweat, her face flushed poppy-red and her large eye winked, making her look more sinister than ever. "You slander me, girl, and I will make you eat your words!"

She advanced and thrust her face into Julie's, who had to force herself to stand her ground.

"Show me your household accounts, then."

Attracted by the shouting, Lucy, Jane and William, three of the other servants, sidled into the kitchen and stood by the door watching curiously. Harry and George disappeared under the table.

"I know nothing of accounts," the woman blustered. "If ought is missing then robbers must have broke in and stolen it. It's a mercy we weren't all murdered in our beds…"

Julie drew herself up and took a deep breath to give herself courage. "I will not call the constable, Mistress Wardle, because you helped me when I was in labour, but you are to leave the house at the end of the day and come here no more."

"You can prove nothing!" screamed the housekeeper.

Julie looked at her with contempt. "Not only are you a thief, but you are also a sloven." She laid the three silver spoons on the table in front of her.

"My curse on you!" Mistress Wardle shouted. "You have dared to call me a thief. You have dismissed and shamed me before the lower servants. I shall not forget, and I promise that you will live to regret it." She tore the keys from her girdle, threw them onto the table and flounced from the room.

Fanny burst into frightened sobs, her tears making pale rivulets down her dirty face. Julie had forgotten the children were still in the kitchen.

She dropped to her knees to comfort the child. "Don't cry, little Fanny, it is not your fault. I am not cross with you."

She wiped the little girl's face clean with a corner of her apron. She thought how very pretty she would be if only she were not so filthy, for she had thick red hair and large eyes the colour of dark honey. Julie filled her hands with raisins from the larder. Fanny sniffed and wiped her nose on her ragged sleeve before sharing the raisins with the eager little boys.

"Can I see your baby, Missus?" she asked Julie, who nodded.

The child leant over the cradle and stroked Isabel's cheek. "She's like the little folk, the fairies I seed on the hill." she said softly, before joining the little boys to play.

All the strength drained from Julie's body. After sending the peeping servants back to work she sat down and blinked away her tears. But it was a victory. When Mistress Wardle had left the house for the last time that evening she felt stronger than before.

Now she wore the keys at her own waist. She engaged new servants and made a list of their duties.

One by one the rooms were cleaned and disinfected with vinegar. She bought linen and engaged a sewing woman to hem them into sheets. She cooked the meals and when she sat down to rest she sewed clothes for the children.

She avoided Edgar and her father, serving them their food in the dining room and leaving the room quickly. Then one afternoon Edgar paid her a visit.

Julie and the boys had been playing and singing "Ride a cock-horse," but at once she sent them to play outside. Edgar looked round. "You have made yourself mighty snug. I vow you are more comfortable here than we are in the parlour."

"That is of no interest to me."

"I came to see your infant. Is that not a friendly thing to do?"

Julie looked at him with revulsion. He was thinner than ever, his chin was unshaven and his eyes were red. She knew from the smell of his breath that he had been drinking.

"You are not welcome here, Edgar. Please leave."

He straddled a chair. "We were close once, Julie, very close, and we could be again."

"I cannot bear the sight of you," cried Julie, picking up a jug of water ready to throw at his head. "I cannot bear it that you try to come to my bed."

He jumped up, shielding his face with his arms. "Do not be so hasty. I meant that we could be friends as we were when we were children. I have no companions. The boys at school did not like me, though I don't know why."

She raised the jug. "Go away!"

"I did you no harm, sister. Yet you ran off with that simpleton, when it was I who loved you…"

Shaking with rage Julie advanced. "Don't dare speak of Jem!"

He went to the door and his voice turned into a whine. "Well then, during the time you were married you and Jem must have put a little money by. I wish to borrow some, for I'm in debt and being chased by creditors."

"They can put you in a debtors' prison for all I care. You are hated everywhere, Edgar, and by me most of all."

His haggard face flushed dark crimson. "Hell and damnation then!" he shouted.

Julie threw the water over him. He staggered from the kitchen, the water streaming down his face and mingling with his tears.

It was another victory, but it gave her no pleasure to defeat someone she despised. Nevertheless he still had the power to ruin her if he told of their incest, for she had no doubt that she would be blamed. And there was the ever-present danger he would realise Harry was his, and take him away from her. If only he would leave and never come back!

In October news came of Nelson's great victory at Trafalgar, and of his death. There was dancing on the green, games, races, wrestling and cockfighting. Edgar as usual attended a fight being held in a barn over at Allerton. When he returned that evening his face was grey, his breath stank and his bowels were in a flux. As a result he spent his time either in the privy or on his chamber pot. He cursed the old pedlar woman at the cockfight who had sold him the game pie. She was tall and thin as a broomstick, he moaned, and from under her old blue bonnet she had stared at him with the black eyes of a witch.

Julie told Edgar sharply that he was talking nonsense, but she secretly rejoiced that Mother Tulley had kept her promise to protect her.

With her brother ill Julie was able to run the house and care for the children in peace.

Then a week later everything changed. A wind sprang up, sending a large fall of soot down the kitchen chimney. Some flakes fell into the beef stew and the rest of it almost smothered the fire. Among the mess of soot on the coals Julie noticed a lump the size of a crab apple. Curious, she shook off the loose black powder. At first she thought it was a crudely made toy, then to her horror she saw what it was – the roughly made model of a baby in a cradle. And that piercing the baby's heart was a long, sharp thorn.

Terror-stricken and shuddering she flung the filthy object from her and sank to the floor weeping. She knew that Mistress Wardle had taken her revenge by putting a curse on baby Isabel.

Chapter Nine

RUSSIA 1807-1825

As soon as he could take leave after the meeting of the Emperors at Tilsit, Sergei sought out other secret liberal groups. They met in country houses, often under the pretence of a birthday party or name-day to avoid suspicion. He also searched for his beloved serfs Platon and Mashenka, but to his distress could find no trace of them.

Meanwhile Napoleon, having invaded Spain, continued his drive through Europe. In 1812 he invaded Russia. Sergei and his fellow officers, however much they wanted reform, then felt a great upwelling of patriotic feeling for their country and their Tsar.

Sergei fought at the battle of Borodino. Once more he was thrown from his horse, injuring his back. While he was recovering from his wound in the Surgeon's tent his skin erupted in boils due to the poor food. To add to his misery he heard the terrible news that Napoleon was in Moscow.

By the time the French retreated from Moscow, leaving it in flames, Sergei's health had improved. He was able to rejoin his regiment to harry the Grand Army from Russia. Abandoned by Napoleon, hungry and despairing, the French soldiers struggled homewards through the cold winter weather.

As his regiment pursued them Sergei thought of his tutor Marcel. He wondered if his friend was one of the hundreds of corpses they found half buried in the snow. He peered at the pale dead faces cobwebbed with frost and felt he hated all war.

In 1815, while spending his leave with his friend Boris at Kiev they heard the good news of Napoleon's defeat at Waterloo. After drinking to Wellington's victory Boris's father by chance mentioned the owner of a near-by estate, whom he disliked. His name was Mihail Rachinskly and he was notorious for buying old serfs and working them to death. It was said that he personally enjoyed watching the punishments meted out to captured runaways.

Sergei's heart gave a lurch. Platon and Mashenka had disappeared many years ago, but he had never given up hope of finding them. He saddled his chestnut mare Dancer and rode over at once to the estate. It was large but neglected and the peasants he saw working in the fields looked ill-kempt and surly.

Rachinsky was a tall, heavy man, with an untidy beard and narrow eyes. He confronted Sergei in his stable-yard, a large black dog at his heels and a riding whip in his hand.

"Yes, I remember them. I bought them, back in '05," he told Sergei. His eyes flashed angrily. "It was a bad bargain. Like all peasants they were too lazy to work and showed no respect for their betters."

"Ah, their betters!" echoed Sergei.

Rachinsky ignored the irony. "They refused to be parted. Such airs they gave themselves, as though they had delicate feelings! The old man was a coward, of course. At the very mention of a flogging he and his fool of a wife took themselves off."

The expression of disgust on Sergei's face enraged him.

"Serfs expect the whip, they will not work without it," he shouted. "It's people like you with your stupid liberal ideas who are ruining Russia. I have nothing more to say to you. You can go now. Good-day!"

As Sergei was about to ride away a young man stepped out from the shadow of the stable and caught hold of Dancer's bridle.

"Wait, Your Excellency, I think your horse is lame."

"No, she is not," Sergei replied, puzzled.

"Please," persisted the man in a whisper, "I beg you, dismount and take a look. I have something to tell you, and I think we are being watched."

Sergei did as he was asked, and together they bent down to examine Dancer's right foreleg.

"My name is Igor Repin, Your Excellency. I heard you speak to the master about Platon and his wife. I am not a bad man, but the old couple were too weak to work and, God forgive me, I could do nothing to help them."

"God damn all serfdom, Igor."

"Shh, Your Excellency, the master spies on us all. He suspects me of having liberal thoughts and I am in danger. But look for your friends in Nizhni-Novgorod, at the time of the great fair. Seek out Katya Federovna Trepov, and may she and God help you find them."

"You are a brave man and I thank you," said Sergei, giving him a handful of roubles. He spurred Dancer on and rode away, glad to be leaving a place of such cruelty. He did not notice Rachinsky emerging from one of the horse's stalls. He could not know that he and Igor would meet again half a world away.

91

"How can Platon and Mashenka survive?" he wondered in despair.

He arrived at the city of Nizhni-Novgorod in August. The annual fair was the greatest in Russia. It drew merchants from many countries to buy and sell in the narrow alleyways. It was very crowded and Sergei felt stifled by the heat, the smell of cooking and unwashed humanity. To cool down he limped to the bank of the river Oka. His right boot was too tight and he cursed the bootmaker who had skimped his work.

The sun glinted and danced on the water. It was crowded with boats, gay with coloured flags, carved and painted with pictures of saints in gold and silver. He noticed that some of the Russian barges bore names such as *The Princess Peerless, The Tsar Sultan, The Princess Olga* and the owners' names, Lensky or Trepov.

"Katya Trepov!" Sergei said to himself as he set off to visit her "So this woman belongs to a wealthy family."

Her house, sited on a hill above the river, was one of the largest in the city. It stood in a well-kept garden shaded with birch trees, its pale yellow walls, white window frames and door giving it a look of cool elegance. After presenting his card Sergei was shown into the richly furnished drawing room by a young, handsome footman in blue livery.

A faint smell of perfumed cigar smoke lingered in the air and he guessed that Madame Trepov's husband must be at home. While he waited for her to arrive he looked round the room. It was crowded with delicate ornaments of glass and procelain, elaborately dressed dolls and spindly walnut tables bearing silver boxes of cigars and sweets. On one of the walls he recognised an icon by Anton Rublev. He was admiring it when he heard the rustle of a silk skirt.

Katya Federovna Trepov was a plump, middle-aged woman, with bright black eyes and thick ringletted hair piled high in the French fashion. She was dressed in a plum-coloured gown and moved in a cloud of French perfume.

"So, Captain of Hussars, please be seated and tell me your business" she said in a low, throaty voice, fanning herself vigorously.

"I – your name was given to me, Madame Trepov –' began Sergei. Sweat ran down his neck into his collar and his foot throbbed. He badly wanted to take his boot off. "The fact is, I am looking for two runaway serfs."

She put her head on one side like an inquisitive bird. "And why do you think I can help you? No, wait, we must have some tea before I expire from thirst." She rang for the footman and ordered tea and cakes. The tray and the silver samovar were brought in by two more handsome servants.

"The tea, Empress," one of the footmen announced, shooting a look of dislike at Sergei.

"Thank you. Now leave us, Ivan, you silly boy," Katya answered smiling, dismissing him with a wave of her lacy fan.

The silver samovar hissed little jets of steam. "Do you know, I think Ivan is jealous." she told him, smiling. She made the tea, passing a glass to Sergei together with a cut-glass dish of jam. "Now, Captain, pray continue."

She listened in silence as Sergei told her of his search for Platon and Mashenka. When he reached the part where the old man was threatened with a flogging he found to his embarrassment that his eyes had filled with tears. They hung on his lashes, refracting the sunlit room into a thousand coloured rays.

"I beg your pardon, Madame Trepov," he stammered, brushing them away with the back of his hand.

To his surprise she rose and put a plump be-ringed hand on his arm. "Captain Andropov, your tears do you credit. Up to this moment I feared you might be a Government informer trying to earn a bounty. But an informer does not weep for his prey, and now I feel I can trust you. This evening you shall dine with me and my guests, and then later we will talk more of this matter."

The dinner guests were ancient relatives of Katya's, her old nurse, a grey-bearded travelling priest, business acquaintances and neighbours. The meal, served in the hot, over-furnished dining room, was rich and indigestible. Beluga caviar, pickled cucumber, stewed mushrooms and smoked salmon were followed by celery soup, little patties, a large sturgeon and roast lamb and Limburg cheese. Glasses were constantly replenished with expensive Hungarian wine. The last course was a towering edifice of ice cream, cream and fruit.

Sergei pushed his food round his plate. He had over-eaten, and was feeling uncomfortably hot. He looked over at his hostess, dressed in a dark green gown with her white shoulders bare, and saw she was eating everything with great relish. There was still no sign of her husband.

The talk, over the coffee in the drawing room, ranged from Napoleon's defeat at Waterloo to a barge that had sunk in the river. The merchants agreed about the laziness of the serfs working on the boats. They were, they said, only interested in filling their stomachs and getting roaring drunk.

"No serf is happy without a master," exclaimed a pot-bellied barge owner. "That is our Russian character, to know our place. I have a hundred souls who all love me and call me their father."

"And I'm sure they call you other names when you cannot hear them," Sergei wanted to shout. Indigestion and a painful right foot made him irritable and it was all he could do to keep his mouth shut. With growing impatience he waited for the guests to leave.

When the last one had gone and the old aunts and uncles had retired to bed, Katya rang for brandy and cigars.

"I could not help seeing your anger," she said, "and I was pleased you kept your feelings to yourself. It proves that you are one of us."

The tray was brought in by the young footman she called Ivan. As he put down the bottle of brandy he bent over her, his oiled curls brushing her cheek.

"Will the Empress need me to massage her feet tonight?" he whispered.

She tapped him with her fan. "No, my dear, not tonight. Don't be so impatient."

To Sergei's surprise she lit a long thin cigar and drew on it with obvious pleasure. With a smile she watched a thin skein of aromatic blue smoke curl up towards the elaborately plastered rose on the ceiling. "They do not call me Empress Catherine for nothing, Captain. I follow her royal example and have many lovers. Do I shock you?"

"No," lied Sergei, thinking that this explained the familiar behaviour of the footmen. "Perhaps a little surprised that you have told me. Your husband is away, then?"

"Dead."

"I am sorry to hear it."

"And I am not. Bogdan Trepov was a nasty old man, grasping and cruel. My father chose him, not I. We women are much like serfs, you see, we have no control over our own lives. Yes, the best thing Bogdan ever did was to slip off a gangplank into the Volga. He got rich by treading down those who stood in his way and he ruined many of his friends. Now I run the business and I try to put right some of his wrongs by helping others."

Sergei began to like Katya. She pleased herself, drank, smoked and spoke her mind.

When she was sure the house was quiet she rose and beckoned him to follow her. To his surprise she led him up a marble staircase to her large bedroom. Dark grape-coloured curtains embroidered with gold thread hung at the windows and round the vast fourposter bed. Sergei hesitated at the door.

"Don't be bashful, Captain." she told him, "but help me with these." She opened a big oak chest and after rummaging among some stiffly beaded gowns and head-dresses lifted out two leatherbound books. Sergei helped carry them to a desk by the window, limping.

"Why do you keep your accounts here?"

She laughed. "It would be a brave man who would dare to look in my bedchamber for evidence of runaway serfs."

In the books were records of her business. Every voyage of every barge, the cargo, the names of the crew, the destination and the date of unloading, the cash transactions, were all written in her firm hand. Sergei followed her plump ringed forefinger as she ran it down the rows.

"Our wonderful river system is their secret escape road. Here, do you see this mark beside the name of *The Vassilisa*? It means a fugitive was hidden aboard. And here I have marked a star at his point of disembarcation. That is as far as our knowledge of a runaway goes, unless he makes contact with the captain of another of our vessels. He must know the password, and of course we change those often to avoid it being discovered."

"Are the runaways ever caught?"

"Unfortunately, yes. I cannot bear to dwell of the fate of a captured runaway serf, but I remember them in my prayers."

Sergei saw other marks beside vessels sailing westwards. "What are these?" he asked idly.

Katya shot him a sideways look out of her dark eyes. "I trust you, so I will tell you. We also help political exiles escape from Siberia. It is hard and dangerous for them, they have but a short time to reach one of our barges before the rivers freeze over, and only a few of the poor souls get home."

Suddenly her finger stopped at a smudged line. "Captain, I have found a Platon and Mashenka Uvarov. The old couple arrived here in Novgorod five years ago at fair time. Fugitives are more easily hidden in a crowd. See here, they were to be smuggled aboard *The Empress Sophia* bound for Astrakhan on the Caspian – oh, my poor fellow!"

Sergei felt his heart constrict. "What is it?"

"This red spot shows that someone informed on them. Yes, I do recall them now, it was so sad. They got wind of the danger and vanished. What happened to them and where they went I cannot tell."

He rose and limped to the window, gazing down at the flaring lights of the fair below. The pain in his heart was intense, as though someone had cut open his chest and torn it out. He knew that he would never see them again. They had disappeared, lost somewhere in the vastness of Russia.

"Perhaps God will care for them," Katya murmured.

When Sergei said nothing she took him by the arm

and led him to the bed. "You are unhappy, my Captain of Hussars, and I shall comfort you. Did you notice how jealous my young men were of you? It is because you are tall and handsome. So let us give them a reason to be jealous. Come and be happy."

Sergei was panic-stricken. He was wretched, he felt hot and sweaty and his foot was agonisingly painful. Making love was the last thing on his mind. But Katya, with swift practised movements, had already removed her bodice and skirt, revealing a vast lacy shift. Surprisingly agile, she flung herself onto the bed and pulled him on top of her.

Sergei tried his best, but it was no use. For all her efforts he could not get an erection with a woman he hardly knew, who did not attract him, who had a strong musky smell, and moreover was old enough to be his mother.

"So the little Hussar will not obey orders and stand to attention."

He suspected she was laughing at him. "I – I am sorry," he stammered. "I am a failure, as I am in most things. And I am in pain from my foot."

She sat up. "No matter. I shall see to your wound and then we shall talk together." She burst out laughing. "Do not look so relieved, my friend, it is not flattering to me."

She examined his blistered foot and after applying a little fragrant yellow ointment bandaged it with capable hands. Sergei kissed her gratefully. Later they lay together on the bed drinking brandy while Sergei told her how Platon and Mashenka had been like beloved grandparents to him. "And shall I tell you what pains me at this moment?"

"What, Captain of Hussars?"

He sat up and put his head in his hands. "It is that

you knew Platon and Mashenka's name, Uvarov. You see, all the years they cared for me I never knew they had one. And I never asked. Katya Federovna, I am no better than the serf-owners we both despise."

She patted his hand. "I am sure they did not mind, Captain, because they loved you. Now we have talked enough. I am going to pack you off to bed in the next room. However, I do not intend to spend the night alone. Before you go please ring for Ivan."

Relieved, Sergei lay awake in the comfortable four-poster bed thinking of the past. If only he hadn't disobeyed his grandmother and sought the serfs' company. If only she had not punished them for disobeying her, if only she had not been so cruel, if only she had not had the power of life or death over her serfs...

He slept at last and dreamed of the Englishman, Richard Bingham, and of the daughter he loved.

After they had breakfasted Katya sent to the fair for a pair of soft moccasins and had a pair of boots made for him from the finest leather. Comfortable at last, Sergei sat smoking one of her husband's long clay pipes, his foot propped up on an embroidered footstool.

"My dear Hussar," said Katya, sipping coffee from an eggshell-thin porcelain cup, "it is as well we did not make love last night. For then you would have been just another handsome boy and been forgotten. But now we can be friends."

They talked all day, discovering that they had mutual acquaintances among the liberals, including the poet Alexander Pushkin. They admired his stirring poetry, but agreed he was too indiscreet to be trusted with any of the society's secrets.

Later, using her name-day as a cover, Katya arranged a meeting of the society where Sergei met the leaders,

Pavel Pestel and Alexander Muraviev. The two men were fiery idealists. Pestel, in particular, argued not only for the end of serfdom and a free Press, but for the abolition of the monarchy and a republican government.

When they had left Katya warned Sergei against Pestel. "Be careful, my friend," she said, "Pavel wants to be another Napoleon. Violence is not the way."

Sergei thought of his father. "Perhaps violence is the only way to bring change, Katya. Tonight Pestel asked me to be part of his inner circle. He wants me to be their treasurer and collect funds for the coming revolution. I am sorry to leave here, but I must go tomorrow."

After they had said an affectionate goodbye Sergei returned to his regiment and did not meet Katya again for many years. However, they wrote regularly, using a code, as they knew letters were opened and read. He did not love her, but the thought of her gaiety and courage warmed his heart.

Chapter Ten

ENGLAND 1805–1824

Although Julie did not see Mistress Wardle for many years she never forgot the housekeeper's terrible curse and her fear for her little daughter made her keep the child close to her.

Isabel was not affectionate like Harry and George. She disliked being kissed or caressed, sliding down from her mother's lap to toddle after her brothers. To Julie's sorrow she would only come to her when she was tired or hurt.

"She is too pretty for her own good," worried Julie, watching the child posturing before the mirror. Isabel's eyes were a deep violet-blue fringed by thick black lashes, and her fair hair gleamed like the finest gold silk. As soon as she could walk she would hold out her little skirts and dance, singing to herself in a sweet, pure voice and curtseying to imaginary partners. Fearful of the child's vanity Julie would always call her to come and lay the table or learn her letters.

To her dismay Harry grew more and more like Edgar, and she was adamant that his hair was brushed over his forehead to hide the telltale widow's peak. He was a delicate boy, but he was quick to learn. George was sturdier, slower at his lessons but mischievous, making her laugh with his tricks. She wanted them to be happy but when she saw the three children playing contentedly together she felt unwanted, knowing this was foolish.

Julie worked hard. When she was not cooking, making their clothes or ordering the household she dug and planted a garden so that they could all have fresh vegetables to eat. The next year she planted six apple, pear and cherry trees beyond the garden so they could have fresh fruit.

Under her care the house bloomed as it had in Aunt Bess's time. The furniture gleamed with beeswax polish and the presses were full of lavender-scented linen. Julie was proud of her skills, but her bitterness at her lowly position as a servant made her avoid her father. When the children played outside in the garden she often saw him watching them from the window. But they did not enter the library, parlour or dining room, keeping to the three rooms she had taken as theirs.

A few years after her arrival back at Starcross Edgar left home. His talents were wasted in a such dull place such as Wychwood, he told his father, and he meant to make his fortune in London. All he needed was some money. Julie was relieved to see him go.

Amy Finch had married Tom and left the parish while she was at Thrushfield. As a girl at Starcross Julie had not been free to make friends and now found it difficult to make new ones. She knew this was because of her position in society, neither servant nor mistress.

In the hope of making friends Julie decided to attend church, leaving Isabel in Lucy's care. One Sunday the new parson quoted in his sermon from the Song of Solomon: "As the lily among thorns, so is my love among the daughters," and Julie thought of her deep love for her own little daughter. She looked at the parson with interest He was slight young man with a curly black beard. For a while she imagined herself in love with him. Each Sunday she wore her new yellow bonnet, lingering by the church door in the hope of talking to him. It was only when he announced his betrothal to an heiress that she rapidly lost interest in him.

One Sunday after the service, as she and the boys prepared to walk home, a man in the scarlet uniform of an officer left the group around the parson and introduced himself. He had large gingery moustaches that curled onto his ruddy cheeks.

"A good sermon, was it not? Though a trifle long for my liking." He gave a little bow. "Captain Grevill, late of the Hussars, at your service, Ma'am."

Julie held out her hand, smiling. "Indeed the sermon was a little tedious. I am Mrs Julie Tulley and these are my children, Harry and George."

"I live with my sister, Miss Jane Grevill, at the Old Rectory, and we are new to the parish. Did I hear you are at Starcross House? Perhaps I can take you home in my carriage"

Julie shook her head. "Thank you, no, we prefer to walk."

He swished his silver topped cane. "Then perhaps I may have the honour of accompanying you."

He walked by her side, decapitating clumps of nettles with his cane, while the boys trotted behind.

"I want my dinner, Mama," shouted George. "I'm hungry."

The Captain smiled wolfishly. "And so am I, young man."

It seemed he was hinting for an invitation.

"I know no-one and should be glad if you and your sister would come and take some supper with me," Julie said impulsively.

The Captain beamed. "My sister and I would be delighted, Mrs Tulley. We shall come next Thursday, sharp at five."

They walked side by side through the park. The Captain swung his silver topped cane and talked of his heroic actions against Napoleon in Egypt, while Julie silently arranged a menu for the coming supper party.

"A fine house and park you have here, Mrs Tulley," he exclaimed, his little eyes shining. "Time of Good Queen Bess and all that. Grand, absolutely grand!"

His smile vanished when he found they were approaching, not the main entrance, but the kitchen door.

"Now then, what's this? Some mistake here, Mrs Tulley. This is the door used by your servants or I'm a Dutchman."

Julie turned to him. "This is the door we use. I am the housekeeper here, Captain, not the mistress."

His face froze into a mask of disdain and he gave a stiff little bow. "Then we have both made foolish mistakes, and I must bid you good day. Of course, you must understand it will not be possible for my sister and I to accept your invitation. Really, I cannot but wonder at your suggesting it."

Julie's face scorched crimson with anger. Her feet itched to kick his shins and her hand to pull his ridiculous moustaches. But before she could think of a stinging reply he had turned and stalked away. Leaving the boys she flew into the privy to relieve her feeling by screaming.

She did not go to church again.

Although she ached with loneliness she tried to make life pleasant for the children. As they usually spent Christmas without her father she always garlanded the rooms with holly, made little presents for them and cooked a goose and plum pudding.

One snowy Christmas she watched the children playing outside in the white wintry garden. They were making a man out of snow with stones for eyes and twigs for arms, shrieking with delight.

"How beautiful they are," she said to herself, with a little glow of pleasure.

When the goose was ready and the gravy made she took a tray in to her father in the dining room.

"Julie, I have a present for you," Richard said awkwardly, rising from his chair and handing her a gown of brown silk. She knew he was trying to reach out to her, but he had rebuffed her for so long she could feel nothing. She put down the tray and took the gown without looking at it, annoyed that he had not thought of giving presents to the children.

"Thank you. I am sorry I have no gift for you," she said stiffly, turning on her heel.

Back in her bedroom she went to the tall mirror and held the gown up against her body. It shimmered softly, brown with golden lights, like her own hair. The collar and cuffs were of rich creamy lace. It was beautiful and she knew she would look well in it. Although she was small she was still slim and her complexion was pink and white, her eyes still bright blue. But in her bitterness she resolved never to wear it.

Soon the boys were at school in the village. Anxious that Isabel should not be left out Julie gave her lessons at the kitchen table.

"It's dull!" the six year-old cried, tossing her slate

onto the stone floor, where it shattered into pieces. "I won't do the stupid sums."

It was no better when Julie tried to teach her simple household tasks.

"Why should I work?" she demanded. "Just because you are a servant don't think I will be the same. I mean to be a lady and have fine clothes to wear."

Julie sighed with exasperation. "I work so that we can have somewhere to live and food to eat. If you do not work you will never be free. You will be dependant on others – on men."

Isabel jumped up. "I am not free now! You never let me go from your side!" She flounced from the kitchen weeping, and Julie's heart ached. She yearned for the companionship of the happy, loving daughter she had dreamed of when Isabel was born. The feeling of rejection was a constant sorrow.

As the years passed Julie came to realise she was no longer the centre of her children's world. When she saw that they were as tall as she was she knew their childhood was over. Harry and George visited their school-friends or worked on neighbouring farms. Isabel spent her time in her room reading novels, trimming her bonnets or designing gowns.

Julie gazed out at the park, watching the land turn brown, then green, then brown again as the seasons and the years crept slowly by. Each autumn she watched the leaves wither and fall.

"I am withering away, as they are," she thought.

Life seemed to have been drained of meaning and a terrible melancholy settled over her like a stifling grey shroud. She could keep busy during the day but when evening came she felt that the world had forgotten her.

"I am only twentyseven, yet I am growing old. Where

has my life gone? All to waste," she said aloud to the empty room. "How did I change from the young girl who laughed and climbed trees and once had a sweetheart called Jem?"

Jem! She had not thought of him for a long time, and now to her dismay she found she could hardly remember his face. If he had lived she knew she would have grown away from him. How strange life was! Everything had changed because a pedlar woman had come to the house to sell ribbons. As a result Aunt Bess had died, and Edgar had been able to take advantage of her grief.

She placed her finger on the steamy window and traced a line from the pedlar to her aunt and then her brother. Then came her pregnancy and her marriage. Then she went back and traced a large elaborate letter R. It had all started when her father had gone away to Russia and she drew her finger down the window from that point. But why was he so altered after that? Everything happened because of something else, she decided, frowning with the effort of thinking about life.

That year, 1815, while England celebrated Wellington's victory at Waterloo, Edgar arrived home for a visit. He looked thin and shabby, but insisted he was in a good way of business. He told his father that he had decided to study law and only needed a loan of twenty pounds for the fees.

"They think very highly of me in London. I have an aptitude for the law. It's likely I shall end up a Justice of the Peace, or even a Judge."

Before he left with a little money from his father he talked to Harry and George. Then he visited Julie in the kitchen to tell her he had met Amy in Covent Garden, where they both had lodgings. Her husband Tom had left her and she was down on her luck.

"If you give me a few pounds I will see she gets it," he said, avoiding her eyes, "I know you have money from father."

"He promised to pay me wages, but he forgets. He pays any bills, but I have nothing of my own, and would not trust you with it if I had. You can tell Amy *she* is always welcome here at Starcross. She was a good friend to me. Now get out of my sight!"

Julie felt more dreary with each year that passed. Harry grew tall, but was delicate and coughed continually. George, on the other hand, became stout and ruddy-cheeked. While Julie was plucking the first grey hairs from her head, her daughter was growing more beautiful, with a glowing complexion, full red lips, even white teeth and large eyes of violet-blue. She liked low gowns that showed off her voluptuous figure and small waist, and spent her time in front of the mirror dressing her golden curls in the latest fashion. She sullenly refused to help her mother in the house.

One day when Isabel was thirteen Julie found her dancing before Richard in the parlour, and a poisonous anger swept over her. Had not she danced for her father when she was young, before he went away and came back changed? For some reason he had withdrawn his love from her and now he had given it to her daughter. She was filled with a bitter jealousy she could almost taste.

"Go to your room, miss!" she cried, pulling at the girl's arm. "You are making an exhibition of yourself."

Isabel wrenched herself from her mother's grasp. "You spoil everything. Why shouldn't I enjoy myself?" She burst into loud sobs and ran from the room.

"I meant no harm, Julie," stammered Richard.

"I will not have you make a pet of her," she retorted sharply. "She is vain and frivolous enough as it is."

"But I am not well, Julie, my heart is weak and … and I fear my mind is going. The Captain lurks in the shadows … he haunts me. I did wrong and he reproaches me … and I think of the boy Sergei. And then I have so few pleasures in life … "

Julie could not contain her anger. "Your life is of your own choosing, Father. You turned away from me and my little ones when we were most in need. You let Edgar rule you. Even now you ignore the boys. I will not have Isabel singled out and her silly head turned."

A few days later Richard approached her as she was polishing the oak table in the library.

"Julie," he said hesitantly, "I wish to alter our arrangements."

"In what way, pray?"

"In future I wish you all to join me in the dining room for meals…"

The bile rose in Julie's mouth. She continued rubbing the already gleaming table. "But *I* do not wish it," she told him coldly. "We are content in our own lowly quarters. All these years we have not been welcome, and now seek no other company but our own."

She marched from the room, leaving her father pressing his hand to his chest. It should have been a moment of triumph, but it felt sour.

"He is old, his heart is bad and he is sick in his mind," she thought dismally. "And I have grown hard and mean."

After this Richard took to his bed each evening as soon as the grandfather clock in the hall struck seven. The house was quieter than ever and Julie fell into a deeper melancholy. She wandered from room to room, sometimes sitting at her father's desk in the library reading his letters and newspapers. From the former she discovered that he had been able to buy Starcross at a good price from a Lord Cross, who had gambling debts. Her father had invested in Canal stocks, which did not bring in much return. From The Times newspaper she learnt about the world. When she read about Napoleon's life in exile she thought about Russia and the mysterious Captain Andropov who haunted her father's dreams. She wondered what had happened to his son, Sergei, the boy who had sat on the stairs in his nightshirt showing his bare toes.

After the newspapers Julie began to read the books on the shelves in the library.

"How little I have known of the world," she thought.

For Harry's sixteenth birthday Julie cooked his favourite supper of roast mutton and apple pie, but she saw that he had little appetite and all day was quiet and melancholy.

"It's because he's in love with that red-headed beauty, Fanny Wardle," George told her, laughing. "And he's not the only one, she has many admirers. He should love 'em and leave 'em, as I do."

"That's enough, George!" said Harry savagely, "At least I don't sniff after the girls like a dog in heat." This was so unlike him that Julie was worried.

The last time she had seen Fanny she had been a little auburn-headed urchin with a dirty face. Now it seemed she was the village belle and had many suitors. But she was Mistress Wardle's grandchild and although Julie had not told anyone, she could not forget the awful curse the housekeeper had laid on Isabel as a baby

"I have good reason for asking you to forget Fanny," she told Harry sharply. "Please take heed of my wishes."

"You misjudge her," Harry answered sadly. "She is the sweetest girl, and we love each other, but I shall never marry."

A few months later they heard that she was engaged to the village blacksmith, Billy Slade.

Harry fell ill and coughed continually, bringing up blood-flecked phlegm. The doctor diagnosed pneumonia and advised rest, and while Julie nursed him they talked of his future. He confided that he and George meant to be farmers.

"But you are not strong, Harry dearest. I hoped you would study for a profession."

He smiled weakly. "George is strong enough for us both, Mother. I will be the brain and he the brawn. These are good times for farmers, the corn law favours us. Besides, there are so many beautiful new breeds of cattle and there are all the new inventions. Steam's the thing, you'll see, it'll be driving the plough and cutting the corn soon. George and I have got such plans! And we want Isabel to live with us."

Julie turned her face away, careful that he would not see how hurt she was. "So I am not included in these plans of yours?"

He took her cool hand in his hot one. "Mother, you have worked so hard for all of us, seen we have good food and clothes of your own making. We are grateful, but we have other needs now. I shall not marry, but George will, though he's a great flirt. And Isabel must, for she's such a beauty. She needs amusement, to attend parties and dances. Yet you deny her every pleasure."

Julie flushed, cut to the heart by her son's criticism. "There is a good reason, Harry," she told him.

It was many years since she had seen her mother-in-law. But in the spring of 1820 a visiting tinker told her that Mother Tulley had wintered over at Allerton and was now too ill to travel the roads. At once Julie set off to visit her. She carried a basket containing a newly-baked loaf, a pot of heather honey, a bottle of cowslip wine and a woollen shawl.

The day was warm and sunny and her spirits rose as she walked through the country lanes. A scented breeze tossed the blossom from the apple and pear trees and blew the lambs-wool clouds across the blue sky.

The workhouse was a grim stone building divided into four rooms. Outside the womens' section one old woman was pegging aprons on the washing line, while another was on her knees scrubbing the stone step.

The Superintendant of the Workhouse was taking his ease in a chair by the door, chewing a wad of tobacco. He was so larded with fat that his stomach hung over on his knees and Julie guessed that he was stealing the food meant for the inmates. They were all as thin as garden rakes.

"Tulley? Taken to her bed. Like all of 'em, too lazy to work and lives off the parish," he answered her query, contemptuously spitting a stream of brown tobacco juice past her into the corner. He jerked his thumb towards the end of the dormitory.

Mother Tulley was lying in a narrow cot covered with a threadbare blanket. Her face was so gaunt that it made Julie think of a skull, and her once dark eyes were milky pale.

"Is that you, Jem's wife?" she whispered, feeling round with her thin hand for Julie's own. "I have longed for you to come. I would have written to you, but I never learnt how, and now I cannot see."

"Mother Tulley, you cannot stay in this dreadful place. Come home to Starcross with me and let me care for you," cried Julie, kneeling beside the bed. "I will be your eyes."

The old woman shook her grey head. "No, my dear,

I know I shall die soon and be with my boy Jem. I was harsh to you once, yet for all that you were kind to me, and now I will not bring sorrow to your house. I wish you to be happy."

"But I am not," wailed Julie. "My children do not need me any more. I am all alone and I have no-one to love me. I am so unhappy."

She felt the old fingers touch her hair. "Listen to me, child. You cannot travel the roads and sleep under the stars as I have done these many years without gaining a little wisdom. Be patient. The world is turning and happiness is coming your way."

She fell silent and they could hear the wind rise and blow round the stone building.

"The world is turning and the wind is blowing," Mother Tulley murmured. "Joy will soon be yours."

She died the next week and Julie mourned that another link with the past was broken.

In 1824 Julie heard that Fanny Wardle was to be married at Birchington, where she was working as a dairymaid. The next day she came across Isabel trimming a lilac-coloured silk gown to wear to the wedding. She was surprised, as she did not know that Isabel even knew Fanny.

"You think I have no friends," Isabel said defiantly, biting off a thread. "But I do and I am going to the wedding with Harry and George."

"No, I forbid you to go," cried Julie, fearful of Mistress Wardle's curse. "The family are evil."

Isabel turned on her in a fury. "You have tried to ruin my life. You have kept me a prisoner, though I have done nothing to deserve it. You have never loved me!"

Julie felt as though she had been struck, and stared at her daughter in dismay. Everything she had done had

113

been wrong. Harry and George, hearing the noise, hurried in and joined their sister.

"We are going to the wedding, Mother." Harry said calmly. "There is no reason why we should not."

"I forbid you!" cried Julie, hating herself but unable to stop.

"You cannot, Mother," said George. "We intend to see Fanny married and go to the dance afterwards. We shall all three of us sleep at our schoolfriend William's house and return the next afternoon."

Harry kissed her. "Mother, do not upset yourself over so small a matter."

The three of them left the room together.

"I have lost them," thought Julie, bursting into a torrent of weeping.

Isabel had begged the use of the carriage from her grandfather. On the morning of the wedding Julie watched from the window as Harry, George and Isabel drove out to Birchington dressed in their best finery. The house servants followed, having also been invited to celebrate the wedding. Julie was in a turmoil of envy and foreboding. In the parlour her father dozed over his newspaper and the house was deathly silent.

"Nobody needs me," Julie said aloud in the echoing silence. "My life is over." She went slowly to Aunt Bess's bedroom and lay down facing the wall.

A little while later there was a loud knock at the door. Rousing herself with an effort, Julie rose, smoothed her apron and went down to open it.

Outside stood a tall young man with corn-coloured hair, high cheekbones and slanting grey eyes.

Chapter Eleven

ENGLAND 1824

It was a long time since Julie had seen anyone unfamiliar. Lost for words, she stood looking up at the tall stranger.

"Is your master at home?" he asked. His voice was low and musical, with an odd foreign accent.

"My Master?" echoed Julie, puzzled.

"I have some business with Mr Bingham," the stranger said patiently. "Please be so good as to announce me. My name is…"

"Julie," called Richard, who had heard voices. "Who is it?" He came slowly across the hall, then stopped and peered at the tall figure. "Captain Andropov," he said in a gasping whisper, his pale face suddenly glistening with sweat, "Captain, you are here…"

He took a few tottering steps towards Sergei. "You have come … forgive me … " His blue-tinged lips opened and shut as he struggled to speak. He clawed at the empty air, then slowly pitched forward. Julie rushed to catch him as he fell, but he slipped from her grasp and crumpled to the floor.

She cradled his head in her lap, patting his clammy

cheeks to rouse him. "He has a bad heart," she cried to the stranger, her own heart thudding fearfully. "Fetch him some water. Hurry!"

He found the kitchen and filled a cup from the pitcher. He tried to force some water between Richard's lips, but it ran out and dribbled down his chin.

"Shall I go for a doctor?"

"Yes, go!" she whispered wildly. "No, no, don't leave me. He is ill, his heart is weak. He has fainted away, that is all."

Kneeling beside the limp body, Sergei undid Richard's shirt and slipped his hand inside. There was no heartbeat. He tried to find a pulse at his wrist and neck, but there was nothing. Julie bent over him and her father's pale eyes stared blindly up at her, his pallid face fixed in a ghastly mask of death.

"He *is* breathing," she whispered hopelessly, stroking his sparse white hair. "Hurry, fetch Doctor Jason, he will make him better."

Sergei searched for a pulse again. "I am sorry," he said slowly, "but I fear that what is needed now is a priest."

Unable to speak, Julie bent over Richard, rocking back and forth in her grief.

Sergei did not know what to do. He only knew to his embarrassment that his bladder was bursting. Mumbling an excuse he rushed outside to relieve himself into the lavender bush. Then he hurriedly searched the house for the other servants, puzzled to find there were none. He had seen death many times in war, but this had the feeling of one of Mashenka's folk tales – the sudden death of the man he had last seen in St Petersburg so many years ago, the deserted house, the servant's wild grief.

When he returned to the hall and saw that Julie had

not moved, Sergei suggested that they should lay the body out on his bed. Nodding consent she led the way to Richard's room, while he carried the body, light as a withered flower. There they laid him, with his hands crossed on his chest.

They sat in silence on either side of the high bed. Sergei waited, not wanting to intrude on her grief. At last, roused by the grandfather clock below striking three she looked up, dazed.

"Who are you?"

"My name is Sergei Dmitryvich Andropov," he told her. "I am from Russia and have come to see your Master about a matter of business."

"And now he is dead," she said dully, not hearing the word master.

"I am deeply sorry he was taken ill and died. I would like to be of service. Shall I go now for a priest?"

Julie shook her head. Her hair, already dishevelled, came loose and fell about her shoulders. "No, no, I wish to be with him a little longer, and the others will be back soon. Perhaps we could talk a little."

Sergei wondered who the others were and concluded they were fellow servants.

"Sergei!" Julie went on, puckering her brow. "My father spoke sometimes of a boy he saw in St Petersburg with that name, one he took a liking to."

"Your father! Mr Bingham was your father! I did not know. Forgive me for thinking you were the housekeeper. I saw the keys at your waist – but no mind. So you are his daughter Julie! Mr Bingham mentioned you with such love. You see, I have reason to remember every detail of that wintry night when your father came to the house, for it was the last time I saw my own father."

They fell silent, each lost in memories of the past.

117

Then a door banged and they heard happy voices and laughter from the hall below.

"My sons and daughter have returned from a wedding," Julie whispered, rousing herself. "I must break the sad news to them. But I would like to know more of your story. Let us continue our talk later."

As she rose she stumbled. It was as though all the strength had gone from her, and she accepted the offer of an arm to help her. It was strangely comforting.

"Mother!" George called up, "the wedding was splendid and Fanny looked beautiful. She and her new husband are going to live over at Illminister, and Mistress Wardle is going with them."

"You should have come, Mother," added Harry. "Oh and a woman spoke to me. Her name was Amy Finch and she said to tell you she has come to live back in Wychwood..."

As Julie slowly descended the stairs leaning on Sergei's arm the young people stared up in surprise, their chatter dying on their lips. Sergei noticed the startled look in Isabel's dark blue eyes as she saw him, and he couldn't help being filled with sudden delight as she took off her bonnet and her golden curls tumbled over her shoulders.

"And who may you be, sir?" cried George, surprised out of his good manners.

"Mr Andropov knew your grandfather," Julie murmured, "and I fear I have bad news." She swayed and almost fell.

Quickly Harry took her arm and settled her in a chair in the parlour. There she told them of Sergei's arrival and of their grandfather's sudden death. Isabel wept briefly, while the boys went upstairs to see Richard's body. Then Harry rode over to fetch Parson Liddle and George walked over to fetch Doctor Jason and see the undertaker.

It was nine o'clock before the three men left, having arranged for the funeral the next day. Soon afterwards the servants returned from the tavern where they had been drinking the bride's health in ale. Isabel helped them prepare a supper of cold beef and potatoes and lay it in the dining room. It was a sombre meal.

Sergei looked round at the family. He watched the lamplight making a shining halo of Isabel's hair and thought how beautiful she was, with her heart-shaped face, velvety skin and full red lips. Julie, he considered, had a sweet face but was not as handsome.

"But then she is herself and does not need to be beautiful," he thought, and immediately blamed himself for thinking of such frivolous things at a time of tragedy.

Seeing their mother's exhausted look Harry and George offered to keep watch by their grandfather's body that night. Julie thanked them but refused, saying she wished to be alone with her father. Upstairs she placed two candles at the head of his bed, while Isabel picked a posy of lavender and lily-of-the-valley and tucked them between his thin hands.

Julie sat alone beside her father's body. She had not prayed for a long time, but now she prayed for his soul to be at rest. She listened to the subdued voices of the young people as they went to bed, and fell into a reverie of the past. How happy they would have been if only her father had not travelled to Russia, if only, if only…

After a while Sergei came in and asked permission to keep watch with her. She nodded. It seemed only right, as he had known Richard long ago. They sat quietly, the candle flames making their shadows flicker on the wall, the flowers filling the room with scent. A little later the candlelight paled as the full moon appeared at the window and lit up a dim corner of the room. At this Julie roused herself and looked at Sergei.

"It is so sad, Mr Andropov. I loved my father very much when I was a child. We have been like strangers for so long, although I know now I did always love him. He tried to heal the breach between us but I was too proud to let him. Now he is dead and it is too late."

"When he came to our house on that terrible night I remember he spoke of you with great love."

"I am glad. As we watch, may I tell you about my life?" Julie asked him in a low voice.

"I shall be honoured to hear it." Sergei wanted to touch her hand, to comfort her.

So Julie told him her story, leaving out only the part about Harry's conception. When she came to tell of her years of servitude she touched her father's cheeks with the back of her hand. His grey skin felt as stiff and cold as clay.

"He was greatly changed when he came back from Russia, as though something was crushing his soul. So he was easily ruled by my brother Edgar. He regretted his harsh treatment of me, I knew, but I rejected all his attempts to put it right."

She began to weep quietly. The moon had sailed further across the night sky and flooded the shadowy room with its radiant light. It gleamed on the polished night-table and the tallboy, it glinted on Richard's silver-backed brushes and dazzled their eyes. It turned Julie's face to alabaster and her tears to pearls. Neither of them ever forgot the magic of that brilliant night-watch in the fragrant room.

"I can tell you why your father changed," Sergei said quietly, "but you may not wish to hear it."

"I do wish."

Starting at the beginning, Sergei told her of his motherless childhood, when he was cared for so lovingly by the two house serfs, Platon and Mashenka. He told her of his happy life with his officer father, of the Army's hatred of Tsar Paul, and his father's part in his assassination. When he reached that fateful night when his father, fearing discovery and arrest, entrusted the money to her father, Julie leaned forward.

"Wasn't that an odd thing to do?" she asked. "They were strangers."

"In Russia all Englishmen have a reputation for honest dealing," Sergei explained. "And it was to be for one night only. The money was to help the conspirators escape with their families. But nothing went as they planned and your father took the money."

"How terrible! My father was a thief."

"On the contrary, I think he was a honest man who gave way to momentary temptation. Only an honest man would be troubled by his conscience ever afterwards, as you say he was. And he paid dearly for his crime if he was haunted by my father's ghost. I think when he first saw me in the hall he thought he saw my father, and it killed him."

The moon drifted away and the room filled up with shadows. Sergei resumed his story, telling of his flight south, his life with his hated grandmother, the terrible news of his father's execution. His voice cracked as he told of his grief, and tears filled his eyes.

"I am so very sorry," she said softly.

After a pause he told how it was only the love of Platon and Mashenka that enabled him to survive, and how they were lost to him forever.

"She comforted me when my mother died. I remember once walking with her at night along the quays beside the frozen river Neva. I was crying. Above us the Milky

Way flowed like a great silver river across the sky. She held my hand and told me to look up, telling me that my mother had gone to live there happily in the garden beyond the stars. After that I used to look out of my bedroom window at night and think of Mama living there among all that glittering splendour. Mashenka was only an old unlettered peasant woman, but she opened windows in my mind, and she comforted me."

His eyes glistened with unshed tears. He rose to go to the window, looking up at the pale stars. Julie got up and stood close beside him. She felt strangely as if a window somewhere in her soul, too, had opened.

"You have suffered so much," she said quietly. Without thinking she reached up and touched him lightly above his heart. "My own sorrow is nothing to it. But why did you come to visit my father now?"

"I will tell you, but it is a very secret matter and you must tell no one. I have seen many terrible things in Russia, both in war and in peacetime, and I belong to a society that wants to bring about change. An uprising has been planned, and for that we need money. I have been in London seeing fellow liberals and collecting funds, and I traced your father from there. The money he took would have been useful to us."

"*Would* have been? We must repay it, it is only right."

Sergei shook his head. "No, I do not want it. Your father bought this house for his family, and it is your home. I hereby cancel the debt and will write and tell Muraviev so. I have told you a great secret, but I know I can trust you. It's odd," he went on, smiling down at her, "but I feel as if I have known you all my life."

In spite of her grief Julie felt warmed. She thought how tall and handsome Mr Andropov was and longed for an excuse to be close to him.

"It is so strange how our lives are twined together, Sergei. May I call you that?"

"If I may call you Julie." He gazed at the sky, where the first glimmer of opal light had appeared in the sky to the east. "We have talked all night and I hope we have not been disrespectful to your father. But there is still so much I would like to hear."

"Then please, will you stay here at Starcross awhile? You have helped me through this dreadful night and I would like to help you in return. Your work for the Society must be dangerous, and here you would be safe."

He smiled again, his eyes crinkling at the corners. "Thank you. I would like to attend your father's funeral. Then perhaps I could have a quiet room, with a desk to write at."

Julie nodded. She found Sergei's hooded eyes on her and she felt suffused with warmth. But by then she was very sleepy. By the time the clock struck four her eyelids began to droop.

Seeing this Sergei quietly removed the lavender from between Richard's fingers and threw it out of the window into the park.

The funeral next day was a lonely affair, for Richard had made no friends in the neighbourhood. Only the family, Sergei and the servants followed the coffin to the little churchyard, where Julie said her last goodbye. Harry had written to Edgar, but he did not return.

After the period of mourning was over the gloom of the past lifted and Starcross became a happy place. When Julie started to clean and cook George followed her into the kitchen and untied her apron strings.

"You are never to wear this again," he told her with a smile. "You are not a servant, and shall live like a lady."

123

He and Harry made a bonfire in the garden and burnt all her aprons.

Harry and George did not pretend to miss the grandfather they hardly knew. They all three liked Sergei, especially Isabel. The boys discussed the latest farming methods with him and asked him about agriculture in Russia. Isabel, no longer sullen, consulted him about the latest fashions. Julie was afraid her young daughter would bore him, but he seemed content to sit beside her describing the elaborate gowns of silk and velvet that had shimmered at the grand balls and soirees in St Petersburg and Moscow.

Julie still felt weak and was advised by Doctor Jason to rest. From her chair by the window she watched as the three of them escorted Sergei round the park. She chided herself for feeling left out.

Then it was decided to visit Amy to ask her to be the new housekeeper at Starcross, and to her annoyance Isabel asked Sergei to go with her.

Julie was glad to see her old friend, but shocked to see how she had altered. Her hair was flecked with grey, her cheeks were sunken and two of her front teeth were missing. There was a large darn in her blue shawl and her shoes had holes in them.

"I have been struggling to live by taking in washing," she told Julie, thankfully drinking the hot tea put before her. "But the work is too hard for me. I have been ill-treated by life through no fault of mine."

"There is a home here for you," Julie told her. "You shall be the housekeeper, the first among the servants. The work will not be hard and the wages good, I promise."

Amy accepted gratefully. She told Julie of her life, how Tom had deserted her in London, how she had met a rich man who said he was a Lord and promised to marry her. How he had introduced her to his friends and said she was to oblige them and how he had vanished when she became pregnant. She met Edgar when she was plying her trade in Vauxhall Gardens and he was holding horses for the gentry. He had a mistress then but she left and they had shared lodgings in one of the rookeries in Covent Garden. Her baby, Rosie, was born there and Edgar had been a comfort to them, though they were both as poor as starveling mice. Then Rosie had died and she had tried to throw herself in the river. She told Julie she would have drowned if Edgar had not rescued her.

"I loathed what I had to do," Amy continued bitterly. "And no doubt you are shocked, and want nothing more to do with me."

"No," lied Julie, "I am so sorry," She put her arm round her friend's thin shoulders. "You have had a sad time."

"How odd life is," she said to herself. "Edgar is a wretched character, yet it seems he was kind to Amy and her poor child. He has some good in him."

There was still no sign from her brother, and Julie began to hope he would not return. For her it was a time of grief and weakness, yet also of lightness and warmth because Sergei was at Starcross.

The next day she came across him in the library busily writing at the desk. She peered over his shoulder.

"How strange, you are writing pages of numbers."

He quickly slid a blank piece of paper over the page.

"I have to copy out my letters to my friends into code, Julie. Our mail is often opened. Please say nothing of this to anyone."

She nodded. "I have been meaning to ask you, Sergei, why you threw away the lavender placed in my father's hands that night we watched together?"

"I pissed on the lavender bush earlier," he confessed, flushing. "It did not seem respectful."

He caught her eye and in spite of themselves they burst out laughing.

"I am like a snail without its shell," she thought. "The shell was my defence against unhappiness, and I do not need it now."

Soon Harry and George returned to their work on a nearby farm, where they were helping with the new breeds of cattle and sheep. Isabel then took charge of Sergei, walking with him everywhere, asking him to go with her to choose a kitten from a new litter at the mill. Julie watched them go with irritation.

It was the same in the evenings when they gathered in the parlour after supper. They all begged Sergei to tell them stories of the war, of Napoleon, of the Tsar, of the world they had never seen. As he talked the room seemed to glow with the gold of the painted iconostasis in the churches. Then it filled with the mingled scent of incense and spicy resin of the forests. They saw through his eyes the cities, the slow-moving rivers, the delicate silver birch trees, the endless steppes, the cold whiteness of its snowy mountains. Julie noticed her daughter gazing up at him, her blue eyes full of admiration.

When the stories were over Isabel would sing in her sweet voice and Julie saw Sergei leaning towards her, entranced.

"Your daughter is beautiful, and sings like an angel," he told her when Isabel had gone to bed.

"She is idle, Sergei, and will learn nothing."

"I think she is not happy."

It was then that Julie decided there was no longer any need to keep Isabel close to home. Mistress Wardle had

126

gone to live with Fanny and the threat of her curse was over. It was time, she thought, that she mixed with friends her own age.

Isabel refused. Neither would she go to bed early and leave Julie alone to talk with Sergei.

"You don't want me to have any pleasure," she said resentfully.

A week later Edgar returned home, claiming that he had only just heard of his father's death. He looked gaunt, his linen was dirty and his coat threadbare. It was clear things had not gone well for him. Julie looked from him to Harry. Her son was taller than Edgar, with clear dark eyes and glossy hair, which he wore brushed forward. No, no-one, she told herself, would guess they were father and son. That danger was over, too.

"I see things have changed here," Edgar told the family, taking up a masterful position in front of the fireplace. "And now I have come into my inheritance they will change again. I shall take my proper position in society here and will become a Justice of the Peace. Yes, things will alter now I am home."

"In what way?" asked Julie, filled with dread. The fragile, rainbow-coloured bubble of her happiness burst.

"I know there is coal under this land and I mean to mine it. I just have to raise some capital. At the moment I have a few debts, having been fleeced by a scoundrel..."

Harry sprang up. "You cannot ruin this land. It is good rich soil and should be farmed."

Edgar smiled complacently. "You crow very loudly, my young cockerel, but I think you will find I can do as I like now I am the master of Starcross. Come, Julie, let us have dinner."

"Mother is no longer a servant," said George, his fists clenched. "Amy is housekeeper here now."

Edgar looked even more pleased with himself. "Then I shall have at least one friendly face to look at."

The next day Mr Findlay, the lawyer, drove up in his carriage. He entered, followed by a small boy almost hidden by the box of papers he was carrying. Julie invited him into the parlour where Edgar and the three young people were assembled to hear him read Richard's will. Sergei, seeing it was a private occasion, retired to the library to write to the Society.

The lawyer coughed importantly and peered at them over his spectacles. "I have Mr Bingham's last will and testament with me, which I will now read to you. 'I, Richard Bingham, being of sound mind, etc, etc, do will and bequeath Starcross House and park to my beloved daughter Julie, and to her heirs. To my son Edgar I leave one hundred pounds. He will know the reason for this. To the servants I leave …'"

Edgar sprang up and thrust his face violently into Julie's. "Traitor!" he shrieked. "You have betrayed me! This is your doing – the estate should be mine!"

"Please restrain yourself, Mr Bingham," said the lawyer, looking at the distraught Edgar with contempt. "The will is signed, witnessed and dated, and cannot be contested. Pray sit down."

"You will pay for this," screamed Edgar, pushing past Julie and stumbling from the room. He shouldered past Sergei, who had left the library to investigate the uproar.

Julie was ashamed that Edgar had so little dignity, but the good news of her inheritance gladdened her heart. She felt that her father had loved her all those years, and that he had wanted her future to be secure.

Later she opened the press in her room and brought out the silk gown he had given her so many years before. She tried it on, pulling in her stomach and twirling before the mirror. Yes, once she had let out the seams and smoothed the crumpled lace it would suit her very well. And she would dress her hair.

That night they celebrated with a festive supper of river trout, roast mutton, fruit tart and cream and a sharp local cheese. They drank toasts to the new mistress of Starcross and to Harry and George's farming enterprise. To start, Julie had given permission for them to plough up the park so they could grow corn. Then Harry proposed a toast to George's new sweetheart, Dorcas, at which George threw a bread roll at him and there was much scuffling and laughter.

As Edgar had not joined them for supper Julie tried to stifle her feeling of revulsion and visited him in his room. She found him hunched over a table by the window writing a letter. As soon as he saw her he threw down his quill and slipped the letter under the ink pot.

"What do you want?" he snapped. "I have important business to attend to."

"I came to tell you I had no notion that father would leave Starcross to me. We never talked of it."

He narrowed his eyes and she thought how like a fox he looked. "I know well that you poisoned his mind against me because you think I wronged you years ago. But I am the rightful heir. Remember that when you put on those fine airs, for you will surely pay for this."

He gave her a look of such malice that she could not help shuddering. She turned and left, slamming the door loudly.

As she was lighting her candle to go to bed Sergei came to see her, looking worried. A letter he had been writing to the Society, which was not yet in code, had disappeared from the desk in the library. He and Julie searched for it, but it had vanished.

"Lucy may have tidied it away," Julie said, not believing it. "I will speak to her." But the letter was never found.

Two days later the lawyer returned to go through her father's affairs with her. "You must invest more wisely, Mrs Tulley," he said, tapping a sheaf of papers to emphasize his advice. "For example, your father bought shares in the Hampshire and Basingstoke Canal. What do the barges on the canal carry? Materials to build the railways that will surely replace it. No, sell all canal shares and invest in steam."

A few days later Sergei told her that he must return to Russia, where he had work to do. "I shall miss you and your sons, and especially your lovely daughter."

"Isabel is very wilful child," replied Julie, irritable that he could not see any fault in her.

On the morning of his departure Julie slept late. She hurried downstairs as the grandfather clock struck nine, anxious to wish Sergei a safe journey. There was no one about. Feeling a growing unease she hurried from room to room. On the desk in the library she found a letter addressed to her.

"My dear friend," wrote Sergei, "I hope in time you will come to forgive me. Isabel is coming with me to Russia. Love such as she has for me is rare and I will do everything I can to make her happy. Please believe me, I did not intend this to happen, nor to deceive you, but Isabel insisted on secrecy. Do not think of me too unkindly. Sergei."

Underneath there were a few scrawled lines in her daughter's hand: "Mother, Sergei and I are going to be married and will live in Russia. Do not think to stop us. My love to Harry and George and to my kitty. I cannot in honesty send you any, for you never had any for me."

Chapter Twelve

ENGLAND 1824

Julie stared speechlessly at the letter, her chest constricting so painfully that she could hardly breathe. Then, like a volcano, fury erupted from deep inside her, red-hot, savage and destructive. Seizing cups and plates from the breakfast table she hurled them violently at the wall.

"How dare they! How dare he!" She heard someone screaming, and did not know it was her own voice.

The uproar brought George running in from the garden. He gaped at his mother, then rushed to stop her. Julie hurled the teapot at him. He ducked so that it crashed into the window, filling the room with flying splinters of glass. George flew to the gap and leant out, bawling to Harry that he was to come at once, as their mother had gone mad.

Amy hurried in, followed by Edgar, half-dressed, their shoes scrunching on the sharp fragments of glass. When Harry arrived Julie picked up a jug to throw at him. Crouching low he flung himself at her, pinioning her arms to her sides. Seeing by her glazed eyes that she did not know him he called her name loudly, then slapped her on both cheeks. At once she collapsed

131

against his chest and began to weep with great shuddering sobs.

"Mother dear, whatever is the matter?" he asked, supporting her to a chair.

Julie could not answer, merely pointing to the letter which had fluttered to the floor. George snatched it up and read it.

"Hell and damnation!" he shouted. "The scoundrel! Isabel has eloped with Sergei."

Harry studied it, his face sombre. "No wonder poor mother is in a fit. We thought he was our friend, we trusted him. Oh, my poor foolish sister."

Edgar turned pale. "He is a traitor – but I did not know – I can't be blamed."

Julie did not hear his words and no one else understood them. George left his mother's side, where he had been tenderly wiping her eyes with his handkerchief.

"Well, I for one will not stand idly by. I shall ride to the village to find which way they went."

He rushed from the room and soon they saw him galloping across the park. Harry, worried for his mother, sent for Doctor Jason, while Lucy swept and tidied the room, tears of sympathy for her mistress running down her cheeks. Exhausted by her outburst Julie's weeping subsided into painful, shuddering gasps.

George returned later, still angry. "They hired a carriage at The Angel, but I'm damned if I know when. They must have left before it was light, because none of the farm workers going to the fields saw hide nor hair of 'em."

When Doctor Jason arrived he tried to give Julie a soothing draught, but she pushed it away. Her heart fluttered and she felt sick.

"Mother," said Harry, stroking her hair, "did Sergei

tell you the name of the ship he was to sail home in?"

She shook her head, dumb with grief. George snatched a piece of bread and folding a thick piece of ham into it, announced that he would travel to London to find Isabel before they sailed and to give Sergei the thrashing he deserved. Harry, knowing his own frailty, did not volunteer, but to everyone's surprise Edgar said he would go with him. He knew London Town, he told them and together they would be sure to find her.

After they had left Julie wandered from room to room, hoping it was a bad dream and that she would come across Isabel reading a novel or copying a new dress from a magazine. In her daughter's bedroom she rummaged among her boxes of lace and ribbons, burying her face in her gowns to catch an elusive whiff of her scent.

A week later George and Edgar returned, limping and with their coats torn. Edgar's head was bandaged with a grimy piece of cloth and he had a scarlet gash on his left cheek.

"Mother, London is a dirty, villainous place!" George shouted, throwing himself into a chair. "We hadn't been there two days before we were set on and robbed…"

"So you did not find them?" Julie asked dully.

"When we asked the way to the dock these three rascals led us down a dark, narrow alley. They called us country bumpkins, knocked our hats over our eyes and beat us black and blue. After they had nearly broken their cudgels on my back and knocked Uncle onto the cobbles they robbed us and fled."

He gulped down the brandy Amy brought them both, but Edgar seemed not to see her and sat quietly staring into space.

"We were helped by a woman, a decent Christian soul, who took us in and bound us up. Her son went to the dock to enquire about ships sailing to Russia. It seems the *The Empress Sophia* left on the morning tide. I'm sorry, mother."

Julie's unhappiness was so deep she could no longer weep. "It is all my fault," she thought. "If only I had let her have more freedom – and now she is sailing away to the other side of the world."

While Amy prepared a warm poultice of comfrey for George's sore back she roused herself to attend to her brother. Underneath the dirty bandage was a black and purple swelling the size of a hen's egg. In the centre of this gaped a red wound like a livid mouth, oozing thick yellow matter. The smell made her retch, but she forced herself to clean it and bandage it with clean strips of linen.

Edgar still said nothing. She peered at him and to her horror found it was like staring through the windows into an empty room. Edgar was no longer there.

"Could you not have looked after Uncle better than this?" Harry asked his brother angrily.

"That is handsome coming from you, who did not meet those ruffians but stayed safe at home," retorted George.

"He could have died," Harry went on, "And you did not find Isabel. You're a fool, George!"

Edgar looked up at him. "But I am not a fool," he mumbled. "I am much respected in the district and am to become a Justice of the Peace."

"Amy, put him to bed and send for Doctor Jason," said Julie wearily.

That night she sat at her window looking out at the park. A beam of light from the crescent moon caught the weathercock on the church spire. It glinted like a little silver star, making her think of her daughter so far away, and her whole being ached with her terrible loss.

She had always dreamed that one day Isabel would stop being sullen and wayward and would become the loving daughter she had always wanted. She would be studious, wise and witty, perhaps even a writer like Fanny Burney, and be much sought after. She would marry the man she loved. As the church bells rang out, so her dream went on, Isabel would emerge beside her husband, a beautiful, radiant bride. Later she would have a baby of her own for Julie to hold in her arms and they would be closer than ever.

Now Isabel was travelling over the rim of the world to a strange land with a man she hardly knew, and none of those dreams would come true.

"The best part of me has been torn away," she thought, "I cannot bear it. I shall die of grief."

Although they missed Isabel, Harry and George soon became absorbed working on plans for the farm, as they had decided to buy additional land. George was in favour of enclosing more of the common while Harry was against it. They appealed to Julie for her opinion, but she could take no interest in their affairs.

She could not sleep. Each summer night she sat alone. The sweet smell of the cut hay from the fields drifted in the window, reminding her of her happy life at the hamlet. She listened to the church clock strike the hours. Once she imagined she heard the ghostly rattle of a coach below and thought she saw Isabel and Sergei arrive and wave up at her…

Sergei! That betrayal was like a knife in her heart. He had been *her* friend. They had watched together that strange night her father had died, had confided in each other, felt the intimacy of their mysteriously entwined lives. She remembered how she had put on the brown silk gown and dressed her hair because he was with them, and she cursed herself for a fool.

"Mother," said Harry, coming into the parlour with a large rolled-up drawing under his arm, "you cannot go on mourning like this, you will become ill. Isabel is not dead, but happy with the man she loves."

"She will not be happy. Sergei is old enough to be her father," Julie snapped.

"She is older than you were when you ran away to marry Jem," persisted Harry. "And in spite of the elopement I believe that Sergei is a good man. I do not blame you, Mother, but you let poor Isabel have so few pleasures it is no wonder she fell in love with the first man who admired her."

"I had to protect her. Mistress Wardle cursed her when she was a baby by making a model of her with a sharp thorn through her heart. And it seems the curse is working, for Sergei is taking her into terrible danger in Russia, of which you know nothing. I will not be criticised by you, whose bottom I wiped not so long ago."

To her annoyance Harry laughed. "If only you had told us of the stupid curse years ago we would have told you it was all nonsense. And I do believe it is jealousy that makes you so angry. Remember this, Mother, in his letter Sergei did not say he loved Isabel, merely that she loved *him*."

It was true. Julie looked at her son and wondered from whom he inherited his calm nature, his good sense. Not from her, and certainly not from Edgar.

Isabel had promised to write to them, but was six months before the postboy walked up to Starcross with the letter.

"Dear Mother," Isabel wrote, "I hope this finds you

well and that you do not bear me any ill-will. Sergei and I were married in St.Basil's Cathedral in Moscow. I was rash in running away, I know that now. I wish I had learnt those skills you tried so hard to teach me. I am not clever, but I am trying to learn this barbaric language because until I do I can have no real friends here. I do not blame Sergei for my loneliness, but he is so often away on some business. He does not tell me what these meetings are about, and I fear he finds me a dull companion because I know so little of anything. I think about my old home a great deal. My love to you all, and to my kitty. I wish I had her here with me. Your daughter Isabel."

Isabel's letter was not hostile like the one she had written before she left Starcross, but Julie was frightened by what she read. It was clear that her daughter was lonely and unhappy and that Sergei was still involved in the dangerous secret Society. That meant Isabel was also in danger. But Isabel had put no address on the letter, and she was unable to reply.

By the autumn of 1825 the new fields had been bought, the park ploughed and sown with wheat. The next spring there were cows in the meadow and pigs in the new sties. Harry and George paid good wages to their men and so were spared the unrest sweeping the rest of the countryside. The price of food rose so high that many poor folk came begging at the kitchen door. Julie remembered Mother Tulley and fed them all.

With Amy's nursing Edgar had seemed to recover, but Julie knew he had changed. He began to drink in secret and she took to hiding the brandy bottles, while Harry encouraged him to help with simple work on the farm.

While her sons were out in the fields all day and with friends in the evenings, Julie spent took to sitting with Amy, gossiping as they sewed.

"Edgar is wretched," Amy remarked, pinning a collar to the neck of a shirt, "Why do you never sit and talk to him?"

"You do not know him as I do," Julie protested. "I do not like or trust him."

Amy threaded her needle. "Yet he was good to my little Rosie. You have lost a daughter to foreign lands, but at least she is alive. My child lies in a lonely grave in Bunhill Fields, far from here."

Julie looked up at Amy's careworn face. "I am sorry. I have been deep in my own sorrow and forgotten yours. But you are happy here with us now, I hope."

"I am grateful that you took me in, but gratitude wears out, as sympathy does." She bit off the thread. "Did you know that when we were near starving together in the tenement Edgar cared for Rosie while I sold myself in Vauxhall Gardens? He was most gentle with her and was with her when she died. Did you know that he asked me to be his wife?"

Julie shook her head, amazed.

"Well, think on this. If we had wed and Edgar had inherited Starcross as he should have, *I* would be mistress here."

A tremor went through Julie. So Edgar had poisoned Amy's mind against her, the one friend she thought was loyal to her! Making the excuse that she was tired she left the kitchen, and for a time on there was a coolness between them.

As a result she spent more time in the library reading books and newspapers. She read of the sudden death of Tsar Alexander in 1825 in Russia, and wondered if the

138

new Tsar Nicholas would free the serfs as Sergei hoped. She ordered a globe of the world and would spin it round until her finger landed on Moscow, where she thought Isabel might be living. It gave her an illusion of being close to her daughter.

In early January 1826 she read with dismay an item about Russia. It was a report of an unsuccessful uprising against the Tsar in St.Petersburg led by a group of liberals. They had been called The Decembrists because it happened in the December of 1825.

In August 1827 Isabel's second letter arrived. This time it was from Siberia.

"My dearest Mama," she wrote, "Please, *please* come. I am ill and so terribly wretched. Sergei was arrested last year for his part in the Decembrist uprising. I did not know it, but he was part of a group of conspirators against the Tsar. Five of his friends have been hanged in the Peter and Paul Fortress, among them his friends Pestel and Muraviev-Apostol. It was so dreadful because even the hanging was botched, the ropes failed and three of them fell down into the pit and it had to be done again. Sergei's life was spared because he was not in St. Petersburg at the time. Still, someone betrayed him and in January he was exiled by the Tsar to hard labour in the silver mine here in Siberia. Of course I followed him. Nerchinsk is a terrible place and poor Sergei has to work all day in the mine although he is not strong. Mama, I fear I have the consumption, I am so weak and always cold. Please come and take me home. Your unhappy daughter Isabel."

The letter fell to the floor and her heart hammered so rapidly Julie felt she would suffocate.

"This can't be true, I am in a nightmare," she whispered to he empty room. Her beloved, foolish daughter was in danger half a world away and she could not help her. After a while she took a deep breath, recovered a little and re-read the letter. "Please come and take me home," Isabel had begged.

A memory of herself as a frightened girl alone on the common at night flashed into her tormented mind. She had found the strength then to save her unborn son and she would find it again to save Isabel.

Calling to Harry and George Julie announced that she was going to Siberia to find Isabel and bring her home.

Chapter Thirteen

ENGLAND AND RUSSIA 1827

Both Harry and George were aghast at Julie's insistance on going to Russia. They said she knew nothing of the world, and that women did not travel such distances. She did not speak the language, she was not strong enough, she would be attacked and robbed. But neither could they go themselves. Harry was not strong enough and George was needed to guard the farm. Unrest in the countryside was increasing, farm workers had smashed new machinery at Allerton and in their own parish of Wychwood ricks had been set alight.

"All the same, I will go," she told them. "Isabel needs me."

She found her father's old Russian grammar and began to learn some words. *Da*: yes, *nyet*: no, *spasseba:* thank you, *skalka*: how much?

By October she had sold some railway shares to pay for her fare and had sewn warm clothes for herself and Isabel. When everything was ready and she was about to leave for London George rushed in from the fields shouting that his uncle Edgar had been attacked by three men he had come across burning hay ricks at a neighbouring farm. He had been struck on the head with a pitchfork and had been carried home on a hurdle unconscious.

Old Doctor Jason was called. He bathed and bandaged the wound on Edgar's forehead, which was deep and inflamed. Then he shook his head sadly.

"This is not the first such blow your brother has suffered, and I fear he may not survive. What is the world coming to, Mrs Tulley?"

When he came to his senses Edgar would not eat. Julie made possets and calves-foot jelly, bringing them to him as he lay propped up in bed. He had been struck in the same part of his forehead as before, and this time the wound would not heal. Petulantly he refused to let her replace the bandage, although blood was slowly leaking from under it and staining the pillow an ugly dark red.

"Why do you never sit with me, as Amy and Harry do?" he asked her querulously, pushing her hand away.

Julie did not tell him it was because she could not forgive him, because the room stank of vomit, and most of all because his accident was preventing her from leaving for Russia.

"I have no time, Edgar, there is so much to do."

He looked at her, his eyes empty. "I am dying, Julie. But I do not mind. I do not care for this world. You do not love me and cannot bear to be in my company."

"That is not true, Edgar," she lied. "And you would get better if you ate something."

He shook his head feebly. "No one has ever loved me. You were Father's favourite when we were children, and Aunt Bess's. I never had a school friend. Even my mistress in the rookery in Covent Garden robbed me and left me for another man."

"Do not dwell on such things. Come, let me change your bandage, it is bloody again."

He was not listening. "Yes, now I think, there was someone, Amy's little daughter, Rosie. She loved me. I cared for her when Amy was pleasuring gentlemen at Vauxhall. Oh, Rosie was such a pretty child. She would sit on my knee and we would sing little songs together, and eat our small dinners in the attic. And at night she liked to sit at the high window and look down on the bright lights and the carriages full of fine ladies and gentlemen. Then when I put her to bed she would not sleep without I told her a story of bears or puss in boots…"

Julie felt suddenly chilly, as though a little child's hand had reached out of the shadows to touch her. "But she died."

He closed his eyes, tears seeping under his sandy lashes and down his fallen cheeks. "Yes, that's the pity of it. London is a cruel place. We could not get her enough food to keep her little body and soul together. She was so thin. One day she lay down and did not get up again."

For the first time Julie felt sorrow for her brother's wasted life.

"Sister," he went on in a whisper. "I have done you a great wrong. More than you know."

"It was a long time ago. All my cares now are for my daughter, and I must go to her."

"You came out best, for all that," Edgar murmured. "You have Starcross, and you have had love and children. I dearly wish that I had a child of my own…"

Julie gazed out of the window at the bare brown fields that had once been the park, and her eyes ached with unshed tears. Edgar was dying. Surely he had a right to know that he did have a son, Harry? As she was about to tell him the truth he muttered something and she bent over to hear it.

"Death may come for me tonight. It would be a comfort if you would read something from my Testament. It is in the oak press."

She rummaged among his musty-smelling clothes in the press, but as she lifted out the heavy Bible two papers from between its pages fluttered to the floor. They were letters, and she saw with a shock that one was in Sergei's hand. With a feeling of dread she took them to the oil lamp and read them both. The first, on thin paper, was indeed from Sergei to his friends in the conspiracy, the letter he had lost before it was put into code. The second, on good thick paper, was headed by a black two-headed eagle and was from the Russian Office in London. It was dated August 1824 and read:

"On behalf of the Nicholas I, Tsar of all the Russias, I would like to thank you for the information about the conspirator Sergei Dmitryvich Andropov. You may be sure that the appropriate measures will be taken."

It was signed by the Russian Minister of Foreign Affairs in London.

Julie read the letter again, feeling as if she had drunk cold poison. So it was Edgar who had betrayed Sergei, who had ruined Isabel's life as well as her own! She was filled with a bitter scalding fury. For a moment she wanted to kill him.

"I have the letters!" she screamed, throwing them in his face. "You betrayed him. Why did you do it? You are evil, a monster, you do not deserve to live!"

Filled with loathing she stumbled from the room. Her heart thumped so violently she felt sick. As she recovered, lying on her bed, she felt Edgar's malignant presence in the next room and recoiled from the evil he had done to her. She did not go near him again, and when he died a few days later she did not attend his funeral. Instead she packed her trunk and prepared to leave.

The day before her departure Amy came to announce she was pregnant and was leaving to marry.

"I did not know you knew anyone. Do you love him?" asked Julie, surprised.

"That's neither here nor there. Unlike you *I* am still flying the red flag and I want to have a child before it's too late," Amy retorted. "I wish I had never swallowed Mother Ferry's dreadful syrup. I know I can never replace my lost darling Rosie, but I can think of nothing else. It's a baby I want, not him, I've had enough of men."

"But who is the father?"

"William. We are going to live at Newmarket where he will help his brother in the racing stables there."

So it was their coachman. Julie had never liked him since she had found him flogging Diamond, their bay mare, and she feared Amy would suffer from his bad temper. There was another regret, too. For the last few years she had only seen spots of red on her rags each month and at times had felt uncommonly hot. Up until that moment she had felt only relief that her childbearing years were over, but now she felt a painful sense of loss. She longed to feel a baby sucking contentedly at her breast again and to bury her face in its soft milkiness.

"Then I wish you well." she said aloud. "I know you think I was harsh with Edgar, but some day I will tell you the reason. I envy you the baby and would like to visit you when I return. Remember that you are always welcome back here if you are not happy in your new life."

She gave her four guineas as a leaving present and a yellow gown with a tucked bodice for the wedding. They embraced and parted good friends, and then Julie set off for London.

Once she had left the stagecoach Julie was confused

by the noisy London crowds and soon lost her way. She was jostled by apprentice boys, drunkards, thieves and prostitutes. She was deafened by the rumble of carriages over the cobbles, the street sellers calling their wares, flowers or oysters, the fetid smells, the many church bells whose ringing filled the air with their clamour.

It was a relief to take a boat on the River Thames from Whitehall stairs. As the surly boatman rowed her to the dock she saw another view of London, with its hundreds of white steeples, the great dome of St.Pauls and London Bridge, and found it beautiful.

At the dock she bought a berth aboard the Merchantman the *King George III* bound for St. Petersburg. It was still being loaded and all day men carried barrels and bales aboard to pile into the hold. Trying not to trip over the coils of rope on deck she watched the sailors with their tarred pigtails who darted barefoot up the rigging at the bo'sun's shouted orders. She listened to the shrill cries of the gulls as they swooped for the rubbish floating on the oily waters of the river, and to the creaking of the ship's timbers. It was all so new and extraordinary.

When she went below she found she was to share a small cabin with a young Russian woman, Sonya Delvig. She had small dark eyes and a thick plait of dark hair wound round her head. Julie was irritated to see the girl had carelessly spread her belongings around the cramped space, explaining that her maid was too ill to travel with her.

"Perhaps you would be good enough to brush my hair?" she suggested, and Julie agreed. Then the girl asked for her supper to brought to her, as she was not well. Julie knew she was being treated as a servant, but said nothing. It was better, she thought, to have the company of a spoiled girl, especially one who spoke English so well, than to travel alone.

Sonya told her that she lived in Moscow and that she had a brother Yuri, a university student, who was to meet her at St.Petersburg. Julie in turn told her she was travelling to Siberia to find her daughter who was married to a political exile, sentenced to hard labour in one of the silver mines.

The girl looked shocked. "But they are all traitors!" She pressed her hands over her ears and begged Julie to tell her no more.

Soon the *King George III* was pitching and tossing in the rough grey seas. Julie was not seasick but Sonya turned pale, then green. Sweat broke out on her forehead and she vomited over the cabin floor.

"I shall die," she moaned as Julie cleaned up the stinking mess and wiped her brow. She would not eat, and pushed the bowl away so hard the soup spilled down Julie's gown. It was all Julie could do not to slap her.

The sea voyage seemed endless. Julie disliked the small stuffy cabin and she had little sympathy when Sonya complained. What were this spoiled girl's sufferings compared to Isabel's and Sergei's in exile?

When at last the ship berthed at the Russian port of Kronstadt Sonya recovered from her sea-sickness. "You've been an absolute angel," she told Julie. "You must meet my brother Yuri and he will give you something for your trouble."

St Petersburg was even more astonishing to Julie than London. The pink granite quays, the wide streets, the canals, the bulbous gold and coloured domes and white walls of the monasteries and churches all bonneted with snow made it magically beautiful.

They were met by Yuri, a slight young man with a fair

147

down like chicken feathers on his chin and wire-framed spectacles that kept slipping down his nose. He wore the dark uniform of a student, with a peaked cap set on the back of his head. After embracing his sister he piled their luggage into a cab and took them to a hotel on the Nevsky Prospekt for tea. There Julie was delighted with the red velvet hangings, the elegance of the decoration, the hissing samovar and the delicious little cakes.

"Madame Tulley wants to travel to Siberia, Yuri. I can't think why, it's such a dreadfully wild place, full of criminals and traitors."

"But I must get there. My young daughter followed her husband, Sergei Andropov, after he was sentenced to exile at Nerchinsk, and she needs me," Julie insisted.

"Shh!" whispered Yuri. "The Tsar has his spies even here. But you have cared for my sister and I would like to help you. All the Decembrist conspirators are heroes to us at the University. And of course I have heard of Andropov."

It was arranged that he would help her book a room, see his sister off to Moscow and then meet her the next afternoon. Julie was not sorry to part with Sonya and waited impatiently for the morrow. At three o'clock she was down in the hotel lobby. As she waited for Yuri she noticed an elderly man with a little pointed white beard sitting in an armchair nearby. He was smoking a cigar and reading a newspaper and also appeared to be waiting for someone. He looked up over the top of the paper as Yuri appeared.

"I will take you to see the sights," the student said, smiling at her and pushing his spectacles back onto his nose. "Take my arm, please, we must seem to be old friends."

He showed her the winter palace, the bronze horseman, the Admiralty, the St. Isaac and Kazan cathedrals and pointed out the sinister Peter and Paul fortress across the Neva. But every now and then he would tug her arm and pull her swiftly down a side road.

"You realise, of course, that we are being followed," he whispered. "The old fellow with the beard. He knows I know. The Tsar doesn't trust any of us students because we like to think for ourselves."

A group of horsemen trotted by down the wide street. The riders were dressed in blue frock-coats and wore tall black sheepskin hats. Long red spears were fastened to their saddles. They were followed by three horsemen in tunics of linked mail wearing burnished helmets topped with scarlet crests. It was an imposing sight and a crowd gathered to watch.

"The ones in front are Cossacks and the others are Circassians," Yuri told her, pulling her by the hand through the crowd. "Handsome fellows. Good, now we've lost our shadow and can talk."

They sat on a bench in the snowy park and Yuri told her that he admired Sergei Andropov. He had not betrayed his fellow conspirators to the Tsar as some others had, and Julie warmed at the thought. He also told her that he had spoken to his friends and they suggested she should pretend to be an English governess travelling to Siberia to teach the language to the children of Countess Sheremetev. That would explain her lack of French and her little Russian. They would supply her with school books to make it look realistic. The Sheremetev family was a good choice, he explained, because the Count was one of those conspirators who did break under questioning. Because he betrayed his friends he was looked upon with favour by the Minister.

"I hope I can carry off the deception, Yuri, I am not clever."

Yuri smiled at her. "I think you are. Anyhow, my friend Vera will go with you as interpreter when you apply for authorisation. That will be helped if you give small donations to the clerks in the Minister's office. It is the way things are done in Russia, unfortunately. Meanwhile I will change your English sovereigns into roubles for you."

They had supper in a steamy room crowded with students all heatedly discussing politics: how they planned for Russia to have a free press, constitutional government and emancipation of the serfs. Later a girl in a red and black embroidered peasant costume sat on a table and played the balalaika. Everyone sang, including Yuri.

"I have been asleep all my life," Julie told him, looking round, exhilarated. "The world is so large and so different from what I've known."

He poured her a glass of vodka and raised his own. "Then we liberals salute your English courage. We admire your country and like to speak your language, as you know. All we ask in return for our help is that you carry letters from their loved ones to the poor wretches in exile. Vera will help you hide them among your clothing."

Julie, with Vera as interpreter, spent many tedious hours in the ante-rooms of the Ministry waiting for the authorisation to travel to Siberia. No one questioned her position of governess and the discreet gifts of money helped. At the end of two weeks the letters were written and stamped. The student committee then brought her letters for the exiles, which Vera helped her sew into the lining of her travelling clothes. They also sewed roubles into the hems. Then together they set off to Moscow.

The sleigh, drawn by three horses, seemed to fly along the highway. They stopped only long enough to change horses, ease themselves and snatch a bite to eat. By sleeping in the sleigh they covered the four hundred and fifty miles swiftly, arriving at Moscow on the fifth day.

Julie liked the city, the bulbous, brightly coloured domes of the churches, the palaces and monasteries and convents. She was especially impressed as they went through one of the great gates in the red walls of the Kremlin and saw the vast square crowded with people buying things at the market stalls. It was a great contrast to the dignity and elegance of St. Petersburg.

Later that evening Vera took her to meet a group of liberals at a house on the Tversky Boulevard, where she was given more letters to deliver to the prisoners at Nerchinsk. One of the girls had written out a list of Russian words and phrases for her to memorise, another student presented her with a bearskin rug for her long journey. Then they had supper of pickled herrings, ham and cheese and coffee. Julie's health was toasted in vodka and for the second time she tried the fiery drink and found she liked it very much indeed.

"How different these young people are from the ones I have known," she said to herself, looking round at their eager young faces. "They risk everything for their beliefs."

The next morning Vera went with Julie to hire a sleigh with a leather cover. Ilya, the old driver who helped load her belongings, had a thick grey beard and most of his front teeth were missing. What is more, he smelt strongly of rum. However, Julie was anxious to leave and with a final embrace Vera waved her off on her long journey to Siberia.

Day after day the sleigh raced eastward, old Ilya flourishing his whip, the harness bells ringing, the three horses sending up great plumes of snow from their pounding hoofs.

"Poidi! – onward!" he shouted.

Julie was exhilarated at the speed, but in great discomfort. Her trunk was in the bottom of the carriage where the space was filled with hay for warmth, but the vehicle had no springs and she felt her bones would be jolted to pieces. There was some relief when they stopped at the black and white striped guardhouses topped by the Imperial eagles. There they changed the horses while she drank glasses of hot tea and Ilya tossed down glass after glass of vodka.

The few inns were so dirty and lice-ridden that she chose to sleep in the sleigh at night. She huddled in the straw, wrapped in the bearskin rug under the leather cover, but even so she was cold to the bone.

On the third day they reached Kazan on the great river Volga. Yuri had told her it was the ancient capital of the Khans of the Golden Horde, which had been captured by Ivan the Terrible. Julie was intrigued by the stories, but disliked the bored officials who kept her standing while they examined her papers.

"Why should a family exiled to Siberia need a governess?" they asked. She wanted to shout the truth at them at them, but held her tongue.

Furious at her treatment Julie begged Ilya to set off at once, even though it was snowing hard. The horses struggled on across the steppe, their bodies white with frost, and it was so cold she thought she would never be warm again. She tried to learn the Russian words and phrases on the list, but ached so much from the jolting she gave up.

Two weeks out from St. Petersburg they reached the Ural mountains. At the sight of the snow-covered peaks her spirits rose, knowing that she had travelled a third of the way to her destination. Beyond them lay the vast land of Siberia, where at her journey's end she would find Isabel.

Julie's yearning to see her was like an ache. She wanted to comfort her and to make up for the girl's unhappy years at Starcross. The cold and discomfort were nothing if only she only could tell her daughter that she loved her.

Once they had crossed the mountains and passed Ekaterinburg old Ilya pointed his whip at a stone monument ahead. At its base a shabby crowd of men and women were gathered, some weeping, some scribbling messages, others on their knees praying. Julie looked closer and saw they were wearing chains fastened to their waists and ankles.

"It is the boundary stone between Europe and Asia," explained one of the guards, coming up as Julie leant out of the carriage. "The prisoners are leaving their loved ones in the west. There will be no going back for them, for when they have served their time in prison they and their children must remain in Siberia."

Her heart gave a painful lurch as she thought of Sergei, who had travelled that same road a few years before. Had he, too, wept at the thought of what he was leaving forever?

Soon they were hurrying on over the endless snowy track that led through the forests and steppe. They swiftly passed the cities of Tiumen, Tobolsk, Omsk and Tomsk.

To Julie, flung from side to side, it seemed as if they were flying along faster and faster, and she hung on to the sides of the sleigh. Ilya, who had drunk too much vodka, lashed the horses into a gallop so recklessly that they slipped on the icy track. With a loud crash the sleigh turned over and broke in two, throwing Julie out into a snowdrift. The three horses wrenched themselves free from the tangled harness and galloped away.

When Julie picked herself up she was white from head to foot. On either side of the track the gloomy pine forest loomed like the dark ramparts of a mysterious city and the silence was profound.

"To the devil with you!" she shouted angrily to the old man, brushing off the snow. "I will find my daughter if I have to walk the rest of the way myself."

Ilya swayed, muttered a curse and took a drink from a bottle. One of the horses trotted back to him, nudging him with its nose. He caught hold of it and tied it to a tree. After gazing soulfully at the wreckage of the sleigh he removed a hunting gun and a lantern. Beckoning Julie to follow him, he stumbled through the trees to an old wood-cutter's hut in a clearing. There was an ancient iron stove in the corner and after cursing loudly he managed to light it with a tinder and flint. With gestures he indicated she was to stay there while he rode to the next village for help. When he pointed out of the tiny window and made a howling noise, Julie guessed he was warning her of wolves. Before he left he gave her the gun, showing her with unsteady hands how to fire it. Then she was on her own.

Julie placed the lighted lantern on a shelf, sat on the rough bench by the stove and waited. The wind rose and outside the hut the tall pine and fir trees murmured together.

She sensed around her the vastness of Russia, reaching to the cold Arctic in the north, to the Baltic Sea in the West, the Pacific Ocean to the east and to the Black and Caspian Seas to the south. How insignificant she was, sitting by herself in a tiny log hut, with only a faint lantern amidst the dark forest. She had the strange feeling that she was quite alone in the universe. The hours went slowly by. Suddenly she heard a sound that made her blood stop in her veins. It was the unearthly howling of wolves somewhere out in the forest.

Stumbling to a corner she grabbed the gun, forced the small window open and pointed it into the darkness. There she waited, shivering, straining her eyes into the gloom of the forest, imagining she saw even darker shapes gliding through the trees, expecting to see their eyes gleaming as they padded towards her shelter. Nothing moved and the only sound was snow dropping from the overloaded branches to the ground. Gradually the eerie sound died away as the wolves went about their secret night prowling.

Shuddering with cold, she shut the window and waited. Suppose the old man never came back? Suppose a bear came prowling round the hut? Suppose brigands or escaped convicts used the hut as a hideaway? Suppose they were set on robbing or raping her? She kept the gun beside her and tried to keep awake.

Before long she fell into a doze, but woke up startled by the sound of steps crunching in the snow outside the hut. Convinced it was brigands she hoisted the gun onto her shoulder, swung round and pointed it at the door.

"Well, I'll be damned!" said a young man, putting up his hands in mock terror.

Julie gaped at him. "You speak English! Who are you? You're not a brigand!"

"Nothing so interesting, I assure you. But I'd be glad

if you would stop pointing that gun at me, so we can be properly introduced."

The young man was laughing at her, so feeling reassured she put the gun away in a corner. The newcomer told her his name was Theodore Johnson and that he was a journalist. He had dark brown curly hair, bright black eyes and dimples in his cheeks. Julie guessed him to be about Harry's age, twentyfour.

"I apologise for my welcome," she told him, "and am glad to have your company."

They sat together by the stove and ate the bread and sausages he brought out wrapped in paper from his pocket. Julie told him of the accident and he told her one of his troika horses had gone lame half a mile further along the track. His own driver had gone to find a replacement.

"So we shall be here all night," he said gaily, passing her a flask of brandy. "Let us be merry and tell each other stories to pass away the time."

Julie told him hers, leaving out the part of Harry's conception. He told her he lived in Kensington in London and was engaged to a girl called Georgina. Their families were friends and they had known each other since they were children. He was a journalist on The Times newspaper in London, a job he loved. He was in Russia because his editor wanted him to write a series of articles for the paper about the conditions of the political exiles in Siberia. Both he and the editor believed that the stories of their barbarous conditions were false. It was only because the Russian Minister of the Interior thought he would write favourable reports that he gave him permission to travel. In fact Theo had been appalled at what he had seen.

"The prisoners are treated like cattle, given thin clothes, unsuitable shoes and bad food to eat. The air they breathe in the prisons is foul, and they are covered in lice. They are chained together and worked to death in the mines. Often they are beaten. I cannot get out of my mind the terrible sight of a woman being flogged for trying to smuggle letters home."

Julie's heart shrivelled, thinking of Sergei and Isabel. "Will you report all this, Mr Johnson?"

"Call me Theo, please, and I will call you Julie. There are no rules of correct behaviour in the wilderness, thank God. No, I cannot report it while I am in Russia, it would be too dangerous for me and for the prisoners, but you can be sure I will do so when I get back home. I am making notes and drawings of everything, which I keep well hidden. I carry forbidden letters for the prisoners in a body belt and in the false bottom of my box. And of course I have still have more prisons to inspect."

In turn they went outside to relieve themselves. It was snowing hard and by opening the door they let in freezing blasts of air. To keep warm they huddled together round the little stove and fell asleep.

When Julie woke she found she had been leaning against Theo's shoulder. Strangely she felt no embarrassment and merely thanked him.

"It was my pleasure, Julie," he told he smiling, and she knew from the way he looked at her that it *had* been a pleasure to him.

It had frozen hard during the night. Outside the hut Julie took a deep breath of the resin-scented air and gazed around, her breath like mist in the freezing air. A pale golden sun sparkled on the myriards of ice crystals on the snow, flashing brilliant red, blue and green points of light as if they were emeralds, rubies, sapphires and diamonds.

"How beautiful it is!" she said to herself. "It is like a

magic jewelled kingdom in a story book. Everything, Russia, the world, is so much more wonderful than I knew."

Theo joined her outside and as she turned she brushed against a branch, so that a cloud of sparkling silver dust settled over her. Theo brushed the ice crystals from her head and shoulders.

"You look as beautiful as a snow queen," he said, smiling. Julie began to love Russia.

She and Theo shared the remaining sausage for their breakfast and drank brandy from his flask. There was no sign of old Ilya, but later Fyodor, the driver of Theo's sleigh, returned riding the replacement horse.

Knowing how anxious she was to reach Nerchinsk Theo suggested to Julie that they should travel together in his sleigh, and she accepted gratefully. Once her trunk had been transferred from the snow-covered wreckage into Theo's sleigh they started off eastwards once more. He had planned to stop and visit prisons on the way, but Julie begged him to travel direct, and against his better judgement he agreed to visit them on his return journey.

"Your driver will follow us to Nerchinsk, and you can settle with him then," Theo told her. "He's probably sleeping off a drunken spree. The lives of Russian peasants are so hard it is not surprising they drown their sorrows in vodka."

They sped past the towns of Kraysnoyarsk and Karsk. Near Nizhni Udinsk Julie carelessly left off her fur mitten and saw to her horror that her hand had turned white. At once Theo clasped it between his own, rubbing it until the colour returned. Her hand burned painfully, but the danger of frostbite was over. Nevertheless he continued to hold her hand in his.

"I am old enough to be his mother, but he is falling in love with me," Julie said to herself. How surprising life was!

The further east they travelled the more Asiatic everything appeared. The Buriat people they saw riding their little blunt-nosed horses had narrow eyes and flat faces, and were dressed in roughly sewn reindeer skins. Later they met Kirghis, Tungus and Chinese merchants from whom they bought bread, brick tea, sugar and rum. They crossed the frozen Siberian rivers by sledge ferries, and at last saw the mountains of Transbaikal. Beyond them lay the great inland sea of Lake Baikal.

Six weeks after leaving Moscow, having covered four thousand miles, Julie and Theo reached Irkutsk, the capital of eastern Siberia. The city on the Angara river was large, with shining domed churches, monasteries, big houses, hotels and shops full of luxuries.

The day after their arrival they had to visit the Governor to present their papers in order to continue their travels. To show his importance he kept them waiting for several days.

When he did receive them he leant back in his carved chair, smoking a large cigar and eyeing them narrowly. As he questioned them he waved the cigar so that the smoke wafted in their faces. It soon became clear he did not want them to travel any further nor to see the conditions of the exiles. Theo was delayed for several days more before he was grudgingly given permission to continue. Julie was refused authorization.

"But Mrs Tulley is my fiancee," Theo said quickly. "We are to be married in Nerchinsk, it is all arranged. As my wife it is clear my travel permit includes her. I know my good friend the Minister of the Interior at St Petersburg would not be pleased if his wishes were disregarded."

He reached out behind his back and pinched Julie's arm and it was all she could do not to laugh. Scowling, the Governor stamped all the letters and as they left arm in arm the clerk wished them happiness.

"I am grateful for your quick wit," said Julie with a smile, when they were outside. "I did not know I was betrothed."

He took her hand. "I wish it were true, Julie. You are the bravest, most wonderful woman I have ever met."

"Thank you, Theo, but it is not true. I am quite ordinary."

As they continued their journey eastward towards Lake Baikal Julie felt a strange and unexpected happiness.

The ice of the great lake was as clear as glass. As the horses galloped across Theo told her that it was the deepest in the world, and that over four hundred rivers flowed into it, but that only one flowed out. The Angara flowed north to the arctic.

He turned to her with a meaningful smile. "They call the Angara river "the bride that got away.'"

Julie smiled back at him, but her thoughts were not of Theo. She was thinking of the six hundred miles they still had to travel before she would see Isabel at Nerchinsk, and wondering what she would find there.

Chapter Fourteen

RUSSIA 1827

As Julie and Theo's sleigh approached Nerchinsk he pointed to small tree-covered islands in the frozen Nercha river.

"Those are the holy places where the shamans live. They're priests, medicine men and prophets, all rolled into one, so I've heard, famous for having second sight. It would be interesting to see them at work."

But Julie was only half listening. She was gazing at the Mongol and Buriat settlements along the river. She stared with foreboding at the prison, surrounded by a stockade and guarded by Cossacks. Around it the forest trees had been felled to stop the prisoners from escaping, and she thought of Sergei confined within its forbidding walls.

As soon as the driver could pull up the horses in the frozen brown mud of the main street she jumped out, ignoring Theo, and asked in halting Russian for the house of the Englishwoman. A man wrapped in a ragged army coat pointed to a small wooden house, whose sagging roof was hung with long icicles.

"Julie, I quite understand that you wish to see your

daughter alone," panted Theo, catching up with her. "I will take a room in a hotel where I can write up some of my notes, and will call on you tomorrow."

A young woman of Isabel's age answered Julie's knock. She was short, with small dark eyes and a beaky nose that made Julie think of a sparrow. The interior of the house was small and dismal, and smelt strongly of fish. When Julie asked after Isabel she pointed up the rickety stairs.

"I am Vera Zulich," she said in broken English. "I am a prisoner's wife also. Together we live here." She shook her head sadly.

The windows of the log house were not of glass, but of fishskin and in the dim light of the bedroom Julie could not see her daughter. There was only a thin, lank-haired woman sitting by the stove who looked up at her with haggard eyes.

"Isabel?" said Julie uncertainly.

"Oh Mama, you have come!" cried the woman, running to her and bursting into a torrent of weeping.

Too shocked for tears, Julie embraced the gaunt figure of her daughter. What had become of her beautiful girl with the voluptuous figure and the golden curls? The child who had loved to sing and dance?

"I have longed for you to come, Mama," Isabel wept, clinging to her mother. "Take me home. I cannot bear it."

"Hush, dearest," murmured Julie, leading the distraught girl to the narrow bed. "You are not well. But I am here now and will care for you and take you home."

"Oh Mama, I have been so alone. I am ill and fear I shall die here and I do so want to see Starcross and Harry and George and my little kitty again..."

Julie helped her onto the bed and lay down beside

her with her arms around her daughter's frail body. She comforted her as she had when she was a baby and soon Isabel fell asleep, her head on her mother's shoulder. Julie stared round the dirty and neglected room. She was frightened at Isabel's emaciated looks, but filled with a fierce joy at having her in her arms.

Later she gave Vera some money to go and buy a chicken and some vegetables in the market. When she returned Julie made them into a nourishing soup and while it was cooking Vera told her of the harsh conditions the exiles' wives had to endure. They were allowed to visit their husbands occasionally at night and as a result some of them had children. The poorer women survived best, Vera told her with condescension, as they were not accustomed to employing servants and were used to hard work. Some of them earned money by sewing or cooking for others, while aristocratic women gave way to despair or illness. It was surprising, she added, that the local shaman had cured several sick women when the doctor could do nothing.

"There is no loyalty nowadays," the girl went on indignantly. "Why, would you believe it, my own maid refused to follow me to Siberia." It was obvious she regretted that there were no serfs beyond the Urals.

Julie looked round at the bare, dirty bedroom in disgust. "Then why do you not clean up and learn to cook properly yourself?"

"That is not work for someone related to the nobility, such as myself," Vera replied loftily. She was offended and a few days later she moved out to share a house with the wife of another prisoner.

"Mama, I am so unhappy," cried Isabel as Julie brought her the hot soup she had made. "I wish I had learnt to cook and sew when you tried to teach me. I wish I had never run away. I loved Sergei so, but I think I bored him. He was always away at his secret meetings and when we were together he was so preoccupied, and I never knew why. I don't think he really loved me."

Tears ran down her thin cheeks. Julie smoothed her hair, dark with sweat. It smelt unwashed, which worried her as Isabel had always been fastidious. She resolved to help her wash it as soon as she could.

Isabel had a fit of coughing. "I don't think you ever loved me either, Mama."

A pain shot through Julie like a knife. "That is not true. I always loved you, my dearest. I know I treated you too strictly, but there was a reason."

She told Isabel about Mistress Wardle's dismissal for stealing and of her revenge, the clay image of the baby with a thorn through its heart.

"I know now how foolish I was to be frightened," Julie went on, refilling Isabel's bowl with soup, "it being nothing but silly superstition."

To Julie's surprise she saw Isabel shrink back into her pillows, her blue eyes darkening with fear. "Oh Mama, I am cursed, I know it! I shall die in this dreadful place..." She was racked again with a fit of coughing.

"That is nonsense," Julie said firmly, "I will clean this house up and care for you and you will get better. I will fetch a doctor."

"Doctors can do nothing. I would like to visit the shaman, he will cure me," whispered Isabel. "He lives on an island in the river. Please, take me to him."

Later she slept again and Julie swept and tidied the room before dressing warmly and walking round the town. It was bitterly cold as she picked her way over the icy mud of the main street to the market, crowded with the colourful figures of Buriats, Tungas and Khirghis buying the frozen meat and vegetables, trading horses, bartering tea for tobacco.

As she prepared to cross the road she heard the thunder of pounding hoofs and saw a sledge flying down the road. It belonged to Leon Dubrovsky, the hated Commandant of the prison. At that moment she also saw a small Buriat child let go of his father's hand and begin to toddle across the street.

Without thinking she flew across in front of the galloping horses and scooped up the chubby little boy in her arms. As she collapsed with him into a pile of grey snow on the other side of the road a chattering crowd of tribesmen gathered round her. One of them took the child from her.

"That was well done," he said in gutteral English. "You have saved my little son the Wolfcub from death."

He was a stocky but dignified figure dressed in a thick coat of reindeer skin fastened with buttons carved from their antlers, and wore a flat fur hat. His round face was plump and his eyes dark narrow slits. He smelt strongly of rancid fat, but he smiled at her and she liked him immediately. He told her he had learnt English and Russian from trading with the prison.

"I am Prince Munku, chief of the Buriat tribe," he told her proudly. "We Buriats do not forget our friends. I shall be glad to be of service to you in return for my son's life."

Julie smiled at the fat little boy in his arms and touched his pink cheeks. "I have sons of my own," she told him. "And a daughter who has followed her husband into exile. She is ill and unhappy. She would like to visit your shaman, as she thinks he may cure her."

Prince Munku set the child down. "That is not to be done lightly. Our shaman speaks to the spirits, he knows the future and he helps the dead on their journey to the other world."

Julie shivered, but she persisted. "I have heard he has cured others. Please take us, I am so afraid for her."

He nodded gravely. "As you ask, so shall it be done. May he give a life for a life."

Theo came to the little house that evening, happy to see her and to meet Isabel. They drank tea together and she told him all that had happened. He had taken a couple of rooms in a hotel at the other end of the town and invited her to supper there before he left to inspect the prison at Chita the next day.

"The prison officials still believe I am writing reports on how good the conditions are. I would be in great trouble if they knew what I was really doing, and that the prisoners were giving me letters to smuggle home."

"Take care, Theo, it is dangerous work."

"I owe it to the poor souls who are suffering, Julie," he went on, gazing at her, "and I know you would like to help me in my task. I thought this evening after supper you might help me arrange the notes and drawings I made of the forwarding prison at Verkhni Udinsk, it was a hell of misery."

She shook her head. "Isabel needs me, Theo, and I must also visit poor Sergei at the prison. I will see you when you return."

Even before he had reached his hotel she had forgotten him.

The next morning Julie set out for the prison. The gate of the stockade was guarded by Cossacks in fur hats and greatcoats leaning on their rifles. Reluctantly one took her to the main door and she was shown into a dark, room. The foul air, thick with the stench of urine and excrement, made her feel sick. Round the wooden walls were sleeping platforms covered in thin grey blankets and above each was a red band which looked like blood, but which she learned were the bodies of squashed bed-bugs. The room was crowded with people, their thin faces and dull eyes betraying their despair.

There was a clanking of chains on the stone floor and a tall, stooping figure came slowly towards her, his legs shackled together by a chain round his waist.

She stared in horror at the grey, lined face, the ash-coloured hair. This could not be the tall, elegant man she had last seen at Starcross. It must a mistake.

"Sergei!"

"Julie, is it you? Truly? I am not dreaming! You have travelled all this way – I never thought to see you – and now you see to what I have come and to what depths I have dragged Isabel. I know you cannot forgive me, and I cannot forgive myself."

It was as though her soul had cracked in two. "Oh Sergei, I was angry because she was so young and knew nothing of the world. She is ill and I am caring for her. But you do not deserve this."

"Our Prison Commandant, Dubrovsky, is a tyrant. He could remove our shackles, but he will not. He espe-cially despises those of us who are not criminals but political prisoners, and I think he hates me most of all. The worst of it is that most of my friends and fellow con-spirators, like Baron Rozen and Nikoklai Bestuzhev, have been sent to the prison at Chita where conditions are more humane. I hear they have organised a carpenter's shop and have a garden where they can grow vegetables. But in this hell I have only one friend, Igor Repin. And he is here because of me. His master sent him here after he tried to help me in my search for Platon and Mashenka."

"Why could you not go to Chita with the others?"

"One day we had finished our work in the mine early and Dubrovsky kept us standing outside on the freezing mountainside instead of letting us return to the prison here. When I protested he said that he despised all soft intellectuals, and I told him that was because he had no intellect himself. So this is my punishment."

Julie felt as if her mouth was full of dust. "And Isabel is ill," she whispered. "How do any of you survive this life?"

He looked at her with his hooded eyes and gave a wan smile. "Igor says that life itself is a gift, and we must not always expect happiness. That is a bonus."

Feeling she would vomit if she had to breathe the fetid air any longer Julie gave Sergei a shirt she had made for him, and hurried outside to take great gulps of the cold air. When she had recovered she trudged back through the snow.

"If he can bear it, then I must," she thought. She stopped at the market and bought candles, a set of painted wooden dolls and some coloured red, yellow and blue silk from a stall. That evening she cut the silk into petals and made artificial flowers to brighten Isabel's room. She knew her daughter had been allowed visits to her husband and had seen how he lived, so she said little of the horrors she had seen.

A few days later she visited Sergei at the silver mine outside the town. After slipping a few roubles to the guard, she was given a tallow candle and was able to climb down the ladders into the gloomy galleries where the prisoners were working. She could make out the shadowy figures drilling holes for the dynamite, and there found Sergei wheeling a load of ore to the hoisting shaft. He told her they were in constant danger from the lack of oxygen, and from the naked lights and the explosives. Hurriedly she handed over the presents of bread and tea to share with the other prisoners, who blessed her and gave her messages to take back home to their families. As she climbed the worn ladders to the surface she felt as though she was escaping from the jaws of hell.

In spite of Julie's cooking and careful nursing, Isabel's health did not improve. She coughed continually and grew thinner than ever. The doctor called but could do nothing for her consumption but prescribe rest. Desperate, Julie sought out the Buriat Prince and begged him once more to take them to the shaman.

"We Buriats do not forget our friends," he replied with dignity. "My sledge will be by the river's edge tomorrow when the sun rises over the mountains."

Their breath smoking in the freezing air, Julie and Isabel rose while it was still dark and dressed in their warmest clothes.

"You are not strong enough," Julie warned her daughter. "This is folly."

As she coughed bright red patches appeared on Isabel's thin cheeks. "Mama, I know he has cured others. I want to go."

They hired a peasant's cart to take them to the riverbank where the Prince was waiting for them. The sun rose higher, shining weakly on the ice and turning it to pale gold. The sledge sped towards one of the islands. There, among a thicket of birch and fir trees they saw the grey felt yurt of the shaman.

Inside the earth floor was covered with green and blue carpets. To one side a white mare's skin was spread, on which stood a big drum, a whip and a rattle. A fire was flickering with yellow flames on a circle of stones in the centre. After a few minutes the shaman entered quietly, dressed in a fringed coat of reindeer skin decorated with silver. Over his coat was a red apron hung with magical amulets and tiny animal skulls, and on his head he wore a tasselled red hat. As they watched in silence he threw a handful of white horsehair into the fire which crackled and glowed fiery red, filling the yurt with an acrid smell.

The young man sat down without speaking and began to play the drum, quietly at first, then louder and louder, rocking wildly until his head began to loll and saliva ran from the corners of his mouth. The two women huddled together and Julie shuddered at the sight of his blank eyes, rolled so far back in his head that only the whites could be seen.

"He is communicating with the spirits," whispered Prince Munku "No one must speak to him until he returns from that far land. It would put him in great danger."

At last the shaman collapsed onto the mare's skin. His eyes closed and he began to speak softly in the Buriat tongue. The Prince listened with bowed head, then respectfully placed a present of tobacco beside the drum before gesturing to the two women to leave.

Julie knew she had witnessed something powerful and strange. She was silent as they walked slowly back to the sledge. As they settled in and covered themselves with the fur wrap Isabel was shivering with the intense cold and had a long painful bout of coughing.

"What did he say?" she whispered to the Prince when she could speak. Julie noticed that after holding her handkerchief to her mouth she quickly thrust it into her pocket.

The prince took up the reins and urged the little horse over the ice.

"I will think on his words. Now it is not the time to speak of what we have seen or heard."

The cold Isabel caught that day made her weaker than ever. Soon she could not get out of bed. Her friends among the other wives came to visit with little gifts, full of suggestions for a cure, but nothing did any good. Then a few days later Julie saw with dread a scattering of bright red spots on her daughter's pillow.

"Mama," cried Isabel, as her mother changed the linen. "Prince Munku has not told me what the shaman said to him. Go and see him. Ask him to tell you when I will be strong again."

Prince Munku met Julie dressed in a blue caftan decorated with silver buttons. He invited her into his yurt, where his wife, who spoke only the Buriat language, welcomed her with smiles and a cup of kvass. The little wolfcub came to her to show her his puppy and Julie gave him a piece of toffee. Then, the courtesies over, she asked about Isabel.

"It is heavy," Prince Munku said slowly. "The spirits have told the shaman that after the year has run its course your daughter will go to join her ancestors. But the child will live to give you joy."

"No, she must not die!" cried Julie in anguish. "But what child? There is no child."

"Our shaman can see the future," he answered, his face grave.

When Julie returned Isabel looked at her searchingly. Seeing her mother's face she wept quietly, knowing there was no hope for her. The next week she told her mother that she was pregnant. Julie did not tell her that the shaman had known, but put her arms round her daughter's thin shoulders and comforted her.

"Mama, I know I am dying," Isabel whispered. "But

171

I must live long enough to have my baby. The children of prisoners belong to the state, but I want you to care for her and bring her up. I feel sure it will be a girl. You must take her home to England, to Starcross. I know now I will never return, but I want her to be safe with you. Promise me."

"I cannot bear it," thought Julie, but she knew she must. She no longer pretended to Isabel that she would recover from her consumption, but promised she would carry out her wishes. That night she lay in bed staring at the ceiling, wondering how she could smuggle the baby to England.

"I shall pretend the baby is mine," she told Isabel the next day. "You must not receive visitors after your stomach begins to swell and I will wrap scarves round my own belly to match yours for size. The officials cannot stop me from taking my own child back to England."

Isabel managed a smile. "But you are not married, Mama. People would be shocked."

Julie smiled back. "I will marry Theo," she said.

The next day she visited Sergei in his cell and told him the news. To her distress he beat his fist on the dirty cell wall.

"A child! I can bear the suffering I brought on myself, but this will kill Isabel. And the child will die. Oh, what have I done, what have I done!"

Julie could only repeat that she was doing all she could for them both, and went back to the little house with tears freezing on her cold cheeks.

When he returned from the prison at Chita Theo was delighted to find Julie so affectionate and so eager to hear the tales of his visit. She explained how upset she had been on their first evening at Nerchinsk, and how much she missed him. They dined together at his hotel, and at the end of the evening she pleaded fatigue and took a room next to his. That night, to his great delight, she came to his bed.

"I have never met anyone else like you, my wonderful Julie," he said kissing her passionately. "I love everything about you, your fierce spirit, your courage and then you are beautiful, so beautiful." He lifted her hair and kissed the little constellation of pockmarks on her temple.

As she lay beside him after they had made love she thought of the past. Long ago she had deceived Jem so as to have a father for Harry. But this time, she told herself, the deception was for Isabel and her grandchild, and she made up her mind to think no more about it. She decided she and Theo would make love each night.

Two weeks later she told Theo her courses were late and she feared she was pregnant. He kissed her, his boyish face shining with excitement.

"Julie, that is wonderful! To think that I am to be a father! Now you must marry me, dearest and make me the happiest man in the whole world."

He poured out two glasses of ruby Crimean wine. "To our baby, who will be as beautiful as you are!"

"Theo, there is a difficulty. You told me you are already engaged."

His grimaced, having already forgotten about Georgina. "I will write and tell her it was a mistake. She is only eighteen and I know she will find happiness with someone more worthy of her."

The next day they announced their engagement, and a week later they were married at the little church at Nerchinsk, with Vera and a few of the other wives present. Isabel could not attend, but she told her mother that she liked her new step-father.

"How strange that I am giving my approval of your

husband, Mama, and not you of mine," she said, smiling. Although she knew she was dying she was comforted to know her baby's future was safe.

Julie liked Theo, enjoyed his company, admired his courage and was grateful for his unwitting help. If she did not love him she revelled in being loved. She made sure she welcomed his lovemaking with enthusiasm.

A few days later Julie told Theo that her courses had appeared and that there was to be no baby. He was disappointed, but kissed her and told her there would be others.

Julie's plan worked. Theo visited Isabel again and was told of her pregnancy. Later, in bed that night with Theo, Julie proposed that they pretend the baby was theirs so they could take it home to England, as though the idea had just occurred to her. Theo agreed at once, sorry for Isabel and willing to do anything that would save her child. He was also happy for Julie, whom he thought was unhappy at the false pregnancy.

"Your mother and I mean to have a large family, and your child will be brought up with all of them," he reassured Isabel.

Isabel caught her mother's eye, knowing she was past childbearing, and Julie flushed. She wished she had not had to deceive Theo.

During Isabel's pregnancy Julie sat at her bedside sewing or reading to her. They talked of the past, of Jem, the father Isabel never knew, of Thrushfield and Starcross. Her despair at Isabel's condition was mingled with happiness at the love they had for each other.

To get relief from the sickroom she shopped in the market or visited the Buriat camp, taking homemade gifts of shirts or cakes. She even learnt a few words of their language, much to Prince Munku's amusement.

The other prisoners' wives congratulated Julie on her condition, secretly surprised that she had conceived so quickly at her age. They offered to visit Isabel, but Julie made the excuse that her daughter was now too ill to receive them.

She visited Sergei at the prison as often as she could, reporting Isabel's condition and repeating messages from her.

"My poor, dear Isabel – but our baby will be safe. How can I ever thank you? Your husband Mr. Johnson has been here to ask us questions about the prison conditions. He was telling me about the few prisoners who have escaped and the safe houses and monasteries that sheltered them, but then Dubrovsky arrived and had him removed. Mr Johnson is a good and brave man and you have done an unselfish thing in marrying him, especially as I think you do not love him."

Julie felt obscurely pleased.

Christmas came and went and she and Isabel celebrated as best they could, exchanging little home-made gifts and singing carols.

By the end of nine months Julie was so swaddled with petticoats and scarves she could hardly walk.

Isabel's baby daughter was born at one o'clock on a cold night in February. It was a long and difficult birth, which left her weaker than ever. Her skin was sallow and her sagging breasts were empty of milk. As she could not feed the baby Julie engaged a Buriat girl as a wet-nurse. Irina had just lost a baby of her own and her large breasts were bursting with nourishing milk. Baby Natasha, who was thin and yellow when she was born, was soon sucking contentedly and growing plump and pink.

When the baby had been fed and her napkin changed, Julie would tuck her into the bed beside Isabel.

"It's strange, Mama, but these months with you have been wonderfully happy, because we love each other. And now I have my little Natasha I am so very happy and do not mind dying. Isn't she beautiful? Promise me you will not be too sad when I am gone. When she is old enough tell Natasha about me and Sergei, and say how much we loved her, and look after Sergei for me…"

She died a few days later. Julie looked at her, her fair hair spread over the pillow and felt as if she could not draw breath for pain. She was filled with bitter regret for all the wasted years when there had been such a distance between them. Since she had come to Siberia they had been so close, had talked with so much love. It seemed to her against nature that her child should die before her.

Isabel was buried in the little graveyard on a hill outside the town, mourned by many who had come to love her. Julie could not speak or eat, lost in a suffocating grey fog of misery. Each day she spent time hunched by the snow-covered grave, hugging her knees and rocking to and fro in her inconsolable grief. The cold wind bit into her, but even then she was unwilling to return home and leave Isabel alone.

Theo arranged their departure, asking Irina to come with them to England to care for little Natasha. The Buriat girl nursed the baby devotedly and was glad not to be parted from her.

"But first I must visit the gold mine and prison at Kara," Theo explained to Julie. "It is notorious for the terrible conditions suffered by the exiles."

"No!" cried Julie, "You cannot! You said yourself we must get Natasha back home as soon as we can."

"Dearest, do you not remember that I neglected to visit Kara for your sake when you were in a hurry to reach your daughter? I owe it to those poor wretches to let the world know of their hellish lives. You cannot balance one little baby against such a weight of suffering."

Julie refused to listen, screaming at him that they owed it to Isabel to get Natasha safely home, and in the end he gave way. He sympathised with her deep sorrow, but couldn't help wishing he had back the lively woman he had married such a short time before.

Before they left Julie visited Prince Munku for the last time, taking him a shirt she had made for him as a parting gift. She had embroidered red roses at the neck and cuffs, telling him they were the emblem of her country in the far west. She gave a carved wooden workbox to the Prince's wife and a paper packet of barley sugar to the Wolfcub.

The Prince had heard of Isabel's death. "Now she is with her ancestors," he told her, "but the shaman has spoken more of this heavy thing. He says that one day you will know great joy."

Then she and Theo, together with Irina and baby Natasha, left Nerchinsk for the long journey home to England.

Chapter Fifteen

ENGLAND 1829

The travellers arrived back at Starcross in the spring. The blackthorn in the hedges was smothered under drifts of snowy blossom, the bushes were misted over with green, yellow oxslips starred the meadows and the scent of the earth and growing things filled the warm air.

"It is truly beautiful," said Theo.

"I wish I was back in Siberia," Julie answered shortly. "Isabel lies there."

He took her arm. "Julie, we cannot change the past, but now you will see your sons for the first time for two years. Can you not be a little glad?

Indoors her spirits did rise, for Harry and George had garlanded the parlour with branches of wild cherry and violets to welcome them home. She embraced them both, noticing that Harry seemed taller and thinner, while George was now ruddy-faced and stouter. She was pleased to see that Amy was there too, having left her husband William and returned to Starcross with her little son Tom the year before.

"This is your new father, Theodore," Julie told her sons. "I am sure you will love each other. And this is our beloved Isabel's child, Natasha, and her nurse, Irina."

It was both a sad and a happy occasion. Harry and George could not forget Isabel, and yet they delighted in the rosy, fair-haired little girl who held out her arms to them. They were merely polite to Theo. He was ill at ease, having to face for the first time that he and his step-sons were almost the same age.

"I call your mother my snow-queen," he told them, slipping his arm round Julie's waist. "In Siberia it was so cold she was often white and silver with frost."

"I wish *I* could have accompanied her," Harry replied curtly. "Of course it came as a surprise to find you had married after so short an acquaintance."

"Your mother had been alone all night in the Siberian wilderness, with the wolves howling from the forest. I lost my heart to her when she pointed a gun at me." His boyish face shone with pride as he smiled down at Julie. "There was no reason to delay the wedding."

After Natasha had been caressed by everyone Irina fed the child and put her to bed, while the others enjoyed the special dinner of river trout, venison, pigeon pie, syllabub and blue cheese that Amy had asked the cook to prepare.

Tired though they were Julie and Theo sat up with Harry and George late into the night recounting their adventures. Theo told them how their mother had made herself appear pregnant, laughing at the memory.

George frowned. "Forgive me, Mr Johnson, for not joining in your mirth. You see, my brother and I have lost a beloved sister and we cannot share your amusement in the story."

A deep red flush covered Theo's boyish face. "Of course, forgive me."

"It will take time for him to become part of the family," thought Julie, looking at her sons' faces in the candlelight. "Both for me and for them." She had not wanted to make love with Theo since Isabel's death, and had not the energy to pretend she did. However, he had been the means of saving little Natasha and she wanted him to feel at home at Starcross.

It was useless. Theo was a journalist and no country-man. Try as he might he could not take an interest in the breed of pigs so fat they could hardly stand, prize cattle, or the latest design of threshing machine. He spent his time alone at a desk in the library putting his notes on the conditions of the Siberian prisons in order. Often he went to London to see the editor of The Times, taking a sample of his work with him. There he was congratulated and asked to write, not only a series of articles, but a book of his experiences. He stayed in London to meet the engraver who would reproduce his drawings.

He also visited his parents at the big house in Kensington. He had written to them from Nerchinsk about his marriage, but they had not forgiven him his treatment of Georgina, and his reception was a cold one.

"This woman is old enough to be your mother, Theodore," said his mother bitterly. "You will tire of her in a few years, but it will be too late. There will be no marriage to a girl of good family then."

"But mother, if you would only meet Julie you would love her as I do," Theo said unhappily. "I know I have treated Georgina badly, but I realise now that I never loved her as I should. And you tell me she is to be married to Gerald Dartford in the summer, so she has not mourned me for long."

"That is not the point, my dear boy," said his father.

"You did not behave like a gentleman. Your mother is right, it is better you do not bring your wife here."

Theo did not mention this slight to Julie, making excuses that his mother was in delicate health. When in London he met many Russian exiles and often found it convenient to stay the night at a hotel. He always asked Julie to come with him, but she was unable to leave Starcross. Little Natasha developed one childish ailment after another and she refused to leave the child's bedside, fearful of losing her as she had lost her daughter.

She imagined she saw Isabel everywhere, in her room before the mirror, in the library reading novels, in the parlour dancing. She saw her in her dreams and woke knowing she had gone forever. Isabel's child was her greatest comfort, though to her annoyance Irina behaved as though Natasha was hers. She nursed her, fed her and sang her Russian folksongs and lullabies. If Julie picked her up she almost snatched the child back from her arms.

"I am being small-minded," Julie confided to Amy. "She lost her own baby, and it was she who suckled Natasha, so it is natural she behaves as she does."

"I found her weeping for her home and the wild cold land where she was born," said Amy. "She says everything here is too small."

After that Julie often sat with the Buriat girl and talked of Prince Munku and Siberia. Later she noticed that George was following Irina round the house and farm.

"She has a lovely voice, hasn't she, Mother?" said George, listening to her sing to Natasha. "She told me she used to help her father with their huge flocks. She knows a deal about sheep and I've asked her to come with us when we buy the new ewes."

"George is sniffing round her skirts like a dog in

heat," said Amy, laughing. "He has difficulty keeping his breeches buttoned."

By this time King William was on the throne of England. Harry and George paid their farmhands eight shillings a week when the other farmers paid only seven, so that with good management and new ideas the farm prospered. The brothers were full of plans to buy even more land. They talked about building a larger barn where the harvest home supper would be held, and discussed the possibility of buying the mill.

That evening they gathered in the parlour after supper. Julie played with Natasha, while Irina sewed the hem of a petticoat for the child and George skimmed through a catalogue of farm machinery. Harry finished adding up a column of figures.

"Everyone knows that Miller Hopkins is a scoundrel who steals some of all the corn he grinds. It would profit us greatly if we cut out the middle man and ground our own ..."

"Julie," interrupted Theo, coming in from the library, "I would like you to make a fair copy of my last chapter. It's about the conditions at the Alexandrofski prison –"

Julie bent down and picked up Natasha's rag doll, making it dance, so that the child laughed. "I will do it later, Theo. Can you not see I am busy?"

As soon as the words had been uttered Julie realised how foolish she had been and wished she could take them back.

"I am sorry you cannot spare me a little of your time, Julie," he retorted, nettled.

George looked up from the catalogue. "And I am sorry you cannot spare a little of your time for the farm, Theo. After all, it provides you with a home and income, does it not?"

"George!" cried Julie, shocked.

Theo turned on him, his face tight with anger. "So you think I am a sponger who does not support his wife! Let me inform you my income will come from my book when it is published, and with which I have had precious little help. In London my work is considered of great importance. Here in this small world it seems to count for very little."

He stood looking at the happy, self-contained little group – Julie, her two grown sons, Irina sewing nearby and little Natasha playing contentedly with her rag doll on the floor. He knew then that he would never be part of it.

"I do not think I am wanted here," he said, with some bitterness.

"Theo!" exclaimed Julie, "do not say such things. You are my husband."

"You got what you wanted, Julie," he went on harshly. "A father for Isabel's baby. I think you would like to discard me now my usefulness is over."

"That is not true!" she cried, springing up and laying her hand on his arm.

He shook it off. "Do you think I do not know why you came to me that night in Nerchinsk? I have been used so that you could get your grandchild home. I do not think you are capable of love ... "

She felt as though a bony hand had reached into her chest and was squeezing her heart. Unable to speak, she sat down suddenly, surprised at the sudden pain.

George thrust his face into Theo's. "Do not speak like that of my mother, or I shall make you suffer for it!"

"Your interest in my work vanished very quickly," went on Theo stubbornly, ignoring George and gazing at Julie huddled in her chair. "I have been cheated twice.

You have not been a wife to me since we returned, and you have cheated me of fatherhood. You knew how I longed for us to have children of our own, yet you chose not tell me you were past bearing them."

The pain in Julie's chest loosened its grip. "I am sorry," she whispered. "It is true, but you have Natasha. She is your daughter."

He swooped down and caught the child up in his arms. "Yes, I do have her. Thanks to your scheming she is mine. She bears my name and legally I am her father. And I am leaving and taking her with me to London, and perhaps to America."

Julie rose unsteadily, shrieking "No, you cannot take her away! You cannot!" She clawed at his arm, trying to get Natasha from him. Theo tightened his grip and moved towards the door. Suddenly everything was in confusion. Harry whispered to George and they both shouldered him out of the way as they rushed from the room.

Theo narrowed his eyes and tightened his grip on the struggling child. "This is your own doing, Julie. I am leaving and I believe Irina will come with me to care for Natasha, for she will not want to be parted from her charge. Will you come, Irina?"

Tears trickled down the Buriat's woman's round cheeks. Murmuring that she was sorry she went to Theo's side, unable to leave the child she loved. Julie, hysterical with grief, tugged desperately at Theo to make him give Natasha to her. The child began to wail, struggling frantically to be free.

"You never loved me, or anyone," went on Theo, keeping Natasha out of Julie's reach. "Not even Jem, of whom you have told me so often. He died before you could grow tired of him, as you have of me."

"How can you be so cruel!" shrieked Julie, knowing it to be true. "I have lost my daughter. You cannot take my grandaughter!"

As Theo's grip on her tightened the child screamed "Papa!" pummelling him with her small fists in panic.

"Harry, George, help me!" Julie called wildly when at last they reappeared. They closed the door behind them and stood with their backs to it.

"Theo," said Harry quietly, "give Natasha back to our mother or you will never see your notes on the exiles again."

Theo stared at them in disbelief. A dark flush spread over his face and his eyes glittered dangerously. "What do you mean? What have you done?"

"It is quite simple, Theo," Harry told him. "We have just been to the library and hidden your work, all your notes and drawings, where you will never find them. Your journey and suffering in Siberia will have been all for nothing. Give Natasha back to mother and you shall have the fruits of your labour again."

There was a long pause, then Theo kissed the weeping child. "Goodbye, little Tasha," he said softly, stroking her hair. "When you are grown to womanhood may you have the courage to carry on the fight for justice." He handed Natasha back to Julie, without looking at her "You are despicable," he told them all. "You know full well I promised those poor exiles I would tell the world of their cruel suffering, and I shall not betray their trust. Give me back my notes and I will leave this house at once. You can all go to the devil! I hope never to see any of you again."

As he turned to go Julie saw that his eyes were brimming with unshed tears. He looked so like an unhappy boy that part of her longed to rush and comfort him.

He paused at the door as if hoping she would call him back. When she did not he walked out. Harry followed him to retrieve his notes from the barn. When he took them to his room Theo was already packing a case.

"I am sorry we had to do this, but we could not see mother suffer," Harry told him, handing him the thick bundle of papers.

Theo packed them away carefully and closed the lid of the suitcase, without looking at him. "I have nothing but contempt for you. Did you think I would betray the trust of those poor lost souls?" he asked coldly.

He left the house without saying goodbye.

Julie, with the crying child held tight in her arms, hurried upstairs to watch him from her window as he crossed the fields to the village to catch the stage for London. She knew her marriage was over and that she would not see him again. Her relief at having Natasha safe could not prevent her overwhelming sense of emptiness and failure.

Chapter Sixteen

ENGLAND 1830

Julie and Theo did not meet again. His book on the Siberian exiles was published a year later, illustrated with steel engravings made from his drawings. The first-hand account of the cruel system, which omitted her part in his travels, aroused great interest and concern. He was asked to give lectures and later made editor of The Times. After reading the book Julie wrote to congratulate him, but he did not reply.

With the loss of Isabel and the wreck of her marriage a grey cloud of depression threatened to overwhelm her. To keep it at bay Julie worked hard in the house and on the farm.

One day, going to cut herbs for the linen press she heard laughter coming from the barn. As she watched Irina slipped out, straightening her gown and brushing off wisps of straw. George followed, calling out to Julie that he had been searching for his dog. A week later she went to George's room to take his nightshirt for washing and found them in bed together. Irina's round cheeks flushed scarlet with shame, but George only laughed at being caught naked. The next day he asked his mother's blessing, as he and Irina wished to marry. He told her what she had already suspected, that Irina was carrying his child.

"You should be pleased," Amy told her. "She will stop him chasing the village girls and they can talk about sheep in bed."

For the wedding Julie sewed Irina a gown of dark red and dove grey, adding a sash to disguise her thickening waist. Amy undid her thick plait of dark hair and curled it into fashionable ringlets. The ceremony at St. Lawrence's church was followed by a breakfast to which all the neighbouring farmers came with their wives. Julie did not forget Isabel, but she enjoyed the bustle and her spirits rose.

Not long after Harry announced that he, too, wanted to marry.

"Marry! Who?" asked Julie in astonishment. He was nearly thirty and she had grown used to the idea of her eldest son remaining a batchelor.

"Why, to Fanny, of course. You remember her – Mistress Wardles' grandaughter."

"But she is already married."

"Not any more," he told her. "Her husband was sent to prison for sheep stealing and he died in a brawl there. He was a bad lot, mother, he used to beat her. She's been working as a dairymaid over at Allerton. I've never loved anyone else and I would like to bring her to Starcross this evening to meet you."

Why had she not noticed that Harry was lonely? "Tell me, dearest, why did you not marry Fanny years ago? You told me then you loved one another."

He put his arm round her shoulders. "Because I knew I was misbegotten. I realised some time since that I was not Jack's son but Edgar's, and had heard children of such families might be – strange. Now Fanny has told me that if we had such a one it would be our special child, whom we would love even more."

She kissed him, both relieved and angry at what he told her. She had struggled for so many years to keep her secret to protect him, while all the time he had known and not told her. Neither did she like the thought of being connected with the sinister Mistress Wardle, nor that one day Fanny would be mistress of Starcross. However, when they all gathered in the parlour that evening she received the girl with good grace.

She had last seen Fanny when she was an urchin with a dirty face and runny nose. Now she was a slim, pretty woman with shining auburn hair and a skin like a ripe peach. She bobbed a little curtsey to them all.

"Mrs Johnson, I have never forgotten how kind you were to me when I was little. I was mighty frightened that day in your kitchen when my grandmother stole your silver spoons. I remember how you comforted me. You gave me raisins and let me see your baby, little Isabel. She was as beautiful as a fairy child."

"She was indeed!" said Julie, warming to her at the mention of Isabel. "And you were not to blame for your grandmother's misdeeds, my dear. She was a thief and did a deal of evil in cursing my baby, but that is in the past now and Isabel is at rest, as Mistress Wardle must be."

"But my grandmother is alive," Fanny said, surprised. "There was a wise woman, Mother Ferry, who had a tumbledown cottage on the common. My grandmother lives there now. Have you not seen her with her pack on the roads? She goes from house to house selling remedies to farmers' wives, and she sometimes carries the post when needed. I tell her she is old and should rest, but she will not listen, saying she has still some special letter to deliver."

Julie's heart began to flutter painfully, as though a bird was somehow trapped in her chest. So the sinister creature was close by! And Mistress Wardle's curse had worked, for Isabel had died young. Then there flashed into her mind an image of the more distant past, of an old woman with a pack slowly limping towards Starcross House, an old woman who had brought disaster and the end of childhood.

As she poured the golden wine into the tall glasses for the toast her hands shook.

Harry and Fanny were married a month later. This time Julie made a dress of lime green silk with bands of dark blue set into the sleeves and skirt. Fanny's red hair glowed under its lace headress and she looked so lovely Julie had to stifle pangs of jealousy. Why was it not Isabel standing before the altar, a happy bride, instead of lying alone far away in the cold waste of Siberia?

But she could not bring back the past. Life went on and soon it seemed the house was full of crying babies.

Chapter Seventeen

RUSSIA 1840

For thirteen terrible years Segei toiled in the Nerchinsk silver mine. The grinding hard labour underground, the poor food and foul air in the prison all sapped his strength, yet not a night had passed without thoughts of escape. He knew that if he did not make the attempt soon it would be too late.

Those prisoners whose wives had followed them into exile survived the best, but Isabel had died and he was alone. By then many of his fellow exiles had succumbed under Prison Commandant Dubrovsky's sadistic rule. Some had lost all hope and had committed suicide, others had made reckless bids for freedom in full view of the guards and been shot. A few had gone insane. These unfortunate prisoners, Sergei noted, were laughed at by the guards but not watched so closely. So he decided play the madman.

Once when they had talked of escaping his friend Igor Repin had whispered to him "Our guards are ordinary men. They are not clever, Sergei. Always do what they least expect of you."

He knew that all attempts at escape had taken place

in summer, when the prisoners thought they might survive in the forest. The guards were not so vigilant in winter, certain no fugitive could survive the bitter cold. So he would take his friend's advice and make his break for freedom then.

If only, he thought, Katya could help him as she had so many others.

Letters were rare. It seemed as if the rest of Russia had forgotten about the Decembrists, which is what Tsar Nicholas wanted. Those letters that did arrive were censored. But at long last, in October 1840 Sergei did receive one from Katya in Nizhni Novgorod.

After giving some news of her imaginary family she wrote:

"Our dear little princess, Olga, will be fifteen in August. We shall be holding her party at our Kazan house, and wish you could be there with us. We all pray the Tsar will grant an amnesty. Thinking of you, I opened the cage of my pet sparrow, and away it flew. I quoted to Olga: "I gave a bird its freedom, doing so brings me consolation," and she actually remembered the rest of Pushkin's verse: "...Why complain to God when I can give a single one of his small creatures freedom?" Is she not clever? No wonder her governess thinks so highly of her. Be of good heart. Your friend Katya."

From this Sergei knew that on 15 August of next year he must be in Kazan, where the barge *The Princess Olga* would take him aboard. Katya had also given him the verse from the poet Pushkin to quote as a password.

Alexander Pushkin had never been one of the inner circle of conspirators. However, he had been in sympathy with their aims and Sergei had been distressed to hear he had died fighting a duel. He shredded Katya's letter and swallowed the fragments, allowing a tiny bloom of hope to flower in the parched desert of his heart.

Every month or so the nomadic Buriats passed through Nerchinsk riding their fast little horses and driving their sheep before them. The prison authorities regarded them as barbarians but allowed them to trade with the prisoners. Whenever the Buriat Prince Munku came to the prison he liked to talk to Sergei of Julie.

"Madam Johnson was a great lady. She saved my son from death, she visited our tents and brought him sweetmeats. She learnt some of our language and made shirts for us. We keep these things in our hearts, Lord Andropov."

"I, too, keep her in my heart, Prince. For this reason I trust you and ask your help, for I am leaving this place of sorrow and going to find her. And I go to find my child, whom I have never seen."

"Her whose hair was the colour of the sun went to join her ancestors. That was deep sadness, and it is right you seek your child," replied the Prince, who loved children. "I know you have incurred the anger of the Great Khan of Russia. But he in his turn has incurred the wrath of our tribe. We Buriats are the descendants of the great Ghengis Khan. We were here long before the Cossacks came. The enemy of my enemy is my friend – for that reason also I will help you. When you flee the prison come to our tents, where we are camped to the south beyond the forest. My son the Wolfcub will wait for you and bring you to us. But do not delay, for we must travel to the border of Mongolia after the moon has shone three times with its greatest face."

Freedom! The thought warmed Sergei like the finest Crimean wine and he began to make plans. To be thought of as a madman he knew he must be seen to lose his wits gradually and he began to study those who were truly afflicted. After a few days he began to copy them and act oddly, as if his mind was giving way. He muttered nonsense to himself, and developed a facial tic. A week later he began to make sudden wild gestures and then began to dance. He even managed to croak a few songs, but was silent when spoken to. His fellow prisoners looked on with pity at his apparent decline, but as he hoped the guards laughed at him for a holy fool. Eventually they grew so used to his madness that they ignored him.

He decided to make his escape on Christmas Eve, knowing that on that Holy night they would all be celebrating as best they could. With any luck the guards would be drunk. When he and Igor talked of escaping their living hell his friend's advice had been to trust no one. So Sergei told none of his fellow prisoners of his plan, not even Igor himself. He knew his friend would understand.

Now that the time was so near he was frightened that his plan would fail. He would have only one chance. He trembled, not only with cold, but with fear when Commandant Dubrovsky threatened to build a high stockade directly in front of the prison windows to cut the prisoners off completely from the outside world.

"He wants to kill us," Sergei thought bitterly. "But if I die it will be as a free man."

In November there was an explosion at the mine which killed five prisoners, including his friend Igor. Horrified as Sergei was at the accident and his friend's cruel death, he had the presence of mind to take advantage of the confusion, and amid the smoke and dust managed to conceal a crowbar down the leg of his trousers. To disguise his stiff-legged walk as they trudged back to the prison he began to hop on the other one and to sing. This shocked even the most hardened of the guards. As a result they left him alone and did not bother to check his chains or search him.

At long last the day of his escape came. Supper on Christmas Eve consisted of slightly larger portions of the thin unappetising stew with a few potatoes, black rye bread, a plum pudding and weak tea. Sergei ate hungrily, but concealed his bread inside his jacket. Then he doubled up, making retching noises and moaning loudly that he was ill. To get rid of him the guards banished him to the infirmary, where he feigned sleep until the two guards had drunk themselves insensible on vodka and kvass.

As soon as one had fallen with a crash from his stool and disappeared under the table and the other sprawled across it, Sergei used the crowbar to force the shackles from his ankles. In his haste he bruised his legs badly, but at last he was free of them. There remained the loose chain hanging from his waist and this he tucked up into his belt. Keeping a wary eye on the drunken men he pulled the two thin blankets off his bed, rolled them up and thrust them into them his knapsack. This had belonged to Igor and Sergei whispered a sad thank-you to his dead friend.

Bidding a silent farewell to the prisoners wounded in the explosion quietly dying beside him, he tiptoed past the guards and out of the stench of the infirmary. They had not bothered to lock the door, knowing the only way prison patients ever left was in their coffins.

Outside a freezing wind was blowing. As Sergei frantically piled pine logs against the fence the wind carried the sound of singing from the main building, where the prisoners were celebrating Christmas as best they could. With another silent goodbye to his fellow exiles he clambered up the unsteady pile, tossed the knapsack over, and threw himself from the top of the fence into a snow-drift on the other side. Then he staggered to his feet and looked around.

Before him stretched the vast Siberian wilderness, silvery white in the moonlight. Stumbling and falling, he began to run towards the dark mass of the forest to the south. For thirteen years he had only shuffled like a shackled animal and the sensation filled him with such wild excitement he forgot to be to be cautious.

"I am free!" he cried in the silence to the snow-covered mountains. "Free!"

Luck was with him, for the wind gusted and blew the sound away and snow began to fall, covering his footprints. But the white powdery snow also chilled and blinded him, dampening his exhilaration and replacing it with fear. If he got lost in the icy wilderness he would never find the Buriat encampment. His frozen corpse would be discovered by a search party the next day. He also realised with horror that he had forgotten an important part of his plan – to make up a dummy to take his place in the infirmary bed. He cursed aloud. How could he have been so stupid? Perhaps the guards were already looking for him. Perhaps they were close behind him.

Out of the whirling whiteness the dark forest reared up like a dark wall and thankfully he hurried out of the freezing wind into the shelter of the majestic snow-covered pines. Progress through the forest was slow and after a while he stopped, terror-stricken. Over the murmur of the trees the wind carried the dreaded sound of the prison bell, rung when a prisoner had escaped. How could his absence have been discovered so quickly? Desperately he wrenched a stout stick from the frozen undergrowth and hurried onward, determined to die fighting rather than face recapture.

Later he heard the sound of voices. The searchers were in the forest. At once he flung himself into a snow-drift, hollowing it out and sealing the entrance, poking his stick through the top so he could breathe. During his stay in the Ural mountains he and his friend Petya had often made such snow houses, but then it had been in play. Now his life depended on it.

He hunched in the cold white tomb, hardly daring to breathe, listening to the cracking of the frozen under-growth as the guards searched for him.

"It's that addle-brain, Sergei Andropov," said one. "He won't survive in this damned weather. He should have waited till summer, like the rest of the fools. Let's go back before my balls freeze and drop off."

"He's quite mad. My guess is he'll try going east. Most of the idiots think they can reach the Pacific and get aboard a ship at Vladivostok. They should save them-selves the trouble, they all get caught."

Sergei crouched in his tiny refuge, clasping his knees in anguish as the snow melted and trickled down his neck and the cold penetrated his bones. "Natasha," he whispered, "I will come to find you."

As he waited for the guards to give up their search he thought with despair of the vast distance through forest and steppe he had to travel to reach England. "But I mustn't think of the thousands of miles," he vowed, "I must think only of surviving each step and each hour of each day." He tried to imagine what his daughter would look like, but he could only conjure up Isabel's face, then that faded and Julie smiled up at him.

The voices became fainter. "If the wolves don't get him those slitty-eyed Buriats will catch and eat him. I hear they like human flesh…"

When at last Sergei crawled out of the drift he found

it had stopped snowing. Desperate to put miles between himself and the prison he began to force his way onward. But which way was south? He broke into a sweat, cursing himself for not taking his bearings. He knew, too, that to sweat was dangerous, for his body would cool down even faster. He must keep moving or he would die. The tall pine trees murmured and rustled all around him, as though they also wanted to keep him prisoner.

Knowing that if he gave way to blind panic he would fail, Sergei forced himself to eat the bread he had inside his shirt and quench his thirst by sucking on an icicle.

Later he stumbled into a clearing, an old logging camp where years before the prisoners had sawed logs to build the infirmary. He knew from the old axe marks on the trees which trail led north to the prison and hurried in the opposite direction. His ankles hurt and the cold made his chest ache but he pressed on, knowing every step he took was one further from the hated jail.

After many hours walking he emerged from the forest into the open just as dawn was breaking in a glory of amber, salmon-pink and gold. Waiting for him was a boy with a reindeer sleigh. It was the Wolf-cub, Prince Munku's son.

"I have been here many nights," he said, helping Sergei into the sleigh and covering him with sheepskins. "You are late."

With a tinkle of bells the reindeer trotted uphill and then down into a hollow. The first Sergei knew of the encampment were the skeins of smoke drifting through the holes in the roofs of the grey felt yurts.

Prince Munku, dressed in a red caftan decorated with bears' claws, welcomed him and led him into the largest tent. After the keen cold air it smelt of unwashed bodies and the meat cooking over the central fire. The floor was covered with striped red and blue carpets, scattered with embroidered cushions and bundles covered with sheepskins. Bows, arrows, spears and fishing gear were fastened to the walls. It was crowded with people, women cooking or sewing skins, men sharpening their arrows, fat little children playing with a litter of puppies. They all gathered round their strange visitor, gaping curiously.

By now Sergei was so frozen he could hardly stand. Seeing this a Buriat woman led him away from the fire, gestured to him that he must lie down and piled fleeces on top of him. Gradually warmth seeped back into his chilled body and he slept. Later the chain round his waist was broken off and his chafed ankles covered with a warm poultice. Then he was given a bowl of meat soup, glistening with globules of fat.

It was too rich for Sergei's stomach, used to poor prison food, and he vomited it all up in a great stream. There was a burst of laughter from the onlookers and they closed in on him, clicking their tongues in wonder at his thin clothes and boots. Later the Prince's wife unrolled a bundle containing a pair of reindeer trousers, a thick sheepskin coat and high boots. Then with pride she held up a cream-coloured woollen shirt embroidered with red roses at the neck and cuffs.

"The Madam Johnson sewed little shirts for my children, but this one she made for me," the Prince told Sergei with pride. "But now I am too stout, as you see." He patted his large stomach, roaring with laughter. "You are to wear it, Lord Andropov. When you find her, tell her it was most valued."

As Sergei put it on he felt its warmth and softness, as though Julie was somehow caressing him from half a world away.

Later he was able to eat a bowl of reindeer meat with millet bread. He knew how necessary it was for him to gain strength for his ordeal and he ate the fat meat with relish. He felt safe with the nomads and was grateful for their loyalty to Julie and Isabel. But he was impatient to be on his way.

To his surprise he saw the Wolf-cub and another boy tearing his prison clothes to pieces, laughing loudly. Then they disappeared outside, returning with a bowl of mare's blood, which they dribbled over the rags.

"My sons will scatter these in the snow. The lords of the prison will think you have been killed by wolves." explained the Prince. "Then they will cease to hunt you."

In a week's time the Buriat camp was dismantled and Sergei travelled with them and their flocks westwards. South of Chita they parted company, as they were to cross into Mongolia. The Wolf-cub was told to drive Sergei to the Lamasary at Goose Lake near Selenginsk, where a relation of Prince Munku was the Grand Lama.

"My cousin does not worship the Bear, as we do, Lord Andropov. He now worships the Buddha, but for all that he is a good man and is expecting you."

He gave Sergei a firestick and a knife with a reindeer-antler handle, wished him well and instructed his son to drive him safely to the Lamasary.

Sergei was sorry to part with his friends but glad to be on his way towards Lake Baikal, towards home. The journey was uncomfortable and dangerous. Wildly excited, the Wolfcub whipped the reindeer into a frenzy so that the sleigh bumped and swayed from side to side. Sergei shouted at him to slow down but the boy pretended not to understand. After hitting a rock the sleigh rolled over, throwing him out into the snow. As Sergei picked himself up he saw that the reindeer had bolted, dragging the broken sleigh behind them. The Wolfcub ran after them shouting at them to stop, eventually disappearing into the distance. Sergei waited, shivering with cold, but the boy did not return.

With a feeling of hopelessness Sergei realised he was on his own. The boy would find his way home to the tribe. Sighing wearily he shouldered his knapsack and taking his stick he trudged on westward.

At first he was able to keep a straight course, guided by the weak sun by day and the brilliant stars by night. He made camp between rocks, lighting a fire with the firestick given to him by the Prince and the tinder he kept dry inside his shirt. Warmed by the fire and the reflected heat from the rocks at his back he ate his solitary supper of reindeer meat. Wrapped in his blankets he gazed up at the black velvet of the sky and thought of his mother in the garden beyond the stars. Too cold to sleep he dozed fitfully, waking to hear the eerie howling of wolves in the forest.

After a few days the weather worsened. Dark iron-grey clouds covered the sky, mist hid the mountains and he lost his bearings. By now his eyes were smarting painfully. He sheltered by a rock shaped like a crouching bear to cool his eyes with snow and found his eyelashes were encrusted with ice. He trudged on, a gaunt solitary figure in the vast frozen wilderness. After two days, aching with hunger and panic-stricken, he found himself back at the crouching-bear rock. Only now to his burning eyes it seemed to be strangely marked in orange and black stripes. His face felt as he had been scorched in a fire, yet when he touched his cheeks he could feel nothing.

"I am travelling round in circles. I am in hell, frost-bitten and going snow-blind," thought Sergei in despair.

"Yet I am only at the beginning of my journey. Is this how it will all end?" Frozen, weak and exhausted, he lay down in the snow.

"Life is the gift," said the dead Igor in his ear. "You must survive."

He dreamed he was a boy again, being carried on Platon's broad shoulders through the moonlit orchard at his Grandmother's estate. Suddenly he was awake and knew that the jolting was real. Through painfully inflamed eyes he saw that he was being carried on a hurdle by two hooded figures and knew they must be monks from the Lamasery.

"So I did not die after all," he said to himself wonderingly. "Perhaps I will survive."

When they saw his eyes were open they pointed to a group of buildings ahead. "Lamasary," they told him. "Goose Lake."

He was put to bed in a cell, where an old monk rubbed his frostbitten face and healed his inflamed eyes with scented ointment. Then he fed him with millet gruel, a little at a time until his famished body could digest solid food.

When Sergei had recovered he looked at his new surroundings with interest, but wondered how soon he could leave. He watched the monks as they scurried about their tasks with little steps, their hands tucked into the wide sleeves of their yellow robes. He saw the many gilded buildings with their tilted roofs, the largest being the great hall where the Grand Lama sat in state.

He was about forty, an imposing figure dressed in a long robe of orange silk embroidered with gold thread. On his head he wore a high, pointed brimless hat of blue felt.

He welcomed his visitor in Russian, asking many

questions about the country west of Lake Baikal. Sergei answered as best he could, even drawing him a rough map of the country in the dust of the hall floor. The next day the Grand Lama showed him the main temple, richly decorated with banners and containing vast bronze statues of the Buddha. Incense smoke wafted from brass trays set among dishes of rice and millet. There were many strange curved trumpets, huge drums and a great bronze gong.

After a week Sergei felt well enough to travel, but to his dismay the Lama seemed in no hurry to let him go.

A few nights later, as he lay dozing in his cell he heard a faint shuffling sound. Alert at once, he feigned sleep and watched through half-closed eyes as a muffled figure sidled into his cell. After taking a quick look at the bed the monk stealthily opened Sergei's knapsack and felt about inside. At once Sergei gave a loud snort and pretended to snore. The monk looked up guiltily and slipped from the room.

As soon as he had gone Sergei searched his knapsack and found his reindeer-antler knife was missing. But which of the monks was the thief? The next day he watched at mealtimes, but no-one used his knife to cut their bread. Feeling increasingly anxious he begged the Grand Lama to help him get to Lake Baikal.

"But you should not leave us, there is much yet for you to see," replied the Lama. "There is our great library which holds many valuable Mongolian and Tibetan books. And you have not meditated nor chanted nor learnt the teaching of the Buddha."

Sergei went cold. Was he to be kept prisoner here, before his long journey had properly begun?

"Yes, I am tempted to keep you and hear more of the great world to the west," went on the Lama, as though he had read his thoughts. "But I see you would not be a willing guest. So tomorrow Kunun will drive you to the Great Lake. From there you will cross the ice alone to Irkutsk and he will return here to continue his devotions."

Early next morning Sergei said goodbye to his host, settled himself in the ornate sleigh and covered himself with a bearskin rug. Kunun, the young monk, climbed into the driving seat and with a crack of the whip they were out of the gates of the Lamasery and onto the road to Lake Baikal.

Although Sergei was relieved to be putting more of the Siberian wilderness between himself and the prison, he felt uneasy. The monk had a sullen expression on his round face, and was strangely silent.

When at last they reached the frozen lake Sergei saw the landing stage was crowded with people hiring sledges for the crossing. But to his surprise instead of going directly there the monk led Sergei to an upstairs room in a small inn, where they drank scalding glasses of tea. His feeling that something was wrong increased, for the inn seemed deserted. After the tea had been drunk Kunun told Sergei to stay there while he went to hire him a sledge to cross the lake. Suspicious, Sergei wiped a clear space in the steamy window pane and watched. Below he saw the monk stop and speak to an official, pointing back at the café. The official put money into his hand and nodded.

Sergei trembled with a violent fury, his heart raced and a bitter taste came into his mouth. He had not come this far, been hunted like an dog, suffered cold and hunger, to be betrayed by this treacherous, greedy young man.

He lay in wait behind the door of the empty room.

Kunun was strong and healthy and he was weak from years of work in the mine, so he would have to get him off balance as he had seen the tribesmen do when fighting. When Kunun returned, a satisfied smile on his round face, he leapt on him, clamping his hands rounds the man's neck. The monk's narrow black eyes bulged as he tried to squirm free, but Sergei kicked his legs so violently from under him that he fell to the ground. Blood flowed from a wound in his head. Unable to stop, Sergei went on squeezing his neck until the man lost consciousness.

Thinking that he had killed him, Sergei felt his neck. No, he was alive. As he rolled him on his side the reindeer-antler knife fell out of his robe to the floor. So he was the thief! In a pouch fastened to his girdle he found five roubles. That was the bounty, all his life was worth! Furiously he tore off the monk's yellow robe and black hat, then tied his legs together with one of his own woollen stockings. The other he tied round the man's mouth as a gag. Then, thinking of the kindly Lama, he dipped his finger into the monk's wound and scrawled "A Thief" in sticky red blood across the man's bare chest, before pushing him out of sight under a bench.

"I didn't know I was capable of such violence," he thought triumphantly, as he put on the young man's yellow robe and black hat. As an afterthought he snatched up his wooden begging bowl.

A few minutes later a monk could be seen walking to the landing stage with short steps and bent head, his hands tucked into his wide sleeves. There he hired a sledge to carry him westward across the ice to the western shore of the lake.

When Sergei eventually reached Irkutsk he was cold and hungry. In the bazaar he bought bread, hard-boiled

eggs and pickled cucumber. Although fearful, it gave him
such grim pleasure to be disguised as a monk while
spending the treacherous Kunun's blood-money that he
forgot to keep his head bent.

As he pressed through the noisy crowd of Kirghis,
Tungas, Mongols and Tartars he almost bumped into
two Russian women buying fur hats from a stall. He saw
with dismay they were the Countess Ostrovsky and her
maid. The Countess had followed her husband into exile
and had been granted permission to visit the hospital in
Irkutsk.

Terrified, Sergei backed away and threw himself
down on the cobbles among the beggars outside the
church, remembering to fling Kunun's wooden begging
bowl in front of him. Then he bent his head on his chest.
The one-legged beggar beside him drank red wine from
a bottle, then coughed and spat.

"This is my place," he snarled. "Everyone knows
Mikhail. Make yourself scarce or it'll be the worse for
you."

Sergei sweated. "I'm sorry, my friend. I'll be going
soon."

The beggar seemed mollified and passed him the
bottle.

From time to time a kopek would land in Sergei's
bowl. Later someone tossed in a bread roll, then came a
ball of paper and a greasy chicken leg. Sergei did not
dare to look up until the crowd in the bazaar had thinned
out. Then he ate the chicken leg and examined the ball of
paper. It was a letter which read:

"Sergei, you do not make a good monk, you are too
tall. Dear friend, your secret is safe with me. It is better
that Dubrovsky thinks you are dead. I am glad to tell you
that he has been dismissed, so the suffering will be less. I

give you what I can. May God smile on your journey. Lisa Ostrovsky. Destroy this."

So she had recognised him! Sergei blessed her and kissed the double-headed eagle on the banknote she had folded in with the letter. And of course she was right, at six foot with westernised features he could not hope to pass as himself off as an Asiatic monk. As soon as it got dark he stripped off the disguise and tossed it into the gutter.

"Give me that," cried Mikhail, darting to pick up the bundle, and Sergei saw that he had been sitting with one leg bent under him. The imposter returned and took up his position on the cobbles again. "You're new to this game. Want some advice? Go to the side door of the monastery, they'll give you a coat there."

Sergei's hopes rose. He had twenty roubles! With it he was able pay for lodgings for the night. He could also buy a rifle and ammunition so that he could hunt for food on his journey, thankful that he was a good shot. The next day he called at the large white-walled monastery of St. Methodius. The grave-faced monks who ministered to the little crowd of beggars asked no questions, but gave each a bowl of thick soup, a piece of bread and a blessing. Sergei was also given a second-hand overcoat. Then he crossed the frozen Angara river, and set off westwards.

Chapter Eighteen

ENGLAND 1841

Natasha grew tall for her age, with a pale oval face and grey-blue eyes that reminded Julie of Sergei. Determined not to make the same mistakes she had made with Isabel, she suggested outings and parties. But Natasha was not like her mother and preferred to study. Julie marvelled at her skill at languages. She read novels in French, and was able to talk in Russian and the Buriat language with Irina.

"I have read all my books," she said, spinning the globe in the library and jabbing at Russia with her forefinger. "I want to know about Siberia, about Papa and Mama, I want to know everything about everything."

Julie's stroked the girl's light brown hair. "Then I think you should go to school, dearest, for I have taught you all I know. I have heard of one in Oxford run by two sisters. I will write to them, and if it is suitable you shall board there and come back to us for the holidays."

Natasha flung her arms round her grandmother. "Write and tell them that I won't eat meat and they mustn't try and make me. Oh, and that I won't do calculating, for I find that dull, and I won't gossip with the other girls about sweethearts, neither, for I shall never marry. And tell them I can't sew, but I must be able to study all I want."

Julie laughed. She had never seen her grandaughter so excited. She kissed her, wrote the letter and two weeks later visited Oxford to inspect the school herself. In what seemed to Julie no time at all Natasha had gone and she felt lonelier than ever.

Then one morning Harry found that Daniel, the shepherd, had not come to work. The next day the pigman and cowherd were absent, their wives sending to say they were ill. Soon afterwards Amy took to her bed with a headache and aching back. When Julie brought her some broth she vomited it up, burning with fever. With a sinking heart Julie saw the dreaded red rash on her arms and knew that smallpox had returned to the parish.

"It shan't happen again," she vowed, remembering her Aunt Bess's death when she was a girl. Her own dose of smallpox had given her immunity from the disease, she knew, and Fanny had had cowpox when she was a dairymaid and would not catch it either. Together they would save as many as they could. They cleared the old barn, disinfected it with lye, laid down straw and brought in clean linen for bedding. After they had moved Amy into the barn word got round the village and other patients were brought to be nursed. She and Fanny kept apart from the family and forbade anyone from visiting. Food was to be left outside the barn for them.

For the next few weeks the two women had little sleep. Together they bathed their patients, cleaned up the blood and vomit, cooled their fevered bodies, burnt the straw and boiled the infected bed linen. Most of the sufferers were racked with muscle pains and pounding headaches, their skin crusted with the scarlet pustules. Amy's arms, legs, back and face erupted and she became delirious, calling piteously for her lost child Rosie.

After four weeks old Doctor Jason came for the first time and pronounced the worst was over. Of the eleven villagers Julie and Fanny cared for in the barn, only three died. Daniel lost his sight but survived, as did Amy. She was weak and thin, having drunk nothing but gruel, and her face and arms were badly pitted.

At last Julie and Fanny were able to return to the house, to be told that the parson, the Reverend Tobias Randal, had arrived to see them.

He sat in the parlour, his waistcoat stretched over his bulging stomach. "The whole parish is singing your praises," he told them. "What you did was noble."

Julie was exhausted, her legs ached and she longed to have a bath and wash her hair. She felt like screaming.

"Noble! It was not noble. It was tiring, dirty, disgusting, stinking, horrible. We listened to folk screaming in agony and then we watched them die. We nursed them alone because no one else would. The sick would have welcomed help from the doctor, the dying would have welcomed a blessing from the Church. Now, my eyesight was not affected, and I did not see you or Doctor Jason there to help us."

The Parson prised himself from the chair. "I will forgive you that intemperate outburst, Mrs Johnson, as no doubt your mind is affected by what you have seen. But remember, a sharp tongue is never an attractive thing in a woman. Now I must bid you good-day."

It was not her mind but her body that was affected by the epidemic. She felt tired however much she rested. Every now and then her arms would tingle and her chest constrict as though someone was reaching into it and was squeezing her heart. While the spasms lasted she could not breathe.

The years passed and the family grew. Fanny and Harry had two daughters, George and Irina three boys and a girl. More fields were bought and planted with corn, oats and barley. The stables were enlarged.

"I mean to breed thoroughbreds, Mother," George told her proudly, as he showed her round the new building. "Our Shires are grand animals, of course, wonderful for ploughing, but these horses will be real beauties. They'll be better housed than some cottagers."

Julie admired the whitewashed stalls, the new mangers and the saddle room. She had always loved the smell of hay, straw and leather.

"Where will you buy the thoroughbreds, son?"

He beamed. "I hear Captain Greville's up to his neck in gambling debts. He's had to sell up, and won't need his stable. We'll get 'em at a good price. He doesn't deserve to have such splendid beasts, he's too fond of the whip and spurs."

Julie had not seen the Captain since he had snubbed her so long ago, but she had heard rumours from Amy of his dissolute ways.

A few days later Harry came into the parlour where she was writing letters to tell her he had seen the Captain driving up to their door.

"He's lost his fortune and now he's come to offer to sell us his mares."

But it wasn't Harry or George he wanted to see, but Julie. His gingery moustaches had been shortened and Julie thought he looked more like a tired old horse himself, with his long face and large stained teeth. He accepted a glass of Madeira, humming and hawing.

211

"Mrs Johnson, I have something of importance I wish to say to you," he began, setting down his glass. "I have long admired you, as has the whole village, for the brave work you and your daughter-in-law did during the epidemic. For myself, I have especially tender feelings for you, as I am sure you are well aware."

Julie bit her bottom lip, gazing at him in disbelief. "Indeed I know no such thing…"

He was not listening. "Now a lady on her own like yourself, one with a large estate to manage, must be in need of guidance…"

Julie felt her temper rising. "You mean, Captain Greville, that you wish to apply for the post of estate manager at Starcross? I am afraid we have no need of one."

He flushed at the insult. "My dear lady, I forgive you your foolish mistake. Of course, you choose to be a tease, like so many of the fair sex. No, I have come, as I expect you must know, to ask for your hand in marriage."

It was all she could do not to fling her glass of wine in his face. She stood up, her jaw so clenched with anger she could barely speak.

"Captain Greville, some years ago, when I was in need of friendship, you chose to snub me. No doubt you thought I was not good enough to be in society. Now that I and my family have prospered by hard work and you have wasted your inheritance by gambling and idleness, you wish to repair your fortunes by marriage. My answer is no, and I bid you good day."

After he had gone Julie did not feel triumphant, but strangely melancholy, as though she had lost something. The noisy family lives of her two sons only increased her sadness.

Chapter Nineteen

RUSSIA 1841

"A leper! I am a leper!"

The little crowd around Sergei shrank back, their ruddy faces suddenly ashen with terror. The stout official who had demanded Sergei's papers raised his stick, wanting to strike but afraid to get close. "How dare you linger here, with your filthy disease. Be gone, or I'll set the dogs on you!" he shouted.

As Sergei rose to leave the frightened villagers fled. Only one young woman returned briefly to leave a small bundle for him on a stone. Inside was a meat pasty, still warm from the oven. As Sergei resumed his journey he blessed her for her charity. Starving, he stuffed the pie into his mouth and swallowed without chewing. Attracted by the smell of the meat a mangy brown and white mongrel pattered behind him. When he had put several miles between himself and the village Sergei sat down again, stroked the dog's rough fur and let him eat the crumbs. He wagged his tail and licked his hand.

"Poor fellow, you are hungry too. I'll call you Nikita, after my grandfather, and we will travel the road together."

Not long afterwards another traveller on the great Siberian road caught up with Sergei. The ragged army greatcoat he wore was too large for him and the black patch over his left eye gave him a sinister appearance. To Sergei's annoyance he settled himself on a nearby tree stump and burst out laughing. "Leper my arse! Mikhail knew you were shamming. Still, you scared those village idiots good and proper. You're learning, my friend. We'll do well together."

Sergei thought he had seen him before. The man laughed again and tore off the eye-patch. "Irkutsk, remember?"

Of course, he was the one-legged beggar, Mikhail, only now he was one-eyed. Sergei did not trust him and did not want to travel with anyone except the dog.

"How did you know I didn't really have leprosy?"

"There's a colony of 'em near Selenginsk…Mikhail stayed there a bit, the monks fed him," the man told him with a smirk. "What fools those monks are, risking their own lives looking after that diseased lot." He touched his face, grinning. "You should've seen 'em, Mikhail had to laugh. No noses, some of 'em."

Sergei shuddered, for the skin on the man's face already showed the white patches of a leper.

"I have become a monster, I feel no pity for anyone but myself," he thought, knowing he would leave Mikhail at the first opportunity. As soon as the sun went down he offered to make a fire and under the pretence of gathering sticks, hurried away deep into the forest.

It began to snow. That night he spent huddled inside a hollow tree, the dog Nikita curled up on his chest for warmth. Next day he reached a village where he begged for bread for them both. Of Mikhail there was no sign.

Together he and the dog trudged on, mile after mile

westward, begging, stealing from villages whose names he never knew. Mostly he kept to the fields and forests like the hunted fugitive he was. Light-headed with hunger, he talked to Nikita, telling him his life story.

"So you see, Nikita, I must survive to see my daughter," he told him.

"I understand," Nikita replied sympathetically, wagging his tail. "Have faith. Every step you take is one step nearer home."

Then one day Nikita disappeared. Distraught, Sergei searched the forest calling his name. No welcoming bark answered him and after two days he sadly resumed his journey. It seemed even more dreary now he was alone.

As well as those on foot the great Siberian road was travelled by long freight wagons carrying logs, furs and goods from Siberia to the west, passing others with goods for the east. Once Sergei saw a train of wagons with an armed escort and knew it was carrying silver from the Nerchinsk mine to Moscow. Panic-stricken, he flung himself into a ditch until it had gone by.

At night the wagon drivers stopped, tethered their mules and ate their suppers round their campfires. Sergei often saw the gleam of the orange and gold flames flickering in the gloom but always approached the little groups with caution, unsure of his welcome. So when he saw a figure huddled by a glowing fire and smelt the meat roasting he watched quietly from the shadows.

Sitting alone was an old woman swaddled in coats and scarves against the cold, her feet wrapped in rags in place of boots. She was basting an animal on a wooden spit resting on two forked sticks.

"If you want to get warm by my fire, sit down. Otherwise be on your way," she snapped, without looking up.

"Then I will join you. A fine rabbit you have here, grandmother," said Sergei. As he sat down his stomach rumbled with hunger.

"If you want some, say so," the old woman answered, licking the grease off her fingers. "Otherwise the devil take you."

Even before it was cooked she tore off pieces, blackened on the outside, red raw within. Her gaunt face was lit by the fire as she chewed at the meat like a famished wolf. Then she tore off a leg and handed it to Sergei. He stared at it, puzzled. "This is no rabbit, grandmother."

"What matter? It's all meat."

He looked round wildly, bile rising into his mouth. There, tossed aside, were pieces of brown and white fur and a small skull. Sick with horror, he flung the meat at her.

"You vile old witch, you murderess, you are eating my dog."

She continued to munch. "I'd eat you if you had enough fat on you. Well, starve if you want, it's nothing to me."

Sergei picked up a stone. He wanted to strike her, to hammer her into the ground. "You're a wicked old woman..."

She looked at him, her beady little eyes full of contempt. "You have only lost a dog. I have lost a grandson. Boris was snatched from his school for listening to some liberal nonsense and banished to Siberia. He was only fourteen, a child. I heard he'd escaped hereabouts and I've been searching for him ever since. He's lost, lost..."

Sergei wanted to howl like a wolf. He sank down and put his head on his arm, weeping for all he had lost himself, his home, his father, the regiment, Isabel, the years of his life in the mine, his faithful friend Nikita, for the lost boy. Then, exhausted by the sobs that had racked his frail body he fell into a deep sleep.

Towards dawn he was woken by a gurgling sound. Through heavy eyelids he saw the old woman stumble away from the fire. "She has gorged herself and is sick," he thought with disgust, before falling back to sleep.

When the sun had risen above the trees he woke to find her gone. He came across her at the foot of a pine tree, curled up as though with cramp. She was dead, lying in the pool she had vomited up – a mess of raw meat, fur, grass and earth. He moved her corpse with his foot and her dead eyes gazed up at him.

"Poisoned!" he said aloud into the silence. "You were poisoned because you ate my dog." The trees around him rustled in reply. He placed a few stones on her corpse to stop the scavengers, then scraped a small hollow in which he placed the pitiful remains of Nikita.

As he stumbled along the road black spots danced like flies before his eyes. His legs felt as though he still wore his prison shackles. After struggling on for a few more yards he collapsed.

"Here," said a gruff voice, "Another poor creature – starved, I shouldn't wonder. Help get him into the wagon."

Unable to speak, Sergei felt himself lifted and placed gently onto straw at the bottom of a wagon. His hiding place was narrow, the heavy logs above his head supported by two transverse wooden beams. It was dim, the only light was from the narrow spaces between the tree trunks. Safe at last he fell asleep, the sweet resinous scent of the pine logs entering his dreams as the incense in church on New Years Day. He dreamed of the golden iconostasis and the glorious singing, happy to be a boy again.

The wagon was driven by his rescuers, Old Peter and his wife Maria. Winter was over, spring had come. Now the heat had baked the mud into hard ruts, making the wagon jolt alarmingly. As Sergei was thrown from side to side he was afraid the logs would fall and crush him. He was relieved when night came and he was helped down from his hiding place. Maria tenderly fed him spoonfuls of vegetable soup and in a few days he was strong enough to eat some of her stew. He found they were part of the long train of some twenty freight wagons pulled by mules carrying timber and furs to Moscow.

When it was safe he liked to sit beside Old Peter as he drove the mule. The old man smoked his pipe and asked no questions.

"Why do you risk your life helping people like me?" asked Sergei one day. "There's a bounty out for me and you'd be in trouble if the police caught you."

The old man puffed at his pipe. "Well, it's quite simple. I'd come out of prison and I was in the church praying for a cottage and a cow, so I could marry Maria. This was in the church at Suzdal. But instead of saying, "Very well, Peter," like I hoped, God said I was to change my life and travel the road helping all his suffering children."

One day they heard the thunder of hooves and in the distance saw a cloud of dust, as a platoon of soldiers rode towards them. Sergei slid into the wagon down under the logs, pulling fir branches over him, listening with pounding heart as the horses were reined in beside the wagon train.

"What have you got there, you old ruffian?" shouted a lieutenant, thrusting his sword between the logs on the wagon in front. Sergei pressed himself into a corner, making himself as small as possible. In terror he saw the flashing silver blade dart between the logs above his head, missing his legs by an inch. Then as quickly it was withdrawn.

"Careful you pick up no escaped prisoners, old man, or it will be the worse for you," the officer shouted. He whipped Old Peter's fur cap from his head with the point of his sword and tossed it onto the road before the platoon rode away laughing.

That evening at supper Old Peter told him that a year ago an officer had thrust his sword between the logs and when it was withdrawn the blade was red with blood. The three of them knelt to thank God for their deliverance, and with those prayers Sergei returned to the faith of his fathers.

He had been travelling with the wagon for nearly three weeks. Unwilling to risk the good old peoples' lives any longer he thanked them for their care and told them he must leave.

"We shall remember you in our prayers," old Maria told him, reaching up and patting his face, tears running down her own withered cheeks. Old Peter clasped his hand. "Take my advice and avoid women, or you will never be safe. You talk in your sleep, and that is dangerous. There is a safe house at Tobolsk, the one with green shutters by the church. God go with you, my son."

Warmed by their simple kindness and courage Sergei left them to walk on through forest, fields and steppe.

As he approached Ekaterinburg he saw a despairing column of prisoners trudging eastward towards their exile, as he had done so many years before. A haggard young woman in a threadbare shawl carrying a child held out her cap to him, and risking his life Sergei darted from his hiding place to gave her his last few kopecs.

He crossed the Urals in the heat of June. He earned

his bread working in the fields. When asked for his papers he shook his head and pointed to his mouth, acting the mute. By July he had reached Orenburg, where he was beaten and robbed of the little money he had earned. Hungry, bruised and exhausted he limped the last few miles to his grandfather's estate.

Nothing was as he remembered it. There was a new avenue of trees and a rose garden, outhouses and sleek horses in the fields. The house itself gleamed white in the sun as though it was made of sugar. Suddenly aware of his filthy rags and verminous body, Sergei stood hidden in the shadow of the cedar trees. As he watched a yellow-painted carriage drawn by four chestnut horses drew up to the door. This was followed by an even grander carriage, black with a gold crest on the door. The men who got out were elegant in their scarlet officers' uniforms, the women gay in gowns of blue silk and green velvet.

Sergei was reminded of all the regimental balls he had attended in a life that now seemed so remote and strange to him.

As more guests arrived two figures appeared at the door to welcome them. The woman was young with silver-blond hair curled elaborately, a pearl necklace round her slender throat. The man at her side was as sleek as a seal, with a balding head and black moustache. Sergei saw with a shock of surprise that it was his childhood companion, Petya. He retreated further to a little wooden summerhouse. Inside were two chairs and a table on which stood a jug of lemonade, a glass and an open novel. He drank, read a few pages of the book and waited. Later he approached a hostile servant and sent a message to his cousin.

"Sergei, is it really you! We thought you were dead,"

Petya exclaimed later. He peered at him, then recoiled sharply. Sergei flushed, knowing it was because he stank. "How on earth did you get away? Well, we must talk later. It's the devil's own luck, old fellow, but you can't stay here just now. Next week I'll arrange something, then you can have a bath and I'll get you some decent clothes to wear. It's awkward, my wife and I are giving a party tonight and my father-in-law Vassily Denisov is here, he's Orenburg's chief of police..."

A frost chilled Sergei's soul. "I understand, Petya, you have your position to think of."

"If only you'd turned up earlier, we could have talked of grandfather and the old days," Petya went on, unperturbed. "My brother Vassily died, you know. And Gregory is in France. He'll be sorry to have missed you." He emptied his pigskin wallet and laid some notes on the table. "Here, take these..."

As he babbled on Sergei thought of the old woman by the fire. "Petya, if you intend to help me, say so. If not, to the devil with you." He turned to go, leaving the pile of money untouched. "Keep it," he said bitterly, "keep your good, safe life. I've met more kindness, generosity and courage from the poorest peasants."

As he walked away he heard Petya's call "Wait, Sergei, wait..." but he did not turn back. On and on he walked, savagely determined that nothing, nothing, would stop him reaching Katya and safety.

At Perm his boots burst. He tossed them away and bound his aching feet with strips torn from Julie's shirt. Then one morning, after spending the night in a shop doorway, he found someone had left a pair of boots beside him. They did not fit and bruised his feet, but he was thankful.

Starving and footsore, thin as a skeleton, Sergei

221

limped into Kazan on the fifteenth of August, 1842. He was just in time.

The great city was crowded, baking in the summer sunshine. He pushed his way through the noisy, smelly mass of people at the riverside, searching among the vessels unloading at the wharves for *the Princess Olga*. Although many of the barges bore the name Trepov, *the Princess Olga* was nowhere to be found. Sweating with anxiety he began to run. Surely it hadn't left without him? No, that wasn't possible, that would be too cruel, God could not let that happen. Stumbling, desperate to find it, he did not look where he was going and cannoned into a short middle-aged man who was arguing with a porter.

"How dare you!" the man cried sharply, reaching out and grasping hold of Sergei's arm. "Have some respect for your betters."

Sergei found himself looking into the man's cruel little eyes. It was Dubrovsky.

The man stared hard at him and tightened his grip. "I know you, Andropov," he said softly. "I didn't think you were dead."

Like the terrible explosion at the mine, a red burning fury erupted in Sergei. He had not come so far and suffered so much to be caught within sight of freedom. With lips drawn back in a snarl he kicked out viciously at the older man's legs, so that he lost his balance and fell heavily onto the stones. Then he drove his boot into the man's side and ran, his heart beating so hard he could hardly breathe for terror. Behind him he could hear Dubrovsky gasping and calling for the police.

Where could he hide? In his ear the dead Igor whispered to him. "He will expect you to run, my friend. Therefore be still."

At once Sergei darted down a narrow alley crowded with stalls selling old clothes. He collapsed onto the cobbles in a trembling, sweating heap, wetting himself with fear. Then, remembering Mikhail at Irkutsk, he tucked his left leg under him, holding out his hand for money and lowering his head onto his chest. His heart thudded so loudly he thought the sound would surely betray him.

Dubrovsky, supported by a policeman on his left, and with his hand pressed to his right side, came limping slowly down the alley.

"I tell you the man's an escaped convict and dangerous," he shouted, not giving a glance to the huddled figure of the beggar at his feet. Sergei waited, perspiring, until they moved away, then he got up and ran panic-stricken further along the bank of the river. And at the very end of the wharf he found the black-painted barge, the *Princess Olga*.

By the landing an old man in a sailor's cap was sitting on an upturned bucket, smoking a pipe and tossing bread to the gulls. He looked the dishevelled Sergei up and down.

"Nice birds," he said casually. "Clever, too. That brown one there, I used to have it in a cage. I gave it its freedom because it gave me happiness." He paused and looked at the ragged figure before him.

Sergei stared, his mouth opening and shutting like a fish stranded on a riverbank. In spite of the suffocating heat sweat trickled in freezing rivulets down his chest. The old man had mangled the first part of the quotation from Pushkin, but what was the rest of it? It was so long since he had received Katya's letter! On board the barge he knew there would be clean clothes, food, forged papers, a new life. If only he could remember the passwords.

Then when he was ready to weep with despair the words came to him and he stammered "..why complain to God when I can give a single one of his small creatures freedom?"

The old man nodded. He rose and went on board the barge. "Follow me," he said quietly, and Sergei knew he was safe.

Chapter Twenty

ENGLAND 1842

As the years passed it became plain that Starcross was too small for Harry and Georges' growing families. So Julie had east and west wings built for them onto the original Tudor house, in the latest Victorian style. She now lived alone in her old home, although there was much noisy coming and going of servants and children between the households.

Julie's two daughters-in-law were very different. Irina, like George, had grown stout and placid, but Julie saw that it was she who ruled the household. She never caressed her children, but nevertheless Julie saw that they were happy and shared her love of the farm and the flocks.

The terrible experience of caring for the sick during the smallpox epidemic meant that Fanny was closer to her, as were her three redheaded grandchildren. Harry's worry that they would have a "special" child had proved unfounded. Fanny worked hard, managing the new dairy and selling the cream and herb cheeses in the markets at Wychwood and Allerton.

One day Julie went through to Fanny's kitchen in the east wing to ask for some sour cream. She wanted to make blinis, because the taste recalled memories of Nerchinsk where she had cooked them for the dying Isabel.

Her daughter-in-law was standing at one end of the table rolling out pastry for a mutton pie. At the other end sat a shabbily dressed old woman drinking tea from a saucer. As the old woman looked up at her Julie saw her right eye droop in a slow wink, and with a sudden shock she saw that it was Mistress Wardle. Fear and anger surged through her and she abruptly left the room.

Later she sought Fanny out in the dairy. It was the part of the farm she liked best, a cool stone room with its slightly acid smell of sour milk and its grey-blue slate shelves piled with ripening cheeses. Fanny, her red hair tucked under a mob cap, was standing at the bench with a green and black crock of milk, skimming the thick cream off the surface with a slotted spoon. Susan, her eldest daughter, was pressing sprigs of rosemary onto rounds of pale yellow cheese, while her sister Ellen churned the butter. The two girls were singing a song to make the butter come. Julie could not suppress a pang of envy – if only she had had such a hard-working, sensible daughter – if only Isabel had not died …

It made her a little short with her daughter-in-law. "Fanny, I forbid you to have Mistress Wardle in my house, she is evil."

"But you forget that the east wing is *my* house," Fanny replied calmly, spooning the mounds of cream into a blue crock. "I do not presume to tell you who you can entertain in yours. I know some folk used to fear my grandmother as a witch and she *was* a thief, but she is old and harmless now. She brought me up when my mother died and I must do what I can for her. I have told you she is earning her bread as a post-woman, carrying letters. I wonder you have not seen her in the village. I have told her there is no need for her to work but she is getting confused, like all old folk and still insists she still has a special letter to deliver to someone."

For a moment Julie had an inner vision of a great and terrible clock ticking towards some fearful, desolate future. She shuddered, feeling as though a chill wind had blown through the dairy. Then Fanny smiled and filled a little bowl of sour cream for her and the vision vanished. She thanked her daughter-in-law, trying to behave as though nothing had happened. And what Fanny said was true, she had the right to see her grandmother. She wondered if Harry had told her of the curse.

"Very well, Fanny dear, but I have my reasons for not wishing to see her, so please make sure she stays in your part of the house."

After that if she saw Mistress Wardle with her pack of letters in the village or crossing the fields she avoided her and returned home. Later she challenged Harry.

"Mother, I am surprised you still believe in that silly curse. You must know it is all superstition."

"Perhaps it is. But you cannot deny Mistress Wardle had her revenge. Our darling Isabel died young."

He put his arm round her shoulders. "My poor sister died of consumption. She and I both had weak chests, but it was the Siberian winter that killed her."

Julie looked at her eldest son. He was tall and thin, and his hair was now brushed back. He looked so like Edgar it startled her. But there was intelligence and kindness in his dark eyes that she had never seen in her brother's. She reached up and smoothed his hair. She did not believe him but felt comforted all the same.

The summer of 1842 was hot and Wychwood slumbered under the golden July sun. The school closed for the holidays and Natasha went to stay with her friend

Louisa, the Squire's daughter, at the big house. Then early one morning Harry and George and all the children went off to the Strawberry Fair at Birchington. Julie never forgot her own years as a servant and willingly gave all hers permission to go and enjoy the holiday.

Without children or servants Starcross was unusually quiet. Julie was able to enjoy the day reading and daydreaming in her chair by the window. She looked out with pride at the acres of ripening golden corn, at the brown and white cattle in the pasture and the sheep in the fields. How hard her sons had worked! If only Isabel were still alive to enjoy it all.

Later she fell into a deep sleep and dreamed of the snowy wilderness, of the vast dark forests and mountains of Siberia, of Isabel and Sergei.

She was roused from her sleep by a knock on the door. As there were no servants in the house she tidied her hair, smoothed her blue gown and went to open it.

Outside stood a tall, stooped figure, dressed in a grey suit. He stared at her in silence and she thought there was something familiar about him ...

"Julie," he said at last, "Julie." He had a low pleasant voice with a trace of accent. "It is I, Sergei Andropov. Do you not know me?"

The colour faded from her cheeks and with a cry she crumpled to the floor. Horrified, Sergei lifted her up and carried her into the parlour, calling for the servants as he did so.

"Please!" he cried, rubbing her hands, "Julie, do not die!"

After a few minutes her eyes opened. She stared in wonder at the beloved face, unable to speak for a surprising, overwhelming joy. Then she murmured "It is true. I am not dreaming, Sergei, you are here."

He smiled down at her. "Yes, Julie, I am here. I am sorry I came without warning."

"Oh, Sergei, Sergei, what happiness! You are no longer a prisoner! Has there been an amnesty for the exiles?"

"No, one was long hoped for, but Tsar Nicholas never granted it. I escaped from the prison and walked home across Russia. I suffered a great deal, but by a miracle I survived. There is so much to tell you..."

She was content to gaze at him. His face was thin but though his hair was now silver it was still thick and a lock still fell across his brow. His slanting grey eyes were shadowed and little lines radiated from their corners.

"I have always loved you, always, always."

"It's so strange, I was dreaming of you and Isabel," she told him.

"Oh Julie, what a terrible wrong I did her. She was so beautiful and so unhappy. She loved me and it was a weakness in me that I thought I returned her love."

"You did not love her."

They fell silent, thinking of her. After a while Sergei asked about Natasha and Julie explained that while the others would return that evening his daughter would be back the next day.

"You will be so proud of her, Sergei. She is not beautiful, like Isabel, but she has lovely eyes and is so clever. She can speak Russian with Irina and French, and loves to study."

"Then you must have brought her up well."

"She is not only part of Isabel, but part of you, my dearest love,"

"I long to see her. But where is Theo? I have read his book and it is splendid. You must be proud of him.

"He left us when Natasha was a baby. I will tell you of it later. First tell me how you survived."

"I nearly died, but I found God in the forest and He protected me. And I could not leave this world before I had seen … my daughter."

"And me. Say you came here to see me."

"Oh Sergei, to think the last time we saw each other you were in chains. And you are still so very thin."

"I want to care for you always."

"I will fetch us something to eat, Sergei."

They ate a meal of bread and butter, cold ham and potatoes and drank glasses of white wine. Afterwards they strolled round the house and orchard. Sergei walked slowly, with a slight limp.

"How beautiful Starcross is, Julie."

"It is beautiful because you are here with me."

"It is the same and yet so different, and the park is a prosperous farm. Your sons have done well. I thought of Starcross often when I was in prison. I used to wonder if you would still be here. And then when you fainted I was afraid my sudden appearance had killed you, as it did your father."

"You cannot blame yourself for his death. His heart was not strong, and I fear neither is mine now. We are both of us older, you and I."

"Let us make the most of what time we have left. Tell me you love me."

The sun was a burnished copper disc high in the blue summer sky. The fields shimmered in the heat and soon they returned to the cool of the parlour. Sergei stretched his long legs out and sighed.

"Julie, you and I have lived too long and suffered too much not to say what is in our minds."

"Say you love me. Say it, say it!"

Just then they heard the sound of excited children shouting outside. The parlour door burst open and

Julie's six grandchildren tumbled in. Little Edmund rushed at her, his mouth sticky with orange barleysugar.

"Look, Grandmama, I have a fairing."

"We saw a sheep with five legs," shouted Bertram.

"Mother," said Harry, as the adults followed. "I have good news. I have met with the Squire and he has suggested I become a Justice of the Peace..."

He noticed the tall figure by the fireplace and stopped in surprise.

"And I have the most wonderful news," Julie told them all. "Sergei Andropov has arrived, after escaping from exile in Siberia."

"The devil you have!" cried George, hurrying to shake his hand.

"Great news indeed," said Harry.

They crowded round him, all talking at once. Fanny and the children were introduced, and then Irina came to clasp his hand and welcome him in Russian.

Visibly moved, Sergei thanked them for their welcome, saying he did not deserve their affection because he had eloped with Isabel, and she had not returned home.

"She loved you," Harry said simply. "We forgave you long ago."

"What tales you must have to tell," added George. "When the children have gone to bed you must tell us your adventures."

"And tomorrow I will fetch Natasha, so she can meet her father," added Harry.

"*But he's mine. I want him to myself.*"

They talked until the grandfather clock struck midnight. Sergei's face was grey and Julie felt his exhaustion as if it were her own. She showed him to his room.

"Tomorrow let us talk alone, Julie," he said quietly. "I

shall meet my daughter for the first time and the day will be hers, but let the night be ours."

"I love you. Yes, my dearest, let the night be ours."

Julie could not sleep. She sat by her open window looking up at the starry sky, brimfull with happiness. It was enough to know that Sergei was under the same roof, that there was only a wall between them, that they breathed the same air. She imagined him in the four-poster, his beloved face in repose, and longed to kiss his closed eyes.

"It is so strange, I have never, ever, felt like this before. I have lived all this time and never knew such feeling existed. Not with Jem and not with Theo. How wonderful life is."

Next morning Harry rode over and brought Natasha back to Starcross. She entered the room shyly, her bonnet dangling from its ribbons in her hand. She was now fourteen, her golden-brown hair curled in ringlets about her oval face.

"So you are my father," she said quietly. "I have longed to meet you. I am so happy. It is a miracle you have escaped."

"The miracle is that I have lived to see this meeting, Natasha. Come, let me look at you," Sergei said, holding out his hands to her. "I tried to imagine how you would grow up and longed to be a true father to you."

They sat side by side and talked as if they had been together all their lives. Later Julie saw them walking through the garden and across the fields together. Natasha had slipped her arm through his, reminding her of the time she had looked out and seen Sergei with Isabel.

"I should be walking beside him. No, I won't be jealous, she has a right to be with her father. Only let night come quickly."

232

The day seemed to go on forever. She listened to the grandfather clock in the hall strike the hours, longing for time to go by so she and Sergei could be to be alone together. When at last the house was quiet they stole like children out into the moonlit orchard.

Julie felt they were in their own enchanted kingdom. Everything was magically, beautifully bright. The leaves glistened, the ripening apples shone like little jewels, and the trunks of the trees made long black shadows on the grass, while the sweet smell of hay and wild roses scented the night air.

"Let time stop now. Let us stay here in the orchard forever."

"Julie, Prince Munku gave me the shirt you made for him and I wore it always. I felt it would somehow keep me safe because you worked on it with your own hands. I felt I had part of you with me."

"You wore it next to your heart."

"And sometimes when I was starving I saw visions. I thought I saw you in the forest. You took my hand and led me to safety."

"Please, take my hand now. I shall die if you do not touch me."

Aloud she said "I thought of you so often. Perhaps my thoughts travelled over the forest and steppe to reach you half a world away."

"Do you remember when we watched together over your father's body that night all those years ago?"

"Yes, I have never forgotten."

"I have thought of it often, my darling Sergei."

He turned and looked at her. "You leant over and touched me here with your fingertips on my breast, just above my heart."

"Yes, I remember."

"Touch my breast, Sergei."

He paused and they sat down on a wooden seat side by side. Julie clasped her hands together to stop herself trembling.

"Julie, no woman, no wild embrace, has ever meant as much to me as that light touch of your hand."

"Because I loved you then, I know it now."

He looked at her. "I am not worthy of anyone's love."

"That is not true, Sergei. You are worth the whole world to me"

"I have failed miserably in everything I tried to do. I could not save my dear old servants, and I was given a medal at Austerlitz, not because I was brave but because my horse bolted towards the French. I failed as a husband, and I failed my comrades in the conspiracy. I was not even at St Petersburg that fateful December because I had a most undignified carbuncle and could not walk or ride."

"Hush, nothing we can do can change the past, Sergei. And Theo was brave and successful, yet I did not love him."

"Say it, say it. Say you love me."

His finger traced the outline of a white lily embroidered on the sleeve of her blue silk gown, not looking at her. "I must say it, yet how can I – you are Isabel's mother, my mother-in-law. But I love you, Julie. I think I always have. Perhaps ever since I heard your father speak of you in St. Petersburg when I was a boy." He took her hand in his. "Is it not strange that our lives have been so entwined?"

His touch was like a shock to her whole body, filling her with blazing happiness. The moonlit orchard bloomed and shone with irridescent silver light as though lanterns had been hung from all the branches. All her life had been journeying towards that moment. She leant over and kissed him on the lips.

"My dearest, my darling Sergei, I know now that I have loved you always. Ever since my father told me of the young boy who ran downstairs to his father and who sat on the stairs with his bare toes peeping out from under his nightshirt. I think I was so very angry when you eloped with Isabel because I was jealous of her. Kiss me."

They lingered in the orchard until a chilly dawn wind blew and the clouds were outlined in silver, then pink, then rose red. Then gold flooded the eastern sky.

They tried not to show their love, but Julie felt his eyes constantly on her. And whatever she did she could not keep away from him, brushing against him as she passed, touching his hand as if by accident. When he walked in the garden with Natasha or round the farm with Harry and George she would go into his bedroom and press his nightshirt to her face.

Each evening the family gathered in the parlour where Sergei told them the story of his long journey from Nerchinsk. He reached the part where he was close to death on the slopes of Mount Altai and was rescued by an old man driving a freight wagon bringing timber from Siberia to the west.

"Old Peter was a true Russian peasant, a good man who risked his own life helping escaped prisoners. He once told me he heard God speak to him in church, and I asked him if he heard it in his head or out loud. He told me he heard it aloud, quite clearly, and that the voice sounded a little like a blackbird singing, but mostly like a girl with a cold. So I asked him if God was a woman, then, and he said that puzzled him, too. So he said to God, "Pardon my impertinence, God, but are you male or female? And God said he was both and neither, but that he wasn't to bother his head about it."

"I like that story, father," Natasha said, amid laughter. "I would dearly like to go with you to Russia."

"Sergei is not returning, he is safe here," Julie said quickly. "He hates Russia."

"That is not true, Julie," Sergei answered sadly. "I love my country with all my heart, and I miss it so much – especially our Churches with their golden iconostatis, the candle-lit processions and the glorious singing."

Julie wished she could put her arms round him to comfort him. Up until that time it had been enough for them to be together in the same room, to catch each other's eyes, to brush hands as they passed. She felt his eyes on her like the sun's warmth. Each evening when the others had gone to bed they walked in the garden, their fingers entwined like young lovers.

"We must tell each other everything," said Julie later. "I want to hide nothing of my life from you."

She told him about Edgar, and that Harry was the child of incest.

Sergei lifted her hand and kissed her fingertips one by one. "I hate to think of your unhappiness, dearest. But we cannot alter the past. Edgar is dead and Harry is a fine young man and a credit to you."

Sergei told her of every detail of his suffering in the mine and prison and the terrible walk to freedom. He told her that when he was starving he had slept with a heavy stone on his stomach to give himself a feeling of fullness, and how he had even eaten grass and earth. He told her that he had been sheltered by a peasant woman, a widow, who took him in when he was lost and whose bed he shared. But his talk was of the past, and he shied away from talk of the future. They both knew they could not marry.

"I feel we are married," she told him, reaching up and pushing the loose tendril of hair from his forehead. "Let us not waste any more of our lives apart."

That night he moved into her room and they made love. The world shrank to the warm space in his arms.

"This is a forbidden love," Sergei murmured into her hair, "my dearest, my heart's darling."

"I shall die of joy," she said. "I don't care what the world thinks."

He kissed her. "I feel as though we are two halves of a whole being and now we are together we are complete."

"Then we must never part. Sergei, promise you will have nothing more to do with these liberal societies…"

He put a finger on her lips. "Hush, my darling, my love."

There were nights when Sergei tossed restlessly, reliving his suffering in his nightmares, waking wet with perspiration. Then Julie held him, soothing him like a child until he fell asleep once more.

"Mother is different," complained George later to his brother as they leant over the gate to the pasture. "Sometimes she does not answer when I speak to her, and she smiles at nothing. It's damned odd."

"Oh George, you are blind," Harry replied, laughing. "It is simple. She is in love."

"The devil she is! Who with?"

"Sergei, of course."

George gaped. "Him? Well, it's not decent. He's her son-in-law and they're both old…"

"They have become children again. Now it our turn to be adults and let them be happy."

Natasha knew. Her father talked to her often of her mother and of Russia, but she saw how his face lit up when her grandmother entered the room.

Although summer was over, the flowers faded, for Julie and Sergei the world still glowed with colour and brightness like the stained-glass windows in the church. He grew stronger, his back straightened and he was able to walk without pain.

Once she brought out a jug of lemonade out to the orchard where he and the children had been picking apples. The red and yellow Beauty of Bath filled the baskets and lay about on the grass, scenting the autumn air.

"Sergei has been telling us a story about the firebird who stole the golden apples," said Susan, taking a bite.

"And one about the frog princess, " cried Edmund. "But I like the one about the wicked witch Baba-Yaga who lived in a hut on chicken legs."

"Sergei has lots of stories," said Julie sitting in the long grass and taking the little boy on her lap.

"Everyone loves Sergei," she thought. "How could they help it?"

"Starcross is your home now, dearest," she told him that night. "Here you are safe. Promise me you will cut your ties with a country that treated so cruelly."

"But my people are still suffering. The press is not free, the serfs have not been freed, Julie. There is so much to be done."

"Then let others do it. You have done enough."

That year they all celebrated Christmas together, twelve round the big table laden with a boar's head and a plum pudding. Julie made herself a gown of violet silk and twined ribbons in her hair. They all played Hoodman Blind and Hunt the Slipper with the children and drank healths in champagne. Julie and Sergei were sure no two people had ever spent a more pleasurable time or been so deep in love.

Time passed and spring came, and then it was

summer again. Sergei had been hers for a year and Julie was secure in her happiness. She felt as though all her life she had been waiting for this wonderful gift of joy.

Then one hot day when she was cutting the pink musk roses in the garden she saw an old woman with a pack slowly coming towards her There was something about the figure that filled her with dread. Hadn't it been an old woman with a pack who had brought disaster so long ago? As the old woman came nearer she saw she was holding a letter in her hand. It was Mistress Wardle.

"Yes, it is I."

Her eye closed in a wink. Julie dropped the roses onto the grass and backed away, her heart beating.

Mistress Wardle came closer. "Here, take the letter. It is a special one and it had to come. You cannot escape for ever."

Her face malevolent, the old woman thrust it into Julie's cold hands. Then with a last slow droop of her eyelid she hobbled away.

When Julie dared to look at the letter she saw it was addressed to Sergei and was from Russia. For a moment she thought she might destroy it, then knew she could not. She handed it to him fearfully and watched as he took it into the library to read. When he emerged his eyes shone with tears.

"What is it, Sergei, bad news?" cried Julie, although she already knew.

He turned to the window, not able to look at her. "They need me," he stammered. "I have to go back."

"No! I won't let you."

"I am so sorry, my heart's darling, my love. It is a matter of honour. My friends died for the cause and I cannot forget that. My soul craves to be with you, but I cannot stay here doing nothing while others suffer. An

239

uprising is being planned. My country's future is more important than my happiness…"

"Our happiness!" she shrieked, rushing at him and beating him with her fists. "You cannot go and leave me."

"There is more. I know Natasha will want to go with me. She has told me she feels Russian and she needs to be part of the struggle. She also wants to see her mother's grave."

"Then I will come too."

He pulled her to him. "Dear heart, we both know you are not strong enough to face … what may come."

"You are an escaped prisoner. They will throw you back into prison. I cannot bear it. You are too cruel, I cannot lose you both."

"I will survive. Katya has arranged a new name and new papers for me."

He held her hands in his, but she pulled away. She felt a searing agony, as if a knife had cleft her in two.

"You are killing me. I shall die of this."

He turned back to the window. "Julie, I feel as if we were part of one soul. Time and distance cannot alter that. We shall always be together, always, always. Wherever in the world I am, we will be joined by a silver thread so strong that nothing can break it. I promise we shall talk to each other, always, as long as we live. And even after death we shall be together."

Julie ran from the room, too deep in grief to cry.

Natasha came to her room that evening as she sat in her chair by the window. She sat at Julie's feet and leant against her knees as she had done so often as a child.

"I am sorry to leave you, Grandmama, but I must go with Papa and help him in the struggle for Russia's freedom. It isn't that I haven't been happy here, but it has always felt like a preparation for my real work there. And

240

I long to see where Mama is buried, she must be so lonely under the snow."

The very air Julie breathed gave her pain, but she kissed her grandaughter and stroked her hair. "I too would give all I have to be able to visit my darling's grave. Yes, my dear child, I see now that you must go with your father. In some ways you are more Russian than English. Go with my blessing and bring him back safely to me."

The girl lingered, talking of the exiles in London and Paris, and of her admiration for Theo. She could not remember him, but had read his books and newspaper articles with great interest.

A month later Sergei and Natasha left Starcross for St.Petersburg to help the cause of freedom, and to face the danger that awaited them.

Chapter Twentyone

ENGLAND 1844

After Sergei had left with Natasha to return to Russia, Julie's heart would not cease weeping. Although Starcross was filled with the bustle of the prospering farm, dogs and noisy grandchildren, the world was without meaning to her.

Harry and George, too, were sad to see them go. They all loved Natasha, and Sergei had become one of the family. They hated to see their mother's brief happiness with him destroyed so cruelly, but they were busier than ever. Their sheep were becoming well-known for their long thick fleeces and succulent mutton and they began entering their cattle in the agricultural show. A month before they had obtained a loan from the bank to buy more land, and had at last bought the mill.

So one winter's day, telling no-one, Julie took the gig and drove over to the hamlet at Thrushfield. Many things had changed since Jonas had driven her and her two little boys back to Starcross to face her long years of servitude. The road had been improved and new cottages built, there were prosperous farms and the cows in the fields looked fatter. She crossed the stream by the new bridge and recognised with a shock the fallen beech tree that had killed Jem in the storm. It looked strangely beautiful, covered in velvety brown fungus and emerald green moss. Suddenly overwhelmed with sadness of a young life cut short she paused for a moment, then shook the reins and drove on to the hamlet.

Soon she saw the hill and the little group of cottages among the high elms, with the rooks circling as they had done so long ago. Leaving the gig she stood watching the silver-white clouds race across the sky, and took deep breaths of the cold, clear air.

"I can breathe here," she told Sergei. "This will be my home."

"I am glad, sweetheart," he answered.

She wandered across the green, strangely overgrown with brambles and nettles, and saw to her surprise that the houses were all deserted. The thatch on Granny's whitewashed cottage was neglected and full of holes, the door was swinging open on its hinges, the little kitchen dusty and littered with dead leaves blown in by the winds.

"Everyone I knew has gone," she said to Sergei, "but I was happy here once. And Granny will be with me, and you and I can talk together in peace, my dearest darling."

Later she drove over to Farmer Grimshaw at Foxton and bought the old cottage.

"You're welcome to it, Mrs Johnson. I bought Zak Elworthy's farm off him when he took to the drink, and I don't need the cottage no more. I'll get it set in order for you. But all the folks from the hamlet upped and left to live in the town. Folks have gone soft, they won't put up with hardship these days. You'll be all alone there."

"I shan't mind. It's what I want."

It was at the hamlet that Julie became an old woman. She was not lonely, and had a stray tabby cat for company. She picked berries to make jams and jellies she did not need. She swept and tidied, talking to her ghosts. She watched little Harry and George playing outside the door making mud pies in a broken cup, and swept them up into her arms to kiss them. She tended Granny Forrester lying upstairs.

"I wasn't a good mother to Isabel, Granny," she told her sadly. "But in the end we became so close, so close." Tears ran down her cheeks. "She died, you know, half a world away, and her grave is under the snow.

"Love among the daughters, that's in the Bible. Maybe only women have the secret of it…" murmured Granny, too quiet for Julie to hear.

"And I know I was not fair to Theo, who was a good man," Julie went on. "But Granny, I did it to save Natasha, for Isabel's sake and for Sergei, whom I loved. And although we talk all the time he is far away over the rim of the world, and I cannot bear it."

"Hush, dearest," Granny said, her voice as faint as the wind in the grass. "Hush. The miles between are nothing to loving hearts, and soon you will be together."

Her voice faded away, but Julie was comforted.

Harry, Fanny, George and Irina drove over to see her and tried to persuade her to return home.

"Why live here like a poor old village woman," complained George, "when you could have every comfort at Starcross?"

"Don't you care about your grandchildren any more?" asked Harry.

"Our special child was born and you were not there," said Fanny. "Baby Alice needs you – all the children do. Ellen cried yesterday because she had toothache and I

244

was busy and she could not run to you. But if you won't come home, why not let Amy and Tom come here to care for you?"

"No, my dears, I like it here alone."

Julie knew she was no longer the centre of her sons' lives, but saw they were puzzled that they were no longer the centre of hers.

"It is too noisy at Starcross," she told them. "I cannot hear things."

"What things, Mother?"

"No matter, private things."

Julie did not tell them that she and Sergei were linked by a silver thread, delicate as a spider's web, that spanned half across the world. That she could hear his beloved voice and that they told each other everything. It was only because of that the world was still home to her.

When they had left she told Sergei of their visit. "They are good sons, and I am proud of them. But Starcross no longer seems quite real to me. Are you well, my darling? And how is Natasha? I worry that you might be in danger and wish so much you were here with me so I could see your dear face once more."

One autumn day in 1847 a boy, barefoot and dirty, called at the cottage with capful of squashed blackberries to sell. Although Julie had picked a pailful the day before to make jam, she invited him in. He sniffed the little raisin cakes she had just taken out of the oven.

"You could give me one of them if you like," he told her.

"You're very welcome, and I daresay you would like a cup of milk as well. What is your name?"

"Jack Elworthy, Missus," he said, through a mouthful of cake.

Julie smiled. "Oh Jonas, I'm glad to see you again.

Do you remember when you drove me and the little ones over to Starcross…"

The boy looked puzzled. "Eh? Starcross? The big house at Wychwood? Are you the lady what lost her man in the storm, him whose back was broke? I've heard my father talk of it. That was my dad what drove the cart. He died a while back, but he told me many a time how good you was to him…"

"And I gave you a penny," Julie broke in.

"Weren't me, *I tole you*. It were my dad."

"You were so young, yet I remember you tried to drive carefully so my baby would not be born in the cart."

The boy scowled and left, but after that he came back every few days to see her. Sometimes he would do odd jobs for her or chop wood for the fire and she would give him a jar of plum jam or a cake. Sometimes they talked, but more often they sat in companionable silence.

"Sergei," she said one evening as she sat alone before the fire with her cat on her knee. "I told you of my return to Starcross, in 1805 I think it was. It's odd, I can't seem to remember things now. But the farmer's boy, Jonas, has come back, and he's so very kind."

"I'm glad, dearest," said Sergei, "he will be company for you."

One day she asked the boy, "Jonas, what did you buy with the penny I gave you"?

"I'm Jack, an' I *tole* you, that were my dad…" the boy began. Then he stopped and looked at her and under-stood. "I spent it on toffee, Missus."

"I thought so," said Julie. "All boys like toffee. When you come tomorrow I will make you some."

That evening she took the rolling pin and began to

pound the sugar loaf, but her heart thudded so painfully she had to sit down. At night she told Sergei.

"I am very tired, my darling, but do not worry for me. As long as I have you I am content…"

He did not answer. She waited, but the world felt somehow different, as if his heartbeat was missing from it. Then she knew he had died far way in Russia, and that her own life was over.

Jack knocked at the cottage door next day expecting his toffee, but there was no answer. When he entered he found her sitting in her chair before the cold ashes of the fire. She did not move or greet him, but he told people later that she was still breathing, and it was strange, but she looked happy.

"Missus, wake up!" he called in her ear, but she did not respond. She had gone to meet her beloved Sergei deep in the Russian forest where he lay after they had shot him.

They would always be together, she knew, and the sigh she gave was one of happiness.

BIBLIOGRAPHY

George Kennan, *Siberia and the Exile System Vols 1 and 2* (The Century Co. NY, 1891)

Kate Marsden, *On Sledge & Horseback to Outcast Siberian Lepers* (Century, 1892)

A.E. Richardson, *Georgian England* (Batsford, 1931)

B.H. Sumner, *Survey of Russian History* (Methuen, 1944)

J. Addy, *The Agrarian Revolution* (Longman, 1963)

I. Collins, *The Age of Progress* (E. Arnold, 1964)

M.D. George, *London Life in the 18th Century* (Penguin, 1965)

A. Wood, *Europe 1815–1945* (Longman, 1972)

H. Green, *Village Life in the 18th Century* (Longman, 1976)

R.J. Cootes, *Britain Since 1700* (Longman, 1977)

Tudor and Strati, *Smallpox and Cholera* (Abacus, 1977)

C. Field, *The Great Cossack* (H. Jenkins)

C. Sutherland, *The Princess of Siberia* (R. Clark, 1985)

C. Kightly, *The Perpetual Almanack of Folklore* (Thames & Hudson, 1987)

Asa Briggs (ed.), *The 19th Century* (Thames & Hudson, 1981)

C. Kightly, *The Perpetual Almanack of Folklore* (Thames & Hudson, 1994)